TOMORROW

The Complete Saga, Volume 1

Arthur Leo Zagat

TOMORROW

The Complete Saga, Volume 1

ALTUS PRESS • 2014

EDITED AND DESIGNED BY

Matthew Moring

PUBLISHING HISTORY

"Tomorrow" originally appeared in May 27, 1939 issue of *Argosy* magazine. Copyright 1939 by The Frank A. Munsey Company. Copyright renewed 1966 and assigned to Steeger Properties, LLC. All Rights Reserved.

"Children of Tomorrow" originally appeared in June 17, 1939 issue of *Argosy* magazine. Copyright 1939 by The Frank A. Munsey Company. Copyright renewed 1966 and assigned to Steeger Properties, LLC. All Rights Reserved.

"Bright Flag of Tomorrow" originally appeared in September 9, 1939 issue of *Argosy* magazine. Copyright 1939 by The Frank A. Munsey Company. Copyright renewed 1966 and assigned to Steeger Properties, LLC. All Rights Reserved.

"Thunder Tomorrow" originally appeared in March 16, 1940 issue of *Argosy* magazine. Copyright 1940 by The Frank A. Munsey Company. Copyright renewed 1967 and assigned to Steeger Properties, LLC. All Rights Reserved.

THANKS TO

Joel Frieman, Don O'Malley, Rob Preston & Christopher Roden

CONTENTS

TOMORROW

CHAPTER 1
THE LOST ONES

DIKAR WAS on his knees, his head bowed against the side of his cot, his hands palm to palm. The fragrance of the dried grass with which his mattress was stuffed was in his nostrils, the rabbit fur of his blanket soft and warm against his forehead. Behind him there were two long rows of cots, eleven in each, separated by a wide space. At every cot knelt one of the Bunch, but the only sound was a low drone.

Dikar's own murmur was a part of that drone. "Now I lay me down to sleep, I pray the Lord my soul to keep. And should I die before I wake, I pray the Lord my soul to take." Dikar used, as all of them did, the prayer they had learned before the terror had come. They had never been taught another.

Dikar stayed on his knees as behind him there was a rustle of lifting bodies, a chatter of voices. One cried out, loud above the others, "Hey, fellers!" Jimlane it was. "Who took my bow and arrows an' didn't bring 'em back?" His changing voice, deep at first, broke into a high squeal. "If I ketch the guy—"

"They're out by the Fire Stone, foolish." That was Tomball. "I seen you leave 'em there yourself. You'll be leavin' your head somewhere one these days, an' forget where. You're sure the prize dumby of the Bunch."

The other Boys laughed, tauntingly. Dikar heard them, and he didn't quite hear them.

He was waiting for a soft hand to stroke his hair, for sweet, low tones to say, "The good Lord bless you, my son, and give you pleasant dreams." He knew they would not come. Hand and voice were vanished in the mists of Long-ago, curtained from Dikar by the dark Time of Fear before which, as he very dimly recalled, everything had been different from what it was now. But always, when he had said his "now-I-lay-me," he waited for them...

"Quit callin' me a dumby," Jimlane squealed. "You gotta quit it."

"Who's gonna make me, dumby? You?"

Dikar rose to his feet, sighing, the burden of his leadership once more heavy upon him.

From the blaze on the Fire Stone, a wavering light came in through the unglazed, oblong openings in the wall of the long narrow Boys' House. It bathed with red the stalwart, naked bodies; nut-brown skin under which flat muscles moved smoothly.

Tomball was out in the space between the cots, his bulging arms hanging loose at his sides, his adolescent, chunky jaw

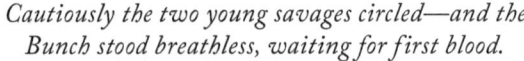

Cautiously the two young savages circled—and the
Bunch stood breathless, waiting for first blood.

black-stubbled, his eyes, too closely set, glittering between slitted lids.

Jimlane faced him and was little more than half his size. Puny, his hairless countenance rashed with small pimples, the kid's upper lip trembled but he stood his ground in mid-aisle as the other advanced, slow and threatening.

"Yes, me," Jimlane answered him bravely. "I ain't scared uh you, you big bully."

"You ain't, huh," Tomball grunted, closing the distance between them as Dikar got into motion. "Then I'll teach you to be."

Tomball had hold of Jimlane's wrist and was twisting it, his shadowed lip curling. The smaller lad's face went white with pain. His free hand twisted, batted at his tormentor's hairy belly. Tomball grinned and kept on twisting. His victim bent almost double, agonized, but still there was no whimper from the youngster…

Dikar's fingers closed on Tomball's arm and dug into the hard muscle. "No fair," Dikar said. "Break!"

TOMBALL LOOSED Jimlane, jerked free of Dikar's hold and swung around. "Says who?" he growled, a redness in his black,

small eyes that was not put there by the light. He was a quarter-head taller than Dikar and broader across the shaggy chest, and his thighs were twice the span of Dikar's. "Oh, it's you!"

"It's me," Dikar said quietly. "And I'm orderin' you to quit pickin' on Jimlane an' on the other little fellows who don't take your guff." Dikar was lean-flanked and lithe-limbed, his hair and his silken beard yellow as the other's was black, his eyes a deep, shining blue.

"There will be no bullyin' here, so long as I'm Boss of the Bunch."

Their code, like their talk, had been preserved unchanged from their young childhood, back before the Days of Fear. Isolated, they had no adult models to copy as they grew to young manhood.

"Yeah?" Tomball said through lips thin and straight beneath their sparse covering of sprouting hairs, and somehow Dikar knew what he was going to say next. It had been coming for a long time and now it was here and Dikar was not altogether sorry.

Tomball said it: "As long as you're Boss." Two gray spots pitted the skin at the corners of his flat nose. "Maybe. But it's time you made room for someone else, Dikar. For me."

By Tomball's increasing unwillingness to obey orders, by his sulking and his endless whisperings with those of the Boys who had to be watched lest they shirk their share of work, Dikar had known the challenge was coming.

He had thought out his answer and was ready with it. "All right," he said, low voiced and very calm. "I'll call a Full Council tomorrow, of the Boys an' the Girls. I'll tell 'em why I think I should keep on being Boss an' you'll tell 'em why you think I should not, an' then the Bunch will decide."

A murmur ran around the ring of Boys that had close-packed about Dikar and Tomball.

"No!" Tomball refused. "It wasn't the Bunch decided you should be Boss in the first place. It was the Old Ones." He paused, and a meaningful grin widened his mouth. "Or so *you* say."

"Maybe," Dikar smiled, surprised he could smile. "Maybe, Tomball, you'd like to ask the Old Ones if they picked me to be Boss when they brought us here and left us. Maybe you'd like to climb down the Drop an' ask 'em whether you or I should be Boss from now on."

The Boys gasped in the ring around them, and Dikar's own skin crawled at the back of his neck.

DOWN, DOWN as far as the Mountain on which the Bunch lived was high, fell the great Drop that fully circled its base. Straight up and down was the Drop's riven rock, and so barren of foothold that no living thing could hope to scale it.

Below, for a space twice as wide across as the tallest of the trees in the forest that robed the Mountain, were tumbled stones as big as the Boy's House and bigger. White and angry waters fumed beneath the stones, and beneath stones and waters were the Old Ones.

Dikar himself had seen these things, from the topmost branch of a certain tree that gave a view of them, but not even Dikar had ever gone out from the concealing curtain of the forest to the brink of the Drop, for of all the Must-Nots the Old Ones had left behind, this was the most fearful; *"You must not go out of the woods. You must not go near the edge of the Drop."*

Thinking of all this as he stared into the red hate in Tomball's eyes, Dikar asked, "Do you dare, Tomball, climb down the Drop an' talk to the Old Ones?"

"Smart," Tomball sneered. "You think you're smart, don't you? You want me to go down there an' that way be rid of me. Well, it don't work, see? I'm just as smart as you are."

Dikar spread his hands. "You will not let the Bunch decide between us, an' you will not ask the Old Ones. How, then, do you want this thing settled?"

"How? How have you yourself ordered scraps between the Boys settled? Dikar! I dare you to fight out with me, fists, or sticks or knives even, who's gonna be Boss of the Bunch—you or me."

"No fair," Jimlane cried out at that. "I say it's no fair. Tomball's bigger than Dikar an' heavier."

"No fair," Steveland yelped. Billthomas yelled, "We cry the dare no fair." But others were shouting, *"Fight!"* Fredalton and Halross and rabbit-faced Carlberger. "They gotta fight it out. It's Dikar's own Rule an' he's gotta stick by it."

Most of the Boys shouted, "Fight!"

"Shut up!" Dikar bellowed. "Shut up, all of you," and at once the yelling stopped. But the ring had shrunk till he could feel their breaths on his back and heard little whimpers in the Boys' throats and read their eyes, shining in the changing light of the Fire. "You dare me fight to decide who'll be Boss," Dikar said to Tomball, taking up the ritual he himself had set. "Do you cry a fight between us two fair?"

A cord in Tomball's short neck twitched. "I cry us equal-matched." (By the Rule, Dikar had a right to appeal to the Bunch from Tomball's lying response.) "If you refuse my dare, Dikar, I will cry you yellow, an' claim the right about which we scrap." Reading the eyes in the ring, Dikar saw that if he appealed and the Bunch said he and Tomball were not equal matched, he might remain Boss in name, but Boss in truth he would be no longer. "That is the Rule you yourself have made." Tomball abandoned the ritual. "And you gotta stick by it."

Dikar's lips still smiled. "That is the rule I have made, Tomball. But this over which we scrap is no bird brought down by an unmarked arrow nor question of whose turn it is to bring water from the spring. Who shall be Boss affects not only you an' me, but the whole Bunch. Is it right that it be decided in the way such small scraps are decided?" Dikar pretended to ask that of Tomball, but his eyes asked the question of all the eyes in the crowded circle, and the eyes had already answered him when Tomball spoke again.

"It is right," Tomball voiced the verdict of the eyes. "It is the only way that is right. You gotta fight me or crawl." There was triumph in his voice, and triumph in his swagger. Tomball had weight on his side, and reach and strength, and he knew he was already as good as Boss.

Dikar knew it too, and his heart was heavy, but he smiled still. "All right," he said. "We fight, Tomball. With bare fists."

The Boys hurrahed, the sound like the bay of the dogpack when they've brought down their prey under the trees. Even Steveland and Billthomas hurrahed, and though Jimlane was silent his pale eyes danced with the dancing red light of the Fire.

Dikar listened, thinking what Tomball would do as Boss of the Bunch; whether he would let his pals shirk work, whether he would see that the corn patches were weeded, and the water tank cleaned, and the roofs of the Boys' House and the Girls' House kept patched against the rains and the snows and the cold.

It was worry about these things and others like them that weighted Dikar's heart. He knew how painfully he had learned, in the long years since the Bunch had come to the Mountain, all the many little irksome tasks that must be done for the good of the Bunch; and he remembered that Tomball had always scoffed at them.

For himself Dikar would be happy to be no longer Boss. It meant being lonely—for the Boss must have no pal, lest he be accused of favoring his friend over any other. It meant carrying a heavy freight of care through the day, and lying sleepless through the night, and never knowing rest. It meant assigning the hunters to the chase, whose joys he never knew; to judging the games and never playing them; to punish when Rules were broken but never breaking Rules just for the fun of it and finding the punishment worth it.

"What are we waiting for?" Tomball's growl broke into Dikar's thoughts. "Come on outside an' let's go."

"No," Dikar said. "We fight tomorrow, before the whole

Bunch. Tonight, now, we sleep. Already it is Bed-Time, an' long past."

"I want to fight now," Tomball insisted, standing his ground. "I don't want to wait till tomorrow."

The smile faded from Dikar's lips, and he felt tiny muscles knot along the ridge of his jaw, beneath his yellow beard. "Bed-Time is not my Rule, but a Rule of the Old Ones. Perhaps, when you are Boss, Tomball, you will let the Bunch break it, but I am still Boss, an' I do not. To bed, Tomball. To bed, all of you. Right away!"

Dikar's eyes locked with Tomball's, and blue eyes and black held for a long minute and there was no sound in the Boys' House, and no movement at all. Then the black eyes fell, and Tomball muttered, "It's the Old Ones I obey, Dikar, not you," and the ring broke up into Boys hurrying to their cots.

Dikar stood spread-legged, the firelight playing on his tall, well-knit form, his chest moving quietly with his slow breathing, the taut hollow of his belly heaving, his eyes somber as he watched the Boys obey him—perhaps for the last time.

He didn't feel Jimlane's fingers squeeze his. He didn't hear Jimlane's whisper, "I hope you win tomorrow, Dikar. Gee, how I hope you win."

Dikar stood there while the curtains woven from slender withes were dropped over the window-openings, shutting out the red light of the Fire that the Girls tended tonight.

He stood there, unmoving, till the excited whisperings along the walls of the Boys' House had faded, and the scrape of the fur blankets along skin had ended, and there were no more creakings. Then he turned and padded to his own cot, and knelt beside it.

Dikar's lips moved, but the words came. He was sending them out through the wall, past the leaping flames on the great, flat Fire Stone, past the Girls' House into the night-darkened woods.

He was speaking to a Presence there, a Someone he had

never seen and never heard, but had always known to be there, because He showed His work in the carpet of the leaves underfoot, in the tall and stately trees, in the wind that rustled through the woods' green roof and the sunlight that shimmered through it.

"I don't care what happens to me tomorrow, Sir," Dikar told Him. "I don't care how much Tomball hurts me, or what he does to me if he wins. It's the Bunch I ask you to take care of. Please, Sir. If Tomball is too strong for me, tomorrow, an' he licks me, please make it all right for him to be Boss. Please make him smart enough to be a good Boss. Please make him be a better Boss for the Bunch than me. They're good kids, Sir, the Boys an' the Girls, an' mostly they obey the Rules the Old Ones left, an' You ought to take care of them. You will take care of them, Sir, won't you?"

Dikar's lips stopped moving, but he stayed on his knees a little while longer, his head bent as if he were listening.

He heard nothing but the soft breathing sounds, and the wind's treetop whisper, and the insect chorus of the night.

When at last he stirred and climbed into his cot and drew his fur blanket up over him he was comforted.

CHAPTER 2
THE NIGHTMARE THAT WAS TRUE

SLEEP'S DEEP emptiness claimed Dikar swiftly and wholly, as always it claims one whose weariness is clean and physical.

A voice came into the nothingness, the voice for which Dikar waited each Bed-Time after he'd said his Now-I-lay-me.

… Mom's voice it was that came through the open door of the dark room where Dick Carr had awakened. Something in

Mom's voice made Dick afraid: tears, and a trying hard to hide the tears, and a smile that he somehow knew hurt Mom more than the tears.

"Take care of yourself," Mom was saying, "and come back soon."

Who was going away? There was only Mom and Dick in the flat, and Henry who was twelve, four years older than Dick, and who took up more than his half of their bed. Dick pushed out to wake Henry, and his hand found only bunched sheets.

Henry wasn't there!

The next minute Dick heard Henry out in the hall. "Sure, I'll come back soon. Don't you worry. This thing will be over in a jiffy, you'll see. We're just being called out because—because the last big drive is on, an' they need us in the rear lines so's all the real soldiers can be free to do the fightin'. There ain't nothin' to worry about, Mom. They can't lick us. Maybe they've licked the rest uh the world but they can't lick the good old U.S.A. We've won every war we were ever in an' we'll win this one—

"Look Mom, I got to run. The radio said for my unit to be at the Eighth Street Armory at eleven o'clock, an' it's four of, now. Goo'bye, Mom."

There was a kiss, and the flat-door slamming shut, and then there wasn't any sound coming in through the door at all and the flat seemed awful empty.

In through the window rang the clatter of feet running in the street. Dick heard it every night, listening to the big boys who didn't have to go to bed early and could play in the street after supper. But Dick knew they weren't playing now, because they all ran the one way and after a little while he didn't hear them any more.

Then Dick lay listening to the thunder that had been in the sky so long he usually didn't hear it. The thunder seemed a little louder tonight, and a little nearer, and more scary. The glass in the window kept rattling and that made Dick look at the window and at the square gold-starred flag that hung in the window.

The star was for Pop. It was to show everybody how proud we were that Pop was a hero. Only Dick didn't quite understand why we should be proud when every window in the block had a flag with a gold star, a lot of them even with two or three gold stars.

What was there to be proud about in your Pop being a hero when all the other kids' fathers were heroes too, and their big brothers, and a lot of their sisters too, being Red Cross nurses and working in ammunishun plants that was blown up and all?

Dick wished Pop would stop being a hero and come home.

Mom and Henry said Pop wasn't ever going to come home, but Dick didn't believe that. Dick didn't believe Pop would go away from them forever and ever.

Now Henry was gone away too. But he was coming back soon. He had told Mom he was, hadn't he? He wouldn't lie to Mom, would he?

Dick heard the sound of feet again, coming down the street. The feet weren't running now. They were marching. Dick knew what feet sounded like when they were marching. He'd heard them before Pop went away, when you could hardly hear them for the crowds shouting and the bands playing soldier-music.

He'd heard the feet marching when Pop went away; there were no bands then, and no hurrahs, and there were hardly anybody in the street, only in the windows a lot of women, waving handkerchiefs, and then holding them up to their faces.

Yes, Dick had heard a lot of marching feet, but they had never sounded quite like these. The sound of them feet wasn't nearly as loud as the others.

Dick pushed back the covers and got to the window. The tops of the street lights were painted black, and the bottoms were blue; so that the gutter was like blue water, deep and awful, and across the street was only a black and dreadful wall.

Down the street came the marchers.

THEY WERE boys like Henry, some of them bigger and some smaller, but none of them very much bigger or very much smaller. Each had a gun slanted across his shoulder. Not one was in uniform. They were dressed in their everyday clothes, caps and jackets and pants. Some of the boys wore longies, most wore knickers or shorts, and a lot were barelegged down to the socks folded over the tops of their shoes. They were like a bunch of boys marching out of school on a fire-drill.

They were not playing soldiers. They were soldiers, real soldiers. The way they marched showed that, straight-backed, not talking or laughing. Their chins were lifted. Their eyes looked far ahead, to the end of the street and the end of the city and farther still, to the dark night out of which came the sound of thunder that never stopped.

Four abreast they marched, four and four and four, as far as Dick Carr could see. And alongside each tenth four marched a man in uniform; a man with one empty sleeve pinned to the breast of his coat: a man whose leg swung stiff so that Dick knew it was not a leg at all: a man whose face was broken so it was ugly and terrible as a Hallowe'en mask.

For a long time the boys and the broken men marched by, to where the thunder rolled and the black sky flickered with a lightning whose flashes Dick Carr could not see...

(And Dikar's dream faded into sleep's nothingness.)

...And into sleep's nothingness came a crash of thunder, shaking the ground. It shook Mom's arms that were tight around Dick Carr, and her body against which Dick's face was pressed. Out of the corner of his eye Dick could see the pin on Mom's black breast. The pin was oblong, and it had a blue border, and on the white inside the border there were two gold stars. There were two on the flag in the window now.

Dick was scared, but he wasn't bawling. He hadn't bawled when the siren waked him up, screaming in through the window, nor when Mom and he had jumped out of bed, all dressed like the radio said they should be. He hadn't bawled when, the siren screaming like a great devil in the black sky, they ran in the dark street, and then stopped running because all the women and kids were carrying them along in a rush faster than Dick could run.

No, Dick hadn't bawled even when he and Mom had fallen down the station steps and the old man had dragged them through the big, stiff curtains into the station.

The station was crowded with women and kids, and it was like an ogre's cave. A couple of electric lights made light enough to see them by, but not enough to keep back the shadows that reached out of the enormous black holes at each end of the station, like black arms pawing out to drag the women and the kids into a night that would never end.

The faces he saw were a queer white, and the eyes were too big; and they were sort of hunched, as if they were waiting for something terrible to pounce on them out of the dark.

It came!

Thunder! Thunder louder than before, thunder so loud that when it stopped Dick couldn't hear himself say, "Don't be scared, Mom. I'll take care of you." But Mom must have heard him, because she squeezed him tighter to her and kissed him on top of his head. Then Dick could hear again. He could hear a woman say, "That must have been one them half-ton bombs. They tell me they can go right down through a ten-story building, and they don't blow up till they hit the cellar, and after they blow up there ain't nothin' left of the building or anyone was in it. Nothin' at all."

The old man, who stood by the brown curtain that hung over where the station steps came in, laughed. His laugh was like the cackle of the hens Dick used to hear when Pop used to drive him and Henry and Mom out into the country.

"Yeah," the old man cackled, his eyes kind of wild. "That's right. Ef'n one o' them things hits overhead here they won't even be little pieces of us left ter pick up."

He had on a uniform, but it wasn't like Pop's uniform. It was very faded but you could see it had once been blue. It was ragged and much too big.

THERE WAS thunder again, not so loud. "Well," said a woman sitting with a suckling baby in her heavy arms. "I wish one *would* hit right over us. That would be God's mercy."

"There ain't no God," someone said. "God is dead." Then whoever it was laughed, and Dick's insides cringed from the laughter. It was a woman in the middle of the platform, and she was standing as still as a rock—her mouth didn't move, and the eyes behind the hair that was down all over her face saw nothing at all. "The End of the World is come and it is too late to repent. We are doomed, doomed—"

Thunder again shattering the laughter, but far away now. The woman who sat next to Mom, with a little girl on her lap and another, brown-haired and brown eyed and pretty, on the floor alongside of her whispered: "Poor thing, I hear tell she escaped from Philadelphia after it was surrendered. She got through the lines somehow. Did you hear how they went through all the houses that was left and dragged out—?"

"Hush," Mom begged. "Hush. The children—"

The little girl's mother laughed quietly. "The children will know all about it soon. Yours too, girls or boys, it don't make no difference to those fiends."

"Not mine," Mom said, very low, and she moved a little to show the other woman what was in her hand. It was a carving knife from their kitchen—

"Attention!" A loud voice shouted out of the place where you used to get your change before the subways stopped running. *"Attention, all shelters!"* Dick looked and he saw there was a radio behind the little hole where your money used to be pushed out. *"The raid is over! The raid is over—"*

"It's over," the old man cackled. "And I'm still alive. Eighty-three years old and not dead yet. I allus said I was born ter be hanged."

"—where you are. Remain where you are. Gas-tests are being made. Remain where you are until gas-tests determine that it is safe to leave. Stand by."

"The Government should of gave us all gas masks," grumbled a fat lady whom Dick knew. "Like they did in England." She was Tom Ball's mother and Tom was behind her, hiding his face in her skirts.

"Much good that did England," the woman with the baby said. "Much good anything did England—"

"Attention!" the radio shouted. "Attention all shelters. Important. An important announcement is about to be made. Stand by."

"Mom," Dick asked. "What is an important annou— what the radio said?"

"News, son. Big news."

"Good news, Mom?"

"Maybe. Maybe we've won the battle. Maybe we're driving Them—"

"Attention! Attention, all shelters. The next voice you hear will be that of General Edward Albright, provost-marshal-general for this area."

"That's Ed Albright," the old man cackled. "I remember when he was a buck private alone o' me, the both of us down with dysentery at Key West. In the Spanish War that was, an—"

"Hush. Hush, you old fool."

The voice Dick heard now, coming into a quiet so deep he could hear Mom's heart beating in his ear, was thin and tired, awful tired. "Our lines are crumbling. Enemy infantry has already penetrated to the outskirts of the city, south and east. The boys, the young women, who have fought so heroically, are still fighting, but there is no longer any hope. Word has come that the columns that were marching to our aid have been completely wiped out by a phalanx of enemy planes."

CHAPTER 3
AFTER ARMAGEDDON

THE VOICE stopped, and there wasn't any sound at all. "We are beaten," the voice began again. "But we shall not surrender. We shall not give over the mothers and the children of this city to the horror that has overtaken the other municipalities that have surrendered.

"My people, when our lines finally break, when the enemy hordes swarm in, I shall press a button on the desk before me to set off mines that have been laid underneath the streets. Every soul in the city will perish in that cataclysm; I, and you, and with us some thousands of those who have made this world of ours a hell."

"Good!" yelled the woman with the babe at her breast. "Good!"

Mom's arms were tight around Dick, and she was crying, but her eyes were shining. "We're going to see Henry soon, son, and your father," she whispered. "Isn't that wonderful?"

And then everyone was quiet again, and the tired voice was still talking.

"To die like that will be, I know, no sacrifice to you who have laid fathers and husbands, sons and daughters, on the altar of your country. But there is one more sacrifice I must ask of you, for your country.

"Somehow, in the maneuvering of the past few hours, a gap has opened in the enemy lines, to the north. It is already being closed, but the terrain is such that a small and determined force may be able to keep it open long enough for a few to escape.

"No troops can be moved from their present positions. We have some arms, some ammunition, available, but no one to use them. No one—except you women who hear me. You mothers."

"That's funny," Mrs. Ball sniffed. "We can escape through a

hole if we get ourselves killed keepin' the hole open. The man must be crazy."

"If you mothers can keep that gap open long enough, we may be able to take your children out through it, the tots who are all you have left.

"We may—the possibility is infinitesimal—be able to get them away to the hills north of the city. The chances are that they will die on the way. Even if they do not, it is possible that they will be hunted down and exterminated, that Nature, though less cruel than these hordes that have come out of the East and across the continent from the West and up from the South, will finish the work of our foes.

"But there is a million-to-one chance that the children will come through, and it rests with you to choose whether we shall give them that chance.

"I know that it is a bitter choice to make. I know, mothers, that you would rather that your little daughter, your little son, when I press this button on my desk, go with you into the Outer Darkness where there is peace at last.

"I know how dreadful it would be for you to die not knowing what fate awaits your children, and I should not ask you to make the choice save for this one thing.

"This is the dusk of our day, the dusk of democracy, of liberty, of all that has been the America we lived for, and die for. If there is to be any hope of a tomorrow, it must rest in them, in your sons and daughters.

"If they perish, America shall have perished. If through your sacrifice they survive, then, in some tomorrow we cannot foresee, America will live again and democracy, liberty, freedom shall reconquer the green and pleasant fields that tonight lie devastated.

"If you choose to give America this faint hope, if you decide to make this sacrifice, leave your children in charge of the warden of the shelter where you are, and come at once to headquarters to receive your weapons and your orders.

"We have no way of telling what your decision is until and unless enough of you come here to make the attempt we contemplate feasible. We wait for you. Will you come? Mothers, the choice is yours."

THE VOICE stopped, and for a long time nobody moved, nobody said a thing. Then, all of a sudden, all the women were standing up. All the women were kissing their kids, and then they were going toward the curtain that hung over the bottom of the steps from the station.

They were pushing aside the brown curtain. They were going up the steps.

They were going fast, fast, and their faces were shining as Dick once had seen a bride's face shine as she walked, all in white, up the aisle.

They were all gone, and in the station there were only the kids, and the old, old man in the uniform of faded blue that was too big for him.

It seemed darker here in the ogre's cave. The dark reached out from the great black holes at the ends of the platform. A small, cold hand took hold of Dick's hand. "I'm frightened," the little brown-haired girl whimpered.

"Aw," Dick said, squeezing her hand. "There ain't nothin' to be frightened about. I'll take care of you."

"Will you," she asked in a very little voice. "Do you promise?"

"Cross my heart," Dick said, "I'll take care of you, always and always," and somehow he wasn't quite so frightened any more. "What's your name?"

"Mary Lee. What's yours?"

"Dick Carr."

"Dikar," she murmured, and moved close to Dick, and her head dropped sleepily on his shoulder.

He liked the way she said it: "Dikar," so he didn't bother to tell her it was two names. He said "Marilee" in his head, making one name out of her two, and he liked the sound of that…

And a shadow moved across Dick Carr… A shadow moved across Dikar, and he stirred and came fully awake out of his dream, and it seemed to him that someone had passed him, moving silently in the night.

CHAPTER 4
WE MEET IN THE NIGHT

DIKAR LAY in his cot, alert. The sloughing of the wind came to him, and the shrilling of the insects of the night and the breathing of the sleeping boys. There was no sound at all out of tune with the harmony of the dark forest.

Yet Dikar was troubled with an uneasy sense of something wrong.

He tried to quiet himself, tried to find sleep again, sleep and the dream out of which he had wakened. Dikar was desperate to find his dream again, for he knew it was one he had dreamed many times. But always before it had slipped from him in the instant of wakening and tonight it was still as vivid in his mind as yesterday.

The small boy of the dream, Dick Carr, was himself in the Long-Ago that had been only a mist of gray half-memories as shapeless as the dawn-haze that drifts in the waking forest. The dream had told Dikar something of himself and something of that Long-Ago, and if he could find it again it would tell him more.

But Dikar could not find sleep again, nor the dream, because his eagerness barred the way, and his sense of something wrong with the night. So he sighed and rose from his cot, making no sound.

He groped for his apron of woven leaves and tied it about his waist, and stole to the curtain of twined withes that closed the door, moving it a little to peer out.

The leafy boughs of a great oak made a roof that joined the

roofs of the Boys' House and the Girls' House, at the end where they came nearest the woods. Beneath it the Fire was burning low on its Stone, and a little distance away from its heat Dikar saw the two Girls whose task it was tonight to tend the Fire.

The two Girls drowsed, arms about each other's waists. They had undone their braids, and the hair that cloaked one was black as the night, and the hair that cloaked the other was brown and shining. The black hair swallowed the light, but tiny red glints from the Fire danced merrily on the wavy fall of the brown.

The Girls wore short skirts of plaited grasses, and circlets of woven leaves covered their deepening breasts; but through their cloaks of long hair a shoulder peeped shyly, and a rounded knee, and curve of a thigh.

Now as long as he could recall Dikar had seen the brown bodies of the Girls as they busied themselves with their tasks or tried to outdo the Boys in the Games, and so it was strange that tonight these small glimpses should set a pulse throbbing in his temples, and stir his breast with a not unpleasant pain.

It was to the Girl whose hair was brown that his eyes clung, to her knee and the soft swell of her throat, and the pale oval of her face.

As he looked out at her, he seemed to feel a small hand in his, to hear a very little voice asking, "Will you take care of me? Promise?" For this was Marilee, the little Girl of his dream. Dikar had forgotten his promise, "I'll take care of you always and always," but now he remembered it.

Remembering, he wanted to hold out his arms to Marilee, wanted to call her to him. He almost did, and for fear that he might, looking at her, not longer be able to hold her name in his throat, he tore his eyes from her and turned them to the Fire. Little flames, blue and yellow and red, licked along the sides of a single log that lay across a great heap of orange glowing embers. That log will not last much longer, Dikar though. I should wake the Girls and tell them to put more on.

Then he thought, no. Let them sleep. I'll do it myself, and with the thought his look went to the pile of logs at the base of the oak.

…To the place where the pile ought to be! There was only one split log there.

Queer, Dikar thought. I sent up enough for the night from where we were cutting them in the woods yesterday—A hand slid past the trunk of the oak, out of the blackness behind! The hand took hold of the one log that was left of the pile and drew it back into the blackness.

A muscle twitched in Dikar's cheek, under his beard.

"Oh," Bessalton exclaimed, the black-haired Girl. "Marilee! We've been sleepin' an' the Fire's almost out. Quick."

THEY WERE running to the Fire, and past it to the oak, and they were looking, dismayed at the base of the oak. "There isn't any," Marilee said, her small face puckered in puzzlement. "You must have put on the last."

"I did no such thing," Bessalton denied. "It was you. You were the last one to put wood on. Remember?"

"Yes," Marilee said slowly. "Yes, I was the last. But there was more here then. I'm sure there was."

"Looks like it," the black-haired Girl came back, "Don't it? If I did something like that—"

"Oh what's the use of scrapping about it? We've got to get more up from the place where the Boys were cutting, before the Fire burns out."

"We?"

"I'll do it, Bessalton. I know where they were," Marilee said, and before Dikar could move or cry out, she had gone past the oak and the night had swallowed her. The night out of which a hand had slid to draw away the logs from the base of the oak!

Dikar sprang to his cot, snatched up his bow and quiver of arrows, was back to the door and out through it. Bessalton stared at the Fire; she neither saw nor heard Dikar flitting by.

Then the damp, fragrant dark of the woods was about him, and the cool softness of its carpet of leaves was under his noiseless feet, and he was a shadow slipping through the forest.

All the Bunch was taught to move in the woods with the silence of its creatures, but Dikar's ears, trained to keenness, caught the barely audible sound of Marilee's progress ahead of him, the flick of underbrush against her legs.

He did not call to warn her, because he needed to know who had lured her into the forest, and why. This was a thing that never before had been done by one of the Bunch and Dikar must find out why it was being done.

Moonlight filtered through the foliage overhead and flecked the night with silver. A small beast scuttered away from beneath Dikar's feet. Marilee was well away from the Houses now. She was almost to the place where the Boys had been cutting—

"Oh!" he heard her exclaim, and then there was another voice ahead there. "Hello, Marilee." Tomball's voice. "I've been waitin' for you."

Dikar froze, as motionless as the tree trunks about him.

"You've been waitin'—" Marilee was puzzled. "Why? Why should you be here, waitin' for me?"

"I wanted to see you alone."

"But—but why do you want to see me alone?"

"Marilee." Tomball's voice was curiously thick. "Do you like me?"

"Of course I like you. I like all the Boys."

"Not that way. Do you like me—like this?" Dikar heard the sound of flesh, and he sprang into the little clearing ahead, and Tomball's hands had hold of Marilee's arms, and he was pulling her to him.

"Stop!" Dikar said, low-voiced, and somehow there was an arrow hooked in the string of his bow, and the string was tight, and the arrow was pointed at Tomball's back. The bow was long almost as Dikar was tall, and the arrow sharp-pointed with stone. Loosed, it could go clear through a deer—or a Boy. "Let go of her."

TOMBALL TURNED on Dikar. Crouched knee-deep in fern there was something about him more animal than Boy. The curling thickness of his lips; the feral look of his black eyes, and the way his neck was tense and corded.

"You—" Tomball grunted. "You again!"

"Me," Dikar said, heavy-tongued with anger. "The Boss. Tomball, you have left your cot before day. You have laid hands on a Girl. For breakin' these Must-Nots you are subject to seven days in the punishment cave, with only water an' dried corn to eat. What's your excuse?"

Tomball licked his lips, and straightened. "Nothin'," he said. "Because you won't give me the punishment."

"Won't I? An' why not?"

"Because I'm not here, that's why. Because I'm in my cot, asleep. Halross will say so at the Council, an' Carlberger."

"They will lie?" Dikar's brow wrinkled. He could not understand. "They will lie, at a Council?"

"Sure, they will. What are you goin' to do about it?"

"But Marilee here will say different, an' I."

"Course you will," Tomball grinned. "Why shouldn't you, the Boss of the Bunch an' the Boss of the Girls? Why shouldn't you say that I left my cot, an' that I laid hands on her, when seven days in the punishment cave on water an' dried corn will leave me so weak you'll be sure to lick me, an' stay Boss? Will the Bunch believe you, Dikar, when I remind 'em of that, or will they believe me an' Halross an' Carlberger?"

Dikar felt sick. That any should lie at a Council, that any should talk as he was hearing Tomball talk, was a new and dreadful thing. "Tomball," he cried. "You're foolin'. You wouldn't really say those things."

"Wouldn't I?" Tomball grinned, licking his lips. "Just try me. You're licked, Dikar, an' you know it."

Dikar knew it, and he knew that a terrible thing had come among them, and he could not think how to fight it. He was licked—

"Dikar!" Marilee's fingers touched his arm. "Dikar. Hold him here with your arrow while I run an' call the Bunch. When they see Tomball here in the woods, he an' his pals cannot say that he is in his cot, asleep." She started away.

"Wait!" Tomball's command halted Marilee. "You can call the Bunch, Marilee," he said. "But when they get here I'll tell 'em that Dikar drew his arrow on me an' forced me to come here. An' Halross will say that, wakin' from sleep in his cot next mine, he saw this, an' that Dikar said he would kill him if he did not keep quiet."

Marilee and Dikar stared at Tomball.

"You can't win," Tomball sneered. "I'm too smart for you, see. An' tomorrow you'll find out I'm too strong for you, Dikar. An' here's somethin' else for you to remember, Marilee. When I'm Boss, you better like me the way I want you to like me!"

He laughed, then, and turning his back on Dikar's arrow, swaggered away; they heard his laugh coming out of the dark woods.

"What did he mean?" Marilee whispered, coming close to Dikar. "He said, 'When I'm Boss.' What did he mean, Dikar?"

Dikar wanted to put his arms around her.

"He meant that we're gunna fight who should be Boss, Marilee. In the mornin', right after Brekfes, you will call a Full Council of the Bunch, an' Tomball an' I will fight who shall be Boss."

Marilee's eyes were upturned to his eyes, her lips were moist and red. "You must win, Dikar," she whispered. "You heard what he said. You *must* win."

The wanting to take her in his arms, the wanting to hold her close to him, was a great ache in Dikar's arms and in his breast, and a weakness in his legs.

"I heard him, Marilee," he said, deep-throated. "I will win."

And then Dikar turned and ran off through the woods, but he looked back over his shoulder at Marilee once and saw the way she stood looking after him, mantled in her brown hair, and he saw the look in her face.

CHAPTER 5
THE OLD ONES

WHEN DIKAR got back to the Boys' House and slipped inside, all was dark there, and quiet, and Tomball was in his cot. Dikar put down his bow and arrow, and took off his apron. He lay down again, and pulled up the blanket of rabbit's fur.

He lay staring up at the black roof of the house, trembling a little. It seemed to him that he saw Tomball's face there, black-stubbled and small-eyed and sneering. And then it was Marilee's face he saw, the red lips moist, the brown eyes holding his, telling something her lips could not. And looking into Marilee's eyes, Dikar's eyes closed and the nothingness of sleep received him… And out of sleep's nothingness formed a sky that flared with blue light, and with red, and was streaked with bright yellow that shimmered and faded; and the sky was filled with rolling, endless thunder. Against that terrible sky loomed monstrous black bulks, huge and ominous, hills that overhung a road and a big truck in which Dick Carr was riding.

In the truck kids were jammed so tight they could not lie down, and just could move a very little. Dick was in a corner so that his back was jammed against the iron sides of the truck, and Marilee was jammed against his side, and her head was on Dick's shoulder, and she slept.

Most of the kids were asleep, in spite of the terrible lights in the sky and the awful thunder. But the old man who was driving the truck wasn't asleep, nor the old woman who sat next to him. Ahead of them on the road were a lot of trucks, and behind them were a lot more trucks, but Dick could tell this only by the noise they made, because none of the trucks had any lights.

Dick knew some of the trucks were loaded high with boxes and boxes of things, but most of them were jammed tight with kids like this one.

"Tom," Dick heard the old woman ask. "Do you think we'll get through?"

"I don't know, Helen," the old man answered. "Only God knows. So you had better pray to God to take us through."

"I can't, Tom. I can't pray any more. I'm all prayed out. God cannot hear our prayers. He has forgotten us, Tom. He has turned His face from us."

"Pray, Helen. Not for you or for me, but for the children in our charge. Pray to God's Son. It was God's Son who once said, 'Suffer ye the little children to come unto Me.'"

"All right, Tom. I'll try."

They didn't say anything more. The truck bounced along, and the red and blue lights flared in the sky, and yellow streaked it, and thunder rolled.

Once the road got steep, climbing up into the sky to what looked like the Jumping-Off Place, and up there against the sky Dick saw things that stuck up out of the top of the black hill. They were just a Bunch of broken poles, black against the blazing sky, but Dick knew that once they had been trees. And to one side there was a chimney sticking up, and Dick knew that was all that was left of a house that the trees used to shade.

Dick started to get sleepy. His eyes closed. The old woman woke him up, yelling something.

"Tom!" she yelled. "Tom! Turn into this side road. Quick!"

DICK'S HEAD banged against the truck side, and the kids fell against him, and Marilee woke up, screaming, "Dikar! Dikar!" Dick grabbed hold of her, telling her it was all right, and then the truck wasn't going any longer, and Dick could hear the other trucks going past, somewhere behind.

"You caught me off guard, Helen, and I did it," the old man said. "But why?"

"I don't know, Tom," she answered, talking slow. "I saw the side road ahead and something told me we must turn off into it. It was like a voice in my ear. No. It was more like a voice in my brain."

"You're all worked up, Helen. You're excited." Tom's back moved, and there was a noise of grinding metal. "Watch out behind. I'm backing up to the highway. As soon as you see a clear space you tell me, so that I can back out and get into line again. If we lose the others we won't know where to—" And then there was a white light in the sky a light bright as the sun floating down out of the sky.

And there was a new sound in the sky, like a bee, like a giant bee, and it became a roar. An enormous black shape came down under the light, and there was a rattling noise, like a lot of Boys were running sticks along a lot of picket fences, but louder, and there were screams and crashes and the rattling noise kept on.

The rattling noise cut off, and the roar faded and became a bee-buzz again and the bee-buzz died away in the sky. There were no more crashes, and no more screams. There was only the rolling thunder overhead, that never stopped.

Old Tom got down from his seat, and went away into the dark. The old woman sat very still, and all the kids sat very still, and nobody moved. After awhile the old man was back, and he was climbing up again to the truck driver's seat.

"Well?" Helen asked, so low Dick could hardly hear her.

"None," Tom said. "Not one of them all. We're the only ones left. If we hadn't turned in here—" He didn't finish.

"I guess," Helen said. "I guess God is still listening, up there above the sound of the guns." And then she said, "Where do we go from here?"

"There's a smashed signpost back there, where this road turns off. One of the boards on it reads, 'To Johnson's Quarry.' Do you remember, Helen, my heading a committee once that tried to stop the Johnson Granite Company from cutting down a Mountain? They were defacing the landscape, you recall, and we wanted to preserve the beauties of Nature for posterity."

He laughed. It wasn't pretty, that laugh. "We failed. Recently I heard that they had blasted away almost the entire base of the Mountain, leaving only a narrow ramp by which their trucks could reach their camp at the top. There are probably quarters for the laborers up there, perhaps some supplies. The Mountain, as I remember, is thickly wooded and there's a possibility we may be safely enough concealed there, at least for a time."

"If only we can get through to it."

"We can try. This is a State Park we are in. There are woods almost all the way, and nothing to attract enemy patrols." The truck started running again.

(Dikar's dream blurred.)

The thunder faded out of it, and the dark, and there was sunlight, with green trees, and a wide cleared space with two long houses each side of it, with cots and a warless house at one end in which there were big stoves, and a lot of tables. There were a Bunch of little kids and there were the two Old Ones.

THE OLD Ones made the kids work. Helen made the Girls make beds and cook and things like that. Tom made the Boys go down the road up which the truck came that first night and hammer deep holes into the hill of rock on top of which the road climbed up to where the trees were. When Tom thought the holes were deep enough he would put fat white sticks into them that he got out of a big red box they had found where the road started to climb up, and little, silvery things on top of the sticks.

When it would begin to get dark, they would all eat, and then the Old Ones would make the Bunch all sit around and they would tell them things.

They called this a Council. At the first Council the two Old Ones told the Bunch a lot of things they should do, and they should not do, and these were the Rules. The Old Ones said Marilee should be Boss of the Girls, and they said Dick should be Boss of the Boys, and of the whole Bunch.

Every morning one of the Boys would climb up high in a tree and watch all day if anybody would come out of the woods on the other side of the fields down there, where Tom and the Boys were working.

The Boys took turns doing this. One day (and this is where Dikar's dream got clear again) Dikar was sitting on top of the tree. The Boys had got through making the holes yesterday, and they weren't down there any more. They were in the front of the house where they slept, and Tom was teaching them how to make bows and arrows. The Girls were in front of their house and Helen was teaching them how to make baskets out of twigs from the bushes in the woods.

Dick was looking at the black smoke, way far off in the sky, that had been there all the time since they came here. He thought about a new Rule the Old Ones had made at Council last night, a Rule they said was most important of all. "You must not go out of the woods," the Rule said. "You must not go near the edge of the Drop."

Wondering why the Old Ones had made that rule, Dick looked down at the edge of the Drop, and at the place where the road climbed up and over it. His eyes went along the road, and across the fields, and he saw someone come out of the woods across there.

The someone looked very little, way down there, but Dick could see he had a kind of dark-green uniform on, and that his face was yellow. Then another one and another one came out of the woods. These were in green too, but their faces were black, and they had guns. All of a sudden there were a lot of them.

Dick yelled down, "Coo-eee! Coo-eee!" and when Tom looked up at him Dick pointed down at the men in the green uniforms and held up his spread fingers and wagged them to show Tom how many there were.

Tom started running into the woods, and then he came out on the other side of them, where the road came up over the edge of the Drop, and he was running down the road. And then Helen was running after him, and Tom saw her. Tom yelled something and she stopped, but she didn't go back.

Tom had a little hammer in his hand.

Dick heard a crack, like a twig breaking, and he looked down and down, and across the fields, and he saw that the men in green had their guns up to their shoulders, and he saw a little white puff of smoke floating away from one of them. Then he saw white puffs come out of all the guns.

Dick looked back at Tom, and just then Tom fell down, but he didn't stop. He was crawling down the road, and Helen was running down it now, running fast.

A lot of cracks came to Dick's ear, and across the fields the air was full of the little white puffs. On the road Helen caught up with Tom and was lifting him up, and then he was leaning on her and the two of them were running down again.

The men in green started running across the fields, stopping every couple of steps to shoot at Tom and Helen, but the Old Ones got down to the bottom of the road, and around inside of where the road started to climb up out of the fields, and the men in green stopped shooting because they couldn't see them any more, but they kept on running.

Dick could see the Old Ones. They were standing near the rocky wall of the hill the road climbed on, Helen's arm around Tom, and the first of the men in green came around to where he could see them.

Tom lifted his little hammer and hit the rock with it. A cloud of dust hid the Old Ones, and Dick heard a boom, and then there was another boom, and another, and one so loud it filled the whole world. The hill the road climbed on leaned away from the rest of the Mountain, and it started to fall.

It fell slowly at first, and then faster and faster, down on where the Old Ones were, and on the men in green, and the noise was so loud Dick couldn't hear any noise at all, and the air was so full of dust it was like night.

The whole Mountain shook, and the tree shook so hard Dick had to grab hold of it to keep from being shaken and his hands started to slip, and…

(Dikar woke.)

CHAPTER 6

SHADOWS AT SUNRISE

DIKAR LAY in his cot, his eyes still closed, remembering his dream, fitting the things it had shown him into the things he knew, seeing how it explained a lot that had always puzzled him.

It explained the Rule that no fire must ever be made except with wood so dry that it would burn without smoke, and the Rule that no fire must ever burn at night except the big Fire on the Fire Stone, and why the big Fire was set not in the center of the space between the Boys' House and the Girls' House but at one end, where it was hidden from the sky by the spreading leafy top of the giant oak. It explained the Rule that when there was a noise in the sky like a bee buzzing, everyone must run into the Houses or into the woods and stay very still until the sound was gone.

But most of all it explained the Must-Not about going out of the edge of the woods, about going to the edge of the Drop.

They were down there, in the woods across the space of tumbled stones at the bottom of the Drop, beneath which the Old Ones lay. Dressed in green, with black faces and yellow faces. They were in the woods, and in all the far country Dikar could see when he climbed the tall tree. If they saw any of the Bunch come to the top of the Drop and so found out that the

Bunch lived on the Mountain, They would come and do to the Bunch what, in his dream, They did to all the kids on that terrible night in the Long-Ago.

Dikar knew now how the Bunch had come to the Mountain, and he knew now that the Bunch could not always stay here on the Mountain. Some day he must lead the Bunch down the Drop, down into the far, green country that stretched away, fold on fold, to meet the sky. And now Dikar was glad that he was Boss of the Bunch, so that he would lead them—

But after this morning he might be no longer Boss!

Dikar remembered that he must fight Tomball over who should be Boss, and he remembered what Tomball had done and what Tomball had said last night, between dream and dream. Dikar threw off his blanket and leaped from his cot, and all down the length of the Boys' House bronzed forms leaped from the cots, and curtains were raised, and the sun streamed in.

But the Boys did not laugh in the sun, and they did not laugh and play jokes on one another as they ran, behind Dikar, out through the door in the wall away from the Girls' House, and through the woods to where a stream leaped from a ledge overhead into a pool below, and ran brawling out of the pool as if eager to reach the edge of the Drop and leap again over it, and smash itself on the tumbled rocks below.

The Boys did not shout as they sprang after Dikar into the icy pool, and none swam near him, and none joined him when he climbed on the stone where the stream came down, and stood there, letting the stream batter him.

But when tingling with the cold of the waters, with the lash of the spray, Dikar ran back through the woods to the Boys' House, little Jimlane came up to run beside him.

"Dikar," Jimlane panted. "Oh, Dikar. They're sayin' Tomball is sure to beat you. They're sayin' he's too strong for you. An' a lot are sayin' it's a good thing, that they're tired of you being Boss, and that when Tomball is Boss we won't have to work all the time, an' we'll have more time for Games, an' for—an' for playin' with the Girls."

Dikar ran along, and from his lithe limbs the drops spattered, shining in the sun, and under his yellow beard his jaw muscles hardened, but he did not speak.

"An' Tomball says he's goin' to fix me when he's Boss," Jimlane whimpered. "An' I'm afraid, Dikar. I'm awful afraid."

Dikar looked down at the little fellow, and he saw the frightened eyes in the pimply face, and the gray, quivering lips.

"Don't worry, kid," he grunted. "Tomball won't win." But Dikar wasn't sure.

SOMEHOW BREKFES was over, and the Bunch was gathered in a circle in the space between the Houses, the Girls on one side and the Boys on the other, and Marilee sat in the Boss's Seat beneath the giant oak, her brown hair still unbraided, mantling her, her small face color-drained. Dikar stood before her, and Tomball stood by his side, and Marilee was speaking.

"You fight," Marilee's clear, sweet voice said, "over who shall be Boss of the Bunch, an' the Bunch will obey as Boss the one who wins. You fight with bare fists, an' you fight fair. You begin when I say the word, you end when one is beaten." Her brown eyes were on Dikar's, and her eyes told Dikar that he must not be beaten. "That is all."

Dikar turned away and walked toward one end of the cleared space about which the Bunch stood murmuring. The grass was cool under his bare feet, and springy.

Marilee had ordered it carefully raked, so that there would be no branches to trip the fighters, and no small stones to bruise them if they fell. Many twigs and leaves and small stones had been raked out of the grass, and so calm was Dikar that he even noted how the stones had been put in a great circle to mark the bounds of the space in which he must fight, and how just beyond the circle the Boys and Girls stood tight-packed.

Dikar came to the end of the space, and turned, and across the space he saw Tomball turning. Fredalton was whispering something in Tomball's ear, and Tomball nodded, grinning with his thick lips.

"Fight!" Marilee cried out.

Dikar started going back toward Tomball, and Tomball came to meet him, half-crouched, his black-stubbled countenance scowling fiercely, great pads of muscle across his shaggy chest, his hairy belly indrawn.

Dikar moved lithely across the raked grass, his beard shining yellow in the sunlight, his limbs dusted with yellow hair.

All at once Tomball was very close, and Tomball's fist struck Dikar's cheek, and Dikar's cheek knotted with the pain of the blow, and his head rocked.

But Dikar's arm jarred with the blow he had landed on Tomball's chest, and then Dikar no longer felt any pain. He stood breast to breast with his enemy, his fisted arms were clubs that pounded the dark face and the hairy body he hated. There was a salt taste in his mouth that was very pleasant, and there was joy in the blows he gave, and joy even in the blows he received.

He made no effort to guard himself from Tomball's blows, nor did Tomball try to guard himself from Dikar's. They fought like the beasts fight, eager only to hurt, eager only to pound the other to submission.

And over them washed the shouts and the screams of the Bunch.

INTO A red haze that was all that was left of his vision, Dikar flung arms so heavy he barely could lift them. Somewhere in the haze was a darker bulk that moved about, and it was at this Dikar flung his arms. Sometimes Dikar found it, more often not, and when he missed the weight of his arms pulled him off balance, and he would start to fall, and somehow not fall.

Sometimes Dikar would be struck, out of the haze, and he would sway on his legs that had no strength in them, and almost go down; but he did not let himself because he must not, though he no longer knew why.

And out of the haze came an endless thunder of shouting.

Dikar pawed once again at the vague bulk that was his enemy, and missed, and swayed, and in that instant the bulk struck him, and Dikar's legs folded, and he sank. His sight cleared, and lurching at him came Tomball's red-bathed body, Tomball's distorted face. Somehow Dikar threw a heavy arm at Tomball and struck him, so that as Dikar settled to the ground Tomball staggered back.

Tomball did not fall, but was steadying. Dikar, sprawled on the grass, knew that when Tomball had steadied he would come in again to finish Dikar, and Dikar did not care—

"Dikar!" he heard a high, clear voice above the endless roar. "No!" *Marilee!* "No, Dikar. No!" And suddenly Dikar cared desperately that Tomball was beating him, and his fallen body trembled as he tried to get up, but he had no strength—

"Oh up, Dikar," a voice squeaked, and Jimlane's pimpled face swam over Dikar, close to Dikar's face, and Jimlane's hand was tugging at Dikar's hand to pull him up. "You can lick him now, Dikar." Dikar came up with the pull of Jimlane's hand, Jimlane's fingers closing Dikar's hand into a fist. And Tomball, grinning through the red that masked him, lurched in to beat Dikar down again.

Dikar lifted a heavy arm and flung it at Tomball, and Dikar's fist fell on Tomball's brow. Tomball crumpled and lay, a still heap on the grass, with Dikar swaying above him, arms hanging by his sides, in his ears a deafening roar.

And out of the roar came Marilee, her cheeks rosy, her eyes alight. "Oh, Dikar."

That was all she said, but Dikar straightened, feeling the strength flow back into him, hearing the hurrays of the Bunch clear in his ears, knowing the hurrays were for him.

Marilee took hold of Dikar's wrist to lift his arm and cry him the winner.

The color fled from her cheeks and from her lips, and the light went from her eyes as they fell to Dikar's still-fisted hand.

Dikar's eyes went down to where Marilee's eyes looked, and they saw what Marilee's eyes saw. In his fist that had pounded Tomball down was clenched a stone, and there was blood on the stone, Tomball's blood.

Dikar knew now why Jimlane had closed that hand into a fist, why Jimlane, tugging him up, had said, "You can lick him now." Jimlane had—

"Dikar," Marilee sobbed. "Oh, Dikar," and then Marilee was lifting Dikar's arm so that all might see what was in Dikar's fist, and the hurrays stopped, and there was a throbbing hush.

Marilee's voice was loud and clear in that terrible hush. "I cry Dikar no fair. I cry Tomball the winner of the fight. I cry Tomball Boss of the Bunch."

Marilee threw Dikar's arm from her, and it was as if she threw Dikar from her, and she turned away. Dikar thought he heard Marilee sob, but she walked away from him head high, back proud. Dikar's mouth moved but no words came out of it, and he knew there was no use of his saying that he had not known the stone was in his fist.

A strange, low sound came from the throats of the Bunch, and it grew louder. A stone struck Dikar on the shoulder, and another, and Dikar saw that all the Bunch was bending to pick up stones, lifting them to throw them at him.

"Run!" Jimlane screamed. "Run, Dikar," and Dikar turned and ran, the stones falling about him; ran, staggering, straight at the hating faces of the Bunch, and the Bunch opened a path for him, and Dikar ran into the woods, the stones spattering about him.

Dikar ran in the dim woods till he fell, and he crawled till he could crawl no longer, and he lay still in the woods, and a sick nothingness took him.

CHAPTER 7
THE FAR GREEN LAND

DIKAR LIVED in the woods as the beasts live, and as the beasts' hurts heal so did his. He set snares for the rabbits and the birds that were so plentiful in the woods, and cooked them over his little fires. He found sharp-edged stones, and used them as knives to make a bow for himself, twisting and drying the gut of the rabbit for string, and he made arrows, feathering them, and a quiver out of the bark of a birch.

He hunted with his bow and arrows, and he lay long hours on the mossy floor of a clearing near the top of the Mountain, watching the little creatures of the forest play, looking sometimes into the great, beautiful eyes of the deer peering out at him from the brush, watching the birds chirp on the tree boughs above him.

It was spring and always the small woods creatures played two by two, and the deer went two by two, and the birds; and seeing this, Dikar would think of Marilee.

Yes, Dikar's hurts healed but the ache within him did not heal.

Sometimes Dikar would climb to the topmost branch of a tall tree that stood on the very top of the Mountain. He would stay there till dark, gazing at the far green land that stretched, fold on fold, away to where the sky came down to meet it. He would think of what he had dreamed the last night he was Boss, and of his thought that some day he would lead the Bunch down into that pleasant land, and his heart would be heavy within him.

Spring warmed into summer, and summer deepened.

Every night Dikar would slip through the woods till he came to where the trees were black against the red glow of the Fire, and he could crouch behind the trunk of some tree and look out into the space between the Houses. He dared not do this till just before Bed-Time, when he knew most of the Bunch were in the Houses and there was little danger of one coming upon him.

Dikar would hear the drone of their Now-I-lay-mes, and he would kneel and say his own with them. With his palms together and his eyes closed, it was almost as if he knelt by his own cot in the Boys' House, almost as if he were still one of the Bunch.

After his Now-I-lay-me was said, Dikar would stay there, listening to the talk of the Boys or the Girls whose turn it was to tend the Fire.

What Dikar heard made his heart heavy. As he had feared, Tomball was letting the Bunch break Rule after Rule, was favoring his pals and laying double work on those he did not like, was shirking many of the little things that Dikar knew were needed if the Bunch was to be warm and comfortable and safe when the cold came, and the snow.

One of the Rules Tomball allowed to be broken was the Rule that none must leave his cot after Bed-Time. Dikar would see Girls come out of the Girls' House and slip off into the woods, and he would see Boys do the same. Often they had not yet come back when Dikar tired of watching had gone back to the shelter he had woven for himself out of twigs. One thing troubled Dikar above all others. He never saw Marilee tending the Fire. That she was never one of those who went into the woods after Bed-Time pleased him, but it was strange that her turn never came to tend the Fire.

ONE NIGHT Dikar heard the reason. He'd heard that, the day he was stoned, Marilee had said that she no longer would be Boss of the Girls, that she had made Bessalton Boss in her place on the promise that she would free Marilee of the duty of tending to the Fire, or of any other duty that would take her away from the other Girls. And that this was because Tomball wanted Marilee to go into the woods with him, and Marilee feared him.

Dikar's throat grew thick when he heard this. Growling, he rose from his haunches to stride out into the light of the Fire and call out Tomball to fight him, not with fists, but with bows and arrows, and knives, in a fight to the death. His rage blinding him, Dikar was caught in a bush he did not see, and before he could get free he heard something else from the tongue of Jimlane, who was tending the Fire with Billthomas and had spoken of Marilee and Tomball.

"If Dikar was Boss again, things would be different, but there's no chance of that, because the minute he shows up the Bunch will stone him again, the way Tomball has ordered, and he would not get away again."

Dikar went cold, remembering the way the stones had spattered about him, and was very still in the bush.

"The Bunch wouldn't stone Dikar," Billthomas said, very low and looking about with frightened eyes, "if you spoke out. Tomball's orders or no, they would not stone Dikar if they knew that it wasn't Dikar's fault he fought no fair."

"I dare not tell them." Jimlane's eyes went big in his white face. "You remember how I told you, an' how you said yourself the Bunch would stone me if I told."

"Yes, I remember."

"Well, I couldn't rest, an' I went to Tomball an' told him, an' Tomball beat me till I could hardly walk. That was the time I said I fell into a hole in the woods, you remember. An' after Tomball beat me, he told me that if I said a word to anyone else he would kill me, an' he would kill anyone I told."

"He did!" Now there was fear in Billthomas's eyes, too, and in his face. "You should not have told me, Jimlane—If Tomball finds out I know—" His voice was still low, but there was a scream in it.

"If only," Jimlane sobbed, "Dikar could some way come back and protect me while I told the Bunch—"

"What's the use of all the ifs?" Billthomas broke in. "Tomball's made sure Dikar would be killed before you had a chance to say anythin'. The best thing we can do is forget about Dikar, like everyone else has."

"Yes," Jimlane whispered. "I guess so. Dikar isn't one of the Bunch any more an' he will never be again."

"Never again," Billthomas agreed.

Now indeed Dikar, rigid in the dark, knew that he was disowned by his kind. He must live out his life alone, a wild beast in the woods—

And then, perhaps from Some unseen Presence in the close-crowding dark, perhaps from within Dikar, a thought came to him. He was no longer one of the Bunch, and so he was not bound by the Rules of the Bunch. He was not bound by the Must-Nots that the Bunch must obey. There was something for him to do, and no Rule to say that he must not.

He drifted off into the darkness, silent as a shadow. But there was no sleep for Dikar that night.

ALL THAT night, and all the next day, Dikar was busy, cutting down long vines from the trees, testing each one for strength. He plaited the vines, never stopping, never resting, till by nightfall he had made a rope long enough for his need.

When dark came Dikar hung his quiver of arrows over one shoulder, and he hung the great coil of green rope over the other shoulder, and he followed the sound of a stream through the black forest till he came to where the woods ended and there was a little space between the edge of the woods and the edge of the Drop, where the stream leaped out into the night.

Here Dikar paused, and laid the rope down, and passed its end around the great trunk of a tree that grew beside the stream, and fastened the rope with many knots, and pulled on it with all his strength to make certain that the knots would hold.

Dikar bent, then, and lifted the coil of rope that he had made from the vines, and carried it to the edge of the Drop, and let it fall into the dark.

At his feet the rope tautened, and quivered, and below him there was the sound of its unwinding coil thumping against the high, sheer rock of the Drop, and the sound of the stream's waters, falling down and down into sightless blackness. And then the rope at Dikar's feet was no longer quivering, so that he knew the coil was all unwound.

Dikar bent again, and lifted the rope, and moved it over so that it lay in the water where the stream leaped out over the Drop, so that when the sun rose again, all the length of the rope that hung down the Drop would be hidden behind the falling waters.

Then, without pause, Dikar had hold of the rope with his hands, and he was over the edge of the Drop, and the icy waters were rushing about him, were battering him, were fighting to break loose his hold and send him hurtling down into the dizzy dark to smash on the rocks below.

Dikar could not see and he could not breathe, and his hands were slipping on the wet rope. He caught a leg around the rope, and slid. He could breathe again because he hung between the rushing waters and the rocky face of the Drop.

Dikar went down and down, endlessly, down into the black and dizzy darkness, down to where the great stones lay tumbled, and the waters raged between them, and the Old Ones slept.

THE SUN was high in the sky, but Dikar was concealed in the leafy shadow of a treetop where he lay outstretched along a thick bough. He was peering at a sight that made of his skin an icy, prickling sheath for his body.

The tree was at the other end of the woods through which Dikar had loped after finally crossing the belt of immense stones that lay about the Mountain where the Bunch lived. Some time in the night, sounds ahead, and moving lights, had alarmed him, and he had climbed the tree to wait for what the day would show him.

Dikar, as comfortable there as on his mossy bed in the Mountain forest, had slept longer than he intended. Into his feet had come the sound of marching feet, and he had thought himself back in his dream of the night before his fight with Tomball. But his eyes had opened and the marching feet had still sounded in his ears, and then Dikar had seen those whose feet made the sound.

The tree in which Dikar wakened was at the edge of the woods and the edge of a great, flat field. Not far from the tree wires stretched, one above the other, twice Dikar's height. Fastened to thin poles, the wires ran away on either hand as far as Dikar could see, and the wires were thick with long, sharp thorns that would tear a Boy's flesh to bits.

Beyond this set of wires was another set just like them, as high and as wickedly barbed, and between the two sets of wires stood, far apart, figures out of Dikar's dream.

They were dressed in green like the men in the dream who had run across the fields that now were covered with great stones, shooting at the Old Ones. Like those, their faces and their hands were black, and like those they carried the shiny sticks that Dikar now remembered were called "guns."

But the sound of marching feet came from inside the second fence. A great crowd of people were marching out of some long, low houses that were very much like the Bunch's Houses. Just as Dikar spied them, they stopped marching and stood in a long, straight line in front of the houses.

They were pretty far away, but Dikar could see them, and he could see that they were very thin, and they were dressed in ragged clothes that hung loose on them. He could see that their faces were white, and that their eyes were sunk deep in their heads, and that they were all stooped over as if they were very tired, although it was only early morning.

A voice yelled something, and the white people turned, so that the lines faced Dikar. Dikar saw that the one who had yelled was different. His face was yellow, and he was dressed in green, but there was something different about his green clothes, and he had no gun.

There were other men in green standing around in there. Some of them were black-faced, and some yellow-faced, some had guns and others didn't. One very big one only had green on below his waist, above that he had nothing on. His body was as yellow as his face, and his muscles were bigger than Dikar's muscles, or even Tomball's. He was holding something in one hand. It was long and thin and black. His other hand was against a thick post beside which he stood.

The man in the different green clothes yelled something again, and then Dikar saw two black-faced ones come out of a smaller house to one side, and between them was a white one who was so weak they had to almost carry him. They came to the thick post, and they shoved the white man up against the post with his face to it, and they tied his arms and his legs around it, and then they tore off his clothes above the waist, and stepped away.

The yellow-faced man yelled a lot to the white people. Dikar could hear him, but he couldn't make out what he was saying. When he finished he made a sign with his hand to the big yellow man.

That one lifted the long, thin thing he held, and it looked like a snake. And he lifted it above his head and it straightened out, and then it came down across the back of the white man who was tied to the post. Dikar heard the crack it made, and he saw the red mark across the white man's back.

And the yellow man lifted the thin, snakelike thing again, and brought it down again, and there was another crack, and another red mark across the white man's back.

Dikar was sick, seeing that. And then he wasn't sick. He was mad. He wanted to yell out, "Stop!" but he remembered his dream now, remembered what the guns could do, and he knew that if he yelled the men between the wires would see him and shoot him down.

Crack, Dikar heard, and *crack* again, and now the back of the man tied to the post was all red, all shining red. But Dikar was on his feet, on the tree branch. He was pulling taut the string of his bow, and an arrow was laid across it.

The big yellow lifted his arm again, but when it fell there was no crack. The big yellow was falling, and the feathers of an arrow were sticking out of his back. Just the feathers.

Dikar didn't see any more, because he was swinging through the treetops, a brown and naked Boy flashing through the tops of the trees, fleeing the death from the guns that he recalled were swifter and farther reaching than any arrow.

Whether the men in green ever thought to look for him in the treetops Dikar never knew.

FAR AWAY from the place of the thorny wires, Dikar lay on his belly in the tall grass that covered a hill, and he looked down through the grass at a place where two roads crossed.

There stood a pole, high as a tall tree, but there was no bark on it, no branches nor leaves, and because at its top five or six cross-sticks were fastened, and a lot of wires ran from these cross-pieces to other cross-sticks at the top of another pole far away down one of the roads.

Dikar was looking at a rope that hung taut from one of the cross-sticks at the top of the pole. Dikar was looking at that which weighed down the rope and kept it taut.

The thing swung back and forth, back and forth, very slowly in the wind, and rags fluttered about it in the wind, and the rags were no grayer nor dirtier than the thing was. And Dikar saw that the thing once had been a man.

… Dikar came to a place where there was a House all of rock, and it was three or four times as high as the Boys' House, and ten times as long. The window openings in the wall of this House were very high and very wide.

Dikar saw a lot of people in there, and there were white men and women. These were thin and gray and sunken-eyed as those in the place with the wires, and they were pushing around things piled high with heavy loads, and they were so weak they could push the things only slowly. And there were men in green standing around, and these had little guns hanging at their waists, and they held black, snakelike things like the big yellow one held.

And Dikar saw a white woman stumble and fall, and he saw one of the men in green raise the thing he held and bring it down on her, again and again till, all bloody, she pulled herself up on the thing she had been pushing and started pushing it again.

And the other men in green laughed, but the white people just kept on pushing, all stooped over and weak, their eyes like the eyes of the woman in Dikar's dream who stood in the subway station and said that God was dead.

Dikar went far and wide that day, a brown shadow flitting through the fields and the woods, a silent shadow none saw. Dikar saw many things that day, and the more he saw the heavier his heart grew within him. For Dikar knew that the white-faced men and women were his people and that this green land belonged to them and to him, and that the black men and yellow men were They whom the voice in his dream had said, "have come out of the East to make this world a Hell."

Yes, Dikar saw the Hell they had made... The sky darkened and the night crept out of the Woods, and Dikar lay belly down in tall grass of a field near the woods, head buried in his curled arm, thinking. Last night he had known that he would never return to the Mountain where the Bunch lived, and now he knew that he could not stay in this land that had seemed so pleasant when he had gazed at it from his tall tree in the forest.

Neither there nor here was there place for Dikar. Nowhere was there place for him—

Fingers clutched Dikar's arm, bruising fingers. Dikar rolled over but the fingers held, and there was a growl of words Dikar could not understand, and in the sunless dusk Dikar saw green-clothed legs, and a green-clothed breast, and a black, fierce face goggling at him.

CHAPTER 8
IN THE TOMORROW

DIKAR KICKED at the black man's legs, and he saw the black man's hand dart to the little gun at his waist. Dikar kicked again, wrenched loose, exploded from the ground.

Dikar's one hand caught the little gun, his other smashed into the black, goggling face. Somehow the black man was on the ground and Dikar was atop him, and Dikar was clutching the black throat with one hand while the other was smashing the little gun down on the black man's head, smashing and smashing and smashing.

When Dikar fled into the night-shrouded woods he left behind him something that had legs and a body and arms, but nothing that was anything like a head.

Deep in the woods, Dikar found a little cave. He crawled into this and lay there a long time, shuddering. But after awhile he stirred, and he became aware that he still held in his hands the little gun, and he sat up, his eyes widening with a sudden thought.

Dikar hid the little gun under a pile of rotting leaves, and he went out of the cave and prowled about till he was certain that no one was anywhere within sound of hearing. Then he went back into the cave with certain things he had picked up and he made a fire, and by the light of the fire Dikar studied the little gun until he had made out how it worked.

Satisfied at last, Dikar put out his fire and buried it with wet earth, and left the cave. That night Dikar traveled far and fast, but careful to leave no tracks by which he might be traced.

Dikar was going back to the Mountain, and he must not leave any trail the men in green might follow.

ONE MORE night Dikar stole down through the dark forest to the Houses of the Bunch, but this night it was long after

Bed-Time that he did so. This night Dikar did not crouch behind a tree, looking out at the Fire, but crept, noiselessly, along the wall of the Boys' House that was away from the Fire till, under a certain window opening, he came to a stop.

Dikar listened, trembling a bit, and all he could hear was the whisper of wind in the trees, and the shrill of insects in the night, and the soft breathing of the sleeping Boys. Dikar lifted, slowly, slowly, till he stood upright. The ground here was banked against the wall so that, standing, Dikar's belly was level with the bottom of the window.

Slowly, he ran his hand over the sill, and touched the curtain of woven withes; and moved it aside. And then he was peering through, and a fleck of red light was dancing on a sleeping face, and the face was rashed with pimples.

Dikar breathed again. He had remembered right. This was Jimlane.

Dikar got his other hand through the window, and then it was tight over Jimlane's mouth, and Jimlane's scared eyes were staring up at Dikar.

"Listen," Dikar breathed. "Listen to me, Jimlane." Dikar spoke so low that barely he could hear himself, but by the look in Jimlane's eyes he knew that Jimlane heard him and understood.

After awhile Dikar stole away, and for the first time since Tomball had challenged him, Dikar was smiling.

THERE WAS green all about Dikar, the dancing, leafy green of the top of the giant oak in which he had spent the rest of that night. He was still smiling when he awoke, but peering through the leaves at the Bunch where they chattered, cleaning up after Brekfes, there was a flutter of some small muscle in the tautness of his belly.

Across the space between the House Dikar spied Marilee talking with Bessalton. Dikar saw how thin Marilee had grown, and how wan her little face, and how her fingers plucked endlessly at her short skirt of plaited grasses, and Dikar's smile faded.

Tomball strode up to the two Girls, black-stubbled as ever. His belly was overlaid with fat, but it was still shaggy with hair, and Tomball's grin was still leering.

Tomball put a hand on Marilee's arm, and Marilee shrank away from him. Under Dikar's yellow beard little muscles knotted to ridge his jaw, and there was a growl in his throat.

Tomball laughed, and then from behind the Boys' House came the loud words of a scrap. "He's mine!" Jimlane's voice piped, and "I say he's mine," squealed the thin voice of Billthomas, and around the corner of the Boys' House the two came, and between them was a half-grown fawn, with a vine wound around its brown neck and trailing, broken, from it.

Jimlane had hold of the fawn's head and Billthomas of its hind legs, and each tugged as if to take it from the other.

"It was caught in my snare," Billthomas piped.

"You lie," Jimlane squealed.

And then Billthomas straightened and cried out. "It's you who lie, Jimlane. I dare you to fight out with me, bare fists, whose snare he was caught in, and whose he shall be."

Tomball's deep-chested laugh came to Dikar's ears, but Jimlane's voice, breaking from squeal to bass and back again to squeal, was answering Billthomas. "You dare me fight whose the fawn shall be?" it said. "Do you cry a fight between us fair?"

And Billthomas: "I cry us equal-matched," and all about were cries of, "Fair. Fair. They're equal-matched!" and the Boys and Girls of the Bunch were running from all over, and crying, "Fight! Let them fight!"

And then the Bunch was crowded in a great circle, and the fawn was tied by the vine about its neck to the Boss's Seat, and Tomball, grinning, was seated in the Boss's Seat, just beneath the oak, and Bessalton was seated beside him, mantled in her black hair, and Jimlane and Billthomas stood before them while Tomball spoke to them.

But Dikar's look was on Marilee where she stood in the crowd, her two long brown braids coming down over her shoulders, her deepening breasts beneath leafy circlets.

Dikar's eyes drank thirstily of Marilee till Tomball was finished speaking and Jimlane and Billthomas were walking slowly, each to their end of the cleared space where they were to fight. Jimlane reached the end of the circle, turned—

The little gun jumped in Dikar's hand, and the fawn, just beneath him dropped, wet-redness streaking the brown neck.

A Girl screamed, high and shrill, and then Dikar was shouting: "Stay where you are or I'll kill each of you as I've killed the fawn. I'll kill the first one that moves."

"Dikar!" Marilee cried, and then she was silent, and all were silent and unmoving, the Boys and the Girls in their jammed circle, Tomball in the Boss's Seat.

"Jimlane," Dikar shouted down into that hush, "tell the Bunch how the stone came into my hand with which I struck Tomball when we fought who should be Boss."

Jimlane, white of face and big of eye, but standing straight, cried out. "I put the stone in Dikar's hand, when he fell at my feet."

"Did I know you put the stone in my hand?" Dikar shouted from the tree.

"You did not know, Dikar. You were blinded with your own blood, an' numbed with Tomball's blows, an' you did not know there was a stone in your hand."

A MURMURING ran around the circle, and a growl, and Dikar saw that the Bunch did not quite believe that he had not known he was striking Tomball with a stone though they had agreed to fight bare fist.

"Jimlane," Dikar shouted. "Have you ever told this thing to anyone?"

"I told it to Tomball," Jimlane cried, "and Tomball beat me for saying that you did not know you fought no fair, an' Tomball said that if I spoke to anyone else he would kill me, an' kill the one to whom I spoke of it."

"You lie!" Tomball shouted, starting from seat. "You lie, dumby!" Jimlane screamed with terror of Tomball, but Dikar's shout beat down Jimlane's scream.

"Back!" Dikar shouted. "Back to your seat, Tomball, or you die." And Tomball went pasty white under his black stubble, and he slumped down in his seat.

And Dikar leaped out from the oak bough on which he stood, and came down, spring-legged, in the clear space around which the Bunch was jammed, and held aloft the little gun.

"This is the thing that kills," he shouted. "Without it I cannot kill," and then he flung the little gun from him, flung it hard so that it went up on the roof of the Boys' House and stayed there.

"Now I cannot kill," Dikar shouted. "No more than any of you."

"Stone him," Tomball yelled. "Stone him, Bunch. He is none of us and we will have none of him." And Dikar saw the Bunch stoop to pluck up stones. Spraddle-legged, bronze-skinned in the sun, he saw this, and his heart within him died, but he would not move.

"No!" It was a high, wild cry in his ear, and it came from Marilee, and Marilee's was beside Dikar. "I cry no fair. I cry the Bunch no fair, all of you against this one."

"He fought no fair," Tomball shouted, "and so has no right to call for fairness. Stand aside, Marilee, and let the Bunch stone him."

"I will not stand aside," Marilee answered. "Be you Boss or not, till you tell the Bunch why you said you would kill Jimlane if he told his tale to anyone, an' would kill anyone he told the tale to. If you still thought Dikar had fought no fair, why were you afraid to let the Bunch hear Jimlane's tale and judge for themselves?"

Now Tomball's little eyes seemed to have grown even smaller, and his mouth was drawn very tight.

"She's right," someone yelled. "Why, Tomball, did you not let us judge for ourselves?"

"Jimlane lies," Tomball answered. "He never told me this tale, and I never—"

"It is you who lie," Dikar cut in. "I say you lie, Tomball. I cry you a liar, Tomball, an' I dare you to fight me whether you lie or not. I cry that I fought fair, an' I dare you to fight me whether I fought fair or not. I dare you to fight me who shall be Boss of the Bunch. I cry us equal-matched, an' if you refuse to fight me I will cry you a liar and yellow an' not fit to be Boss of the Bunch an' not fit to be one of the Bunch. Will you fight, Tomball, bare fists?"

There was only one answer Tomball could make. "I fight you bare fists, Dikar. I fight you here an' now."

AND THEN they were fighting, were clubbing at each other with fisted arms, lips drawn back from white teeth, eyes hating. But Dikar was gaunt and hard-bitten, and toughened by the life he had led since he'd been stoned from the Bunch, and Tomball was fat and slow, and short-winded, and so the fight did not last long. Dikar beat Tomball down, laid him rolling at his feet, and there was scarcely a mark on Dikar when he stood above his beaten enemy and heard the shouts of the Bunch.

"Hurray for Dikar. Hurray for the Boss. Hurray and hurray and hurray."

Dikar scarcely heard the hurrays. He was peering about for Marilee and he saw her, and he motioned commandingly for her to come to him. She came to him, her white and slender body shining in the sun, her eyes shining more brightly than the sun, and then she was beside Dikar, and Dikar's arm was around her, and he was holding her close to his side.

Under the thunder of the hurrays, Dikar spoke to Marilee. "Marilee," he said. "In the time I have been alone in the woods I have learned many things—an' one of the things I have learned is that each creature has his mate, the birds an' the small beasts of the woods, an' the deer. I learned that He who made all things meant this to be so, an' meant that we too, each of us, shall have his mate. Marilee, I want you for my mate." He was looking down into her face, and now he waited, with a tightness growing in him that was both keen happiness and fear.

Marilee's red lips spoke. "Oh, Dikar. This that you have learned only now, I have known always. Dikar, always I have wanted you for my mate."

A great joy leaped within Dikar, and he raised his hand and roared, "Shut up! Shut up, all of you." And the hurrays died away, and the Bunch was hushed, and Dikar was talking into that smiling hush.

"There are many things I have to say to you, an' many Rules I shall have to change. All this will come later. Just now I have something to say, but not to you, though I wish all the Bunch to hear it, all the Bunch, an' Another."

Then, in that hush, Dikar turned to the giant oak, and to the forest beyond the oak, and his voice was low, and slow, and awed.

"You Whose voice is the whisper of the wind in the trees, an' the ripple of the water in the streams an' the song of the insects in the night! You, who watch over us by day, an' by night! You to Whom we say our Now-I-lay-mes at Bed Time! Sir! Look upon me and upon this Girl, an' hear me. In your sight an' your hearin' I take this Girl to be my mate, an' none other than this Girl, an' to You an' to her I promise that all my life I will take care of her an' let no harm come near her. I promise that all my life she shall be bone of my bone an' flesh of my flesh, all my life an' all her life, an' always an' always."

"Hear me, Sir!" Marilee's clear, young voice rang out. "I shall be this Boy's mate, an' none other's, an' he shall be bone of my bone, an' flesh of my flesh, always an' always."

And it seemed to Dikar that a soft hand stroked his hair, though it might have been the wind. How could it be the wind, though, that said in his ear, in sweet, low tones, "The Lord bless you, my son, an' the Lord bless my daughter."

Dikar had climbed to the topmost branch of the tallest tree in the forest, and Marilee had climbed there with him. For a long time, clasped in each other's arms, they had gazed out on the green land that stretched, fold on fold, to the sky, while Dikar told Marilee of his dream that was not a dream, and of the terrible things he had seen down there.

"Some day, Marilee," Dikar ended. "I shall lead the Bunch down there. I have to, because down there is the America of which the man spoke, an' this is the Tomorrow he talked about, an' we are the children of yesterday who will reconquer those green and pleasant fields for democracy, and liberty, and freedom."

And all at once there was a light shining on the land down there, a great and golden light that cast no shadows.

CHILDREN OF TOMORROW

CHAPTER 1

NIGHT WINGS

"DIKAR," MARILEE said, low-voiced. "Of all the day between sunrise and sunrise, I am most happy in this quiet hour just before bedtime." Lying on the grass beside him, the warmth of her love enfolded Dikar like the warmth of the fire behind them and the scent of her in his nostrils was sweet and clean as the breath of the woods that enclosed the wide, long clearing. "I am so happy that I'm afraid," Marilee went on. "Something out there in the night hates to see me so happy."

Dikar's great paw tightened on the slim, small hand of his mate, but he said nothing. "I'm afraid," Marilee's gray eyes widened, "that someday it will take you away from me, and leave me all empty."

Dikar's high forehead was deeply lined with thought, his lips pressed tightly together within his blond, silken beard. From the logs on the Fire Stone the crackling flames leaped high, reaching always for the leafy canopy a giant oak held above them, never quite touching it. The ruddy light of the flames filled the clearing, from the long Boys' House on one side to the Girls' House on the other, from the Fire Stone at this end to the table and benches under the pole-upheld roof of the eating place at the other. The light played on the brown, strong limbs of the Boys of the Bunch, on the slender bodies of the Girls, as they walked slowly or lay, like Dikar and Marilee, in pairs on the grass, murmuring.

54

Over the clearing the purple-black Mountain hung, and the forest enclosed the clearing with night. The forest was silent with its own queer silence that is made up of countless little noises; the piping of insects, the chirp of nesting birds, the scurry of small beasts in the brush, the babble of streamlets hurrying to leap over the edge of the Drop.

Dikar thought of the Drop, of how its high wall of riven rock completely circled the Mountain, so barren of foothold that no living thing could hope to scale it unaided. He thought of the tumbled stones below the Drop, stones big as the Boys' House and bigger, and of how the water of the streamlets foamed white and angry between the stones, and of how beneath stones and water slept the Old Ones who brought the Bunch to the Mountain in the Long-Ago Time of Fear that none of the Bunch remembered clearly, most not at all.

"Dikar!" As Marilee's head rolled to him, a gap formed in the rippling mantle of her soft, brown hair and a round, naked shoulder peeped through. "You won't let it take you away from me, will you? Will you, Dikar?"

Beyond the tumbled stones, as far as Dikar could see from the topmost bough of the tallest tree on top of the Mountain, stretched the far land where they lived from whom the Old Ones had hidden the Bunch on this Mountain.

"Why don't you answer me, Dikar?" There was sharpness in Marilee's voice. "Don't you hear me? Dikar! What are you thinking about?"

Dikar smiled slowly, his blue eyes finding Marilee. "I am boss of the Bunch, Marilee," he rumbled. "And I've a lot to think about. You know that."

"Yes," she whispered. "I know. But sometimes you could think about me."

"I do. Always." Dikar loosed his hand from Marilee's and, sliding it under her supple waist, drew her close to his great body. "Whatever else I think about, I am always thinking about you too." The trouble within him was a little eased as he looked into her bright and lovely face. "Do I have to tell you that?"

"No," she murmured, nesting warm against him. "You don't have to tell me." She sighed with contentment. Her eyelids drooped drowsily, but Dikar's remained open as his gaze returned to the Boys and the Girls in the clearing.

TALL THE Boys had grown in the long years since the Old Ones brought them here, their cheeks and chins fuzzed, their flat muscles banding torsos naked save for small aprons of green twigs split and plaited. Slim the Girls had grown, slim as the white birches in the woods, and graceful as the fawns that bedded in the forest.

Their loose hair fell rippling and silken to their ankles but as they moved Dikar glimpsed lean flanks, firm thighs brushed by short skirts woven from reeds, ever-deepening breasts hidden by circlets woven of leaves for the unmated, of gay flowers for each who had taken a Boy as mate.

Near the middle of the clearing three or four of the younger

And all around them lay the ruin
that could destroy the unwary....

Boys knelt, playing with small, round stones the game called aggies. They were beardless as yet, their faces rashed with small pimples, and as they argued about the game their voices were now deep as Dikar's own, now broke into thin squeals.

Abruptly their chatter hushed, and then one of them was on his feet, was running towards where Dikar lay. He was Jimlane, thin-faced, puny, but keenest-eared of all the Bunch.

Dikar put Marilee out of his arms and was rising when Jimlane got to him. "I hear one, Dikar!" the kid gasped. "It's far away, but I hear it."

"Shut up, everybody!" the boss called aloud. "Listen."

There was no sound in the clearing, save for the crackle of the fire. For a long time Dikar heard no sound except the crackle of the flames behind him, the tiny noises from the woods. And then there was another sound, so faint that he was not quite certain he heard it. In the star-prickled sky, it was a buzz like the buzz of a bee although no bee flies at night.

"There!" Jimlane pointed. Where he pointed a star moved, a sparkle of light like a star. "See it?"

"I see it," Dikar said, quietly. Then, more loudly but just as calmly. "Out the fire, Bunch. Quick."

They came running toward him, the Boys and the Girls, and

past him into the edge of the woods and then out again, and now each had in his hands a birch bark bucket of earth. Marilee snatched a burning stick from the fire and darted with it into the woods, and the others threw earth on the fire, till the flames flickered and were gone, and the clearing was dark as the forest.

Dikar stared into the sky.

The buzzing was louder now, and nearer. The dot of light came nearer and nearer, moving among the stars, and about it the stars blotted out, and shone again behind it, and now Dikar could make out a black shape in the sky.

"In the houses, Bunch," he ordered, and he heard swift movement in the darkness, the padding of many feet. He was alone, standing under the canopy of the great oak, with the hot smell of burned wood in his nostrils and of baking earth.

The noise in the sky was no longer a buzz but a great roaring and the black shape was very distinct now; its spread wings, its long body, the yellow light at its very tip. Like a bird, it was, but larger than any bird. Its wings lay flat and without motion, like a soaring bird's, but no bird soared so long without wing flap, no bird soared so straight. It was a plane and there were men in it, and it was flying straight toward the Mountain. At the height it flew, it would just clear the tall tree that stood on the tip of the Mountain.

The roar of the plane beat at Dikar. The plane was almost overhead now and Dikar was afraid.

Dikar was afraid as he was in the dream that so often came to him in his sleep, dream of the dark Time of Fear when he was a very little boy called Dick Carr, and the sky over the city would fill with screaming of sirens, and he would run hand in hand with his mother to crouch in the subway, the ground heaving and rolling under their feet. A dream it was, but also a memory so vague Dikar could not be sure which was memory, which dream. But this was no dream, this rattling thunder that clubbed at him out of the sky.

"It will go by," he said to himself. "They always go by."

EVERY ONCE in awhile a plane would fly over the Mountain. At the first sound of it the Bunch would hide—if at night, first outing the fire. The Bunch knew, not quite knowing how, what the planes were, but they were not afraid of the planes. They hid from them because it was one of the musts the Old Ones had left, and the musts of the Old Ones must be obeyed.

No more than the rest of the Bunch Dikar had been afraid of the planes until the day not long ago when he had gone down into the far land from which they came.

Dikar had gone far and wide that day, a shadow flitting through the fields and the woods, a silent shadow none saw; but who had seen white men and women huddled within fences of thorn-covered wire, had seen them beaten by yellow men till the blood ran. He had seen a thing, dried and gray, swing from a tall pole at the end of a rope, and the rags that fluttered about the thing had told him it once had been a man. He had seen white men and women working, thin and sunken-eyed and so weak they could hardly stand; when they fell, had seen them lashed to work again by men dressed in green, black men with yellow faces.

Dikar had seen many terrible things that day, and he had learned how terrible they were who ruled the far land that had seemed so pleasant from his perch on the Mountain's tallest tree.

It was they who rode in the planes, and Dikar knew what it would mean to the Bunch if they found out the Bunch lived on the Mountain, and this was why Dikar was afraid when there was a roar in the sky and a plane flew overhead. But this plane was now hidden from Dikar by the oak's canopy, and the roar in the sky was lessening.

"It's gone by," he said to himself, "like they always—" The roar in the sky was loud again, the plane, lower now was again blotting out the stars—A white light blazed in the sky, a great white light like the sun! It floated down, making the woods green, filling the clearing with brightness!

Terror was ice in Dikar's veins.

This too was out of his dream, a white light floating down out of the sky, a noise like hundreds of sticks rattling along a hundred fences, screams and crashes, the screams of kids who were fleeing a destroyed city, the crashes of the trucks in which they fled. The truck in which was eight-year-old Dick Carr, in which were Mary Lee and the other kids who now were the Bunch, rocking to a halt on a tree-roofed side road. The two Old Ones stiff with terror on the front seat of the truck…

That white light floating down, showed only an empty clearing, weather-grayed houses about which there was no sign of life. The light was fading. The black plane was turning again to its course, was blotting the stars no longer, itself was blotted by the purple-dark Mountain. The roar in the sky became the buzz of a monstrous bee. Dikar wiped cold sweat from his forehead with the edge of his hand.

From the plane, held high by the tall forest and steep slope, they had seen nothing of life in the blaze of their white light and they had flown away. But why had they turned back? Why had they lit the clearing with their white light? Always before the planes had flown straight on, over the Mountain.

The bee-buzz in the sky faded to nothingness. The shrilling of insects in the woods began again. Dikar cupped hands about his mouth and called, "Come out. Come out wherever you are."

Forms began to come out of the doors of the houses. Dikar turned to face the woods. "Come out, Marilee," he called through his cupped hands. "M-a-a-arilee."

His shout rolled away into the purple-dark woods, seeking the cave where Marilee hid with the burning stick that must light the fire again, as was her job when a plane came in the night. "M-a-a-rilee." Behind Dikar the Bunch chattered, but no light from Marilee's flaming stick moved among the black tree trunks.

"Ma-a-rilee," Dikar called again, sending his shout into the whispering night of the woods. The woods sent his shout back to him. "Ma-arilee," hollow and mocking, and that was all the answer that came to his shout.

CHAPTER 2
TO FIGHT NO-FAIR

BREATH PULLED in between Dikar's teeth and he was lunging past the oak's enormous bole, plunging into the dark woods. Earth was cold and wet to the soles of his feet. Cold, wet-earth smell was in his nostrils and the green smell of the woods and the smell of mouldering leaves and of the pale things that overnight grew among the leaves. Faintly in his nostrils, too, was the sharp tang of smoke, and that could only be from the stick Marilee had carried off to the cave.

Even to Dikar's eyes, keen as they were, there was no light here, but he moved swiftly, never stumbling, avoiding tree trunks and bushes with the sure deftness of the small woods creatures, no more aware than they how he did so. The ground lifted under his feet, and then there was no longer ground under his feet but rock.

Dikar stopped, sensing walls about him, a roof above him, and so knowing he was in the cave he sought. "Marilee," he called into the sightless blackness. "Marilee. Where are you?"

No answer came. But in his nostrils the smoke-tang he'd followed was sharp, so Dikar knew that Marilee had been here. In his nostrils was the warm, sweet smell of his mate, so that Dikar knew she was still here, somewhere in this blackness-filled cave.

He started moving again, slowly, groping with his feet in the dark. And his feet found her, found her form outstretched on the cave's rocky floor, unmoving even when his feet thudded against her.

"Marilee!" Dikar choked and went to his knees beside Marilee, gathered her into his arms.

She stirred in his arms! "Dikar." Breath gusted from Dikar's great chest at that uncertain murmur, breath he did not know till now had been caught in his chest, "Oh, Dikar."

"What happened to you, Marilee? What—?"

"I—Someone sprang on me from behind, just as I reached the cave and hit me! Dikar! The fire stick! Where—?"

"Not here. Or if here, gone out. No. Not here. Even if gone out its smell would be stronger—"

"The fire, Dikar!" Sudden terror in Marilee's voice, of life without fire, of food without fire to cook, of winter without fire to warm. She was out of his arms and on her feet. "I've lost the fire, Dikar."

Dikar whirled out of the cave, was running through the woods, Marilee at his side. They burst out of the woods into the clearing and Dikar was shouting, "Get the dirt off the fire logs, everybody. Quick."

Dikar went on without stopping, darting to the door of the Boys' House, into it. He lifted an axe from its pegs on the wall, was out in the open again, was running toward where the Bunch were scooping earth off the piled logs on the Fire Stone.

He shoved through the Boys and Girls, made out, by the dim light of the stars, a log they had uncovered, black, lifeless. His axe swept up, smashed down.

Chunk!

The log split open. Red sparks flew, stinging Dikar's legs. He did not feel them. He was staring at the redness from which they had flown, the glowing red heart of the log that still had life in it, the life of the fire, the life of the Bunch. "Dry leaves," he commanded. "Bring dry leaves. Quick! Bring dry twigs. Billthomas! Halcross! Build up the fire. Fredalton! Take this axe and split up one of those logs into little sticks."

DIKAR WATCHED Billthomas put dry leaves on the glowing redness, watched the leaves take flame from the log's heart. Watched Halcross feed little dry twigs to the leaves and the twigs catch flame from the leaves, and the sticks from the twigs.

The fire grew again on the Fire Stone, and the light of the fire grew again in the clearing, but Dikar's forehead was deep-lined and his eyes were no longer blue, and in the darkness of them was a red light that did not come from the fire.

Dikar's eyes moved over the red-lit faces of the Bunch that stood about the Fire Stone watching the fire grow again; and his eyes seemed to ask a question of each face and pass on. They came to one face, and stayed on it, Dikar's brow-lines deepening.

That face was chunk-jawed, black-stubbled, the eyes too small, too closely set, but what held Dikar's gaze was the odd, leering grin that sat on the thick lips.

Tomball had had little to grin about since the day Dikar had returned from the far land and ended Tomball's short time as Boss, forcing him to confess to the Bunch how he had tricked his way to being Boss in place of Dikar. Why, then, was he grinning now?

"Do you think it was *he* who hit me?" Marilee whispered in Dikar's ear, "and ran away with the fire stick?"

"Who else of the Bunch would do a thing like that?"

"But why should he, Dikar? He's smart enough to know that if we lost the fire it would be as bad for him as for the rest of us."

"That's what I don't—Wait! I've got a hunch. Look. Walk along with me like we were just talking about nothing important. Laugh a little, you know, and hold on to my arm."

Marilee's fingers were cold on Dikar's arm, but her laugh rippled like a little stream running over pebbles in its bed. They walked slowly away from the fire reached the shadowy edge of the woods, were closed around by the forest darkness.

"Now!" Dikar said, and he was flitting through the forest night, Marilee a silent shadow behind him. It was like her to stay close behind, like her to ask no questions as he ran through the woods to the cave again.

At the cave-mouth Dikar stopped a moment, sniffing the

air. "Yes," he said, more to himself than to Marilee. "I can still smell the smoke of the fire-stick. The wet night air holds smells a long time." Then he was moving again, following the sharp tang of smoke in the air, following it away from the cave and away from the clearing.

The scent-trail led him downhill. Soon the laugh of a stream-let came to his ears and then Dikar pushed through tangling bushes and came out into starlight on the edge of the brook that he heard. The smoke smell was very strong here—

"Look, Marilee!" Dikar pointed to a black something at his feet, half in, half out of the water. "Here is your fire stick." He squatted to it.

"He brought it here to put it in the water," Marilee said, squatting beside him.

" 'No," Dikar answered, his voice a growl deep in his chest. "No. He slipped on a wet stone and fell, and the water outed it. See. Here are the marks of his knees on the bank. But he brought it here because this was the nearest open place in the woods, the nearest place where its light could be seen from the sky."

"From the sky? Dikar! What do you mean?"

"I mean that I know now why the plane turned back." Even in the dimness Marilee could see that Dikar's face was hard and still, his lips tight and gray. "If he hadn't slipped and dropped the stick in the water, so that they were not sure they'd seen—" Dikar stood up. "Come," he said, grimly.

When they came again into the clearing, it was filled once more with the wavering light of the fire and everything was as it had been before Jimlane had heard the plane. Dikar paused beside the Fire Stone, stood there straddle-legged and glower-ing, a muscle twitching in his cheek.

Marilee laid finger tips on Dikar's arm. "There's Tomball," she whispered. "Talking to Bessalton down there near the eating place."

Dikar's gaze moved to where she had said. Bessalton was

Boss of the Girls and tallest of them, her cloak of hair black as deepest night, her legs long and slender, her hips wide. Tomball was heavy-built beside her, bulging arms hanging loose almost to his knees, great chest black-matted, his belly black with matted hair. Black-haired was Tomball, and squat. He was strongest of the Bunch, and there was shrewdness in him too, a shrewdness Dikar already had learned to fear.

The little muscle twitched in Dikar's cheek. "Marilee," he said, low-toned. "Find Jimlane and Billthomas, and tell them to come to me first chance they can without anyone seeing them."

She slipped away. Dikar watched her, slim and lovely, the fire's red light caressing her, and there was pain in his arms and his chest, sweet pain of the knowing that she was his.

Tomball too watched Marilee, small eyes following her, thick lips a little parted. Seeing this Dikar felt a tightness in his neck and across the back of his shoulders. His hands closed into fists. If he wasn't boss of the Bunch!

Dikar's hands opened and lifted, cupping around his mouth. "Ho Bunch!" he called through his cupped hands.

THE TALK in the clearing stopped, and the strollers turned to him. "Bedtime, Bunch," Dikar shouted. "A good sleep and happy dreams to you all."

"A good sleep to you, Dikar!" they cried to him, but Tomball did not cry Dikar a good sleep as he went toward the Boys' House with the others of the mateless Boys, while the mateless Girls went toward the Girls' House, and the mated pairs went hand in hand past the end of the eating place and into the dark woods behind. Dikar saw Marilee waiting for him by the eating place, but he did not go to her till Steveland and Halross, pimply-faced youngsters whose turn it was to stay awake the night and watch the fire, had taken their places on the smooth bench-rock near the Fire Stone.

"Be sure that one of you stays always awake," he told them.

"Be sure to listen always for the sound of a plane in the sky. If you hear one wake the Bunch right away to out the fire."

"Yes, Dikar," Steveland said, his blue eyes wide. "We get you. A good sleep, Dikar."

"A quiet night to you both," Dikar said and went to join Marilee and go with her to the little house in the woods behind the eating place that, when they took each other for mates, he had built from logs to be theirs and theirs alone.

"Dikar," Marilee said, her eyes puzzled in the ruddy dusk that sifted through to her from the fire. "Why didn't you tell the Bunch about Tomball's hitting me and taking the fire stick to where the plane could see it? Why didn't you punish him for it?"

"Would it be fair, Marilee, to say to the Bunch that it was Tomball, when we do not know that it was? Would it be fair to punish him for doing it, when we do not know that he did it?"

"But we *do* know!"

"No, Marilee. We do not. You saw nothing and I saw nothing that would make us sure it was him. Or did you see something—something you have not told me?"

She stopped, Dikar stopped, looking at her face on which the dim red light fell leaving the rest of her in shadow, thinking how lovely her face was, the red light tangled in the cloudy softness of her hair, her gray eyes grave and thoughtful, her small mouth puckered.

"No-o," Marilee breathed at last. "No, I saw nothing that would make me sure it was Tomball. But I am sure, and you are sure, because we know that Tomball is the only one of the Bunch who would do a thing like that. Look, Dikar. Tomball wants to be Boss, and if he cannot be Boss of the Bunch he would destroy the Bunch, and he would stop at nothing to do it. You know all that as well as I do."

Sadness came into Dikar's face, and trouble in his eyes. "Yes, Marilee, I know that as well as you do. Tomball has always wanted to be Boss, and when he couldn't get to be Boss by fighting fair he fought no fair, and now that he knows he can't get to be Boss by fighting either fair or no fair, he would destroy the Bunch rather than have me or anyone but him be Boss. But it would not be right for me to fight him any other way than fair."

"Why, Dikar? If Tomball wants to destroy the Bunch, it seems to me it would be right for you to fight him any way you can, fair or no fair. Why isn't it?"

THE LINES were back in Dikar's forehead. Very clearly he knew the answer to what Marilee asked, but it was very hard to think of how to say it in words. "Look, Marilee," he cried. "When we were littler we played lots of games, and we always picked someone for umpire to see that everybody played according to the rules of the game, because if there were no rules there would be no game. Remember?"

"Yes, Dikar. I remember."

"Now sometimes the umpire himself would be no fair, letting one side break the rules. And then the other side would break the rules too, and pretty soon the game would bust up because with all the rules broken there was no game any more. Right?"

"Yes. But I don't see—"

His gesture stopped her.

"You will in a minute. Look. The life of the Bunch is no game, but it is lived according to rules, because if there were no rules, if every one of the Bunch did just as he or she wanted to, all the time, there would be no Bunch. Now, I don't think you or anybody else would say that if we hadn't lived all these years as a Bunch; sharing what we had, sharing the work, each doing what he can do best, all helping one another; any but the strongest of us would be alive and happy today. Would you?"

"No. We are all alive and happy after the long years here on the Mountain because we have helped each other."

"And played fair with each other. You call me Boss and obey me, but you really obey the rules the Old Ones left us and the rules the Bunch has made for themselves, and all I am is an umpire to see that everybody obeys the rules, to see that everybody plays fair. Now, suppose I played no fair myself. Suppose, whenever I felt like it, I broke the rules. What would happen?"

She answered slowly:

"Everybody else would break the rules too. I see. Because if the umpire is no fair, all the ones playing the game feel it's all right to be no fair too."

"Exactly. And pretty soon there would be no rules any more, and the Bunch would bust up. If Tomball is trying to destroy the Bunch, I've got to fight him. But if I fight him no fair, that will destroy the Bunch, sooner or later, much more surely than anything Tomball could do, or anything they who live in the far land can do. Now do you understand, Marilee?"

"I understand," Marilee said. And then she cried, "But you've got to do something, Dikar! You can't let him—" She stopped short, twisted to a noise in the brush behind her. "Dikar! There's somebody—!"

Dikar thrust her behind him. "Who's there?" he demanded, his neck thickening. "Who is it?"

Shadows moved in the shadows of the brush, where the red light from the fire could not reach.

CHAPTER 3

THE GUN ON THE ROOF

"WHO'S THERE?" Dikar cried again, and then the shadows were coming out into the light, and they were Jimlane and Billthomas.

"Marilee told us you wanted us," Jimlane said. "We waited till everyone was asleep in the Boys' House."

"Did anyone see you come here?"

"No. They were all asleep."

"All right," Dikar said. "Listen, Jimlane and Billthomas. I have a job for you, but I am not going to order you to do it. I'm going to ask you to."

"We'll do it, Dikar," Billthomas said. He was shorter than Jimlane, yellow-haired, blue-eyed, his skin as smooth as any of the Girls', his movements as graceful. "We'll do anything you ask us."

"Anything at all," Jimlane agreed.

"Wait, youngsters," Dikar warned, "You may not be so ready to promise that when you hear what it is. I hate asking you to do it, but it needs to be done, for the good of the Bunch. It won't be easy. You may be hurt doing it, you may even be killed. Nobody but Marilee and me will know that you're doing it."

Two pairs of bright eyes were fixed on his face. "If it's for the Bunch, we'll do it," Jimlane said. "Whatever it is. Tell us what you want us to do, Dikar."

"Before I tell you, you must promise, cross your hearts and hope to die, that you will say nothing about it to anyone. Whether you will do it or not, you will always keep silent."

"Cross my heart and hope to die," Billthomas said solemnly. "I will say nothing." Jimlane said the same and then the two spat over their left shoulders to show that they could never take back what they had said.

"Now listen," Dikar said when they had done that. "The job is to watch Tomball, by day and by night. You sleep in the Boys' House with him, and I'll always make sure to put you on the same jobs with him, so that part ought to be easy.

"If he slips off any time, day or night, by himself, I want you to follow him without his knowing it. Do you think you can do that?"

"We once followed a deer all day," Jimlane said, "All over the Mountain, and it never knew we was anywheres near."

"I know that," Dikar nodded. "And that's why I picked you to ask first to do this job. I also know you two are champeens of the Bunch at shooting with bonarrers, an' that's another part of the job."

The eyes of the youngsters widened, but they said nothing.

Dikar went on. "Keep your bonarrers near you all the time, and if Tomball does go off by himself, take 'em along. If you see him start to make a fire where it can be seen from the sky, or from the kind of woods that will make a smoke go up through the tops of the trees, shoot him in the legs, right away, and out the fire. If he starts to go out of the woods to the edge of the Drop, in the daytime when they who live in the far land might see him, shoot him in the legs and drag him back. Stop him if he does anything else that might show Them that someone lives here on the Mountain. Do you get me?"

"We get you, Dikar." Billthomas looked puzzled. "But all those things are Must-Nots of the Old Ones. Why do we need to shoot him to stop him from doing them? If he tries to, the Old Ones would wake from their sleep under the rocks at the bottom of the Drop and strike him down. He wouldn't dare to do 'em, and if he tried, the Old Ones wouldn't let him."

"LOOK, BILLTHOMAS." Dikar put his hand on the kid's shoulder. "Do you remember the time when the Bunch stoned me away from the clearing and made Tomball Boss?"

"And you came back with a little gun that made a noise and killed our fawn, and you made the Bunch listen to you while you proved why we shouldn't have stoned you away. And then you threw the gun up on the roof of the Boys' House and fought Tomball who should be Boss, and licked him. Sure I remember."

"Well, between the time I was stoned away and the time I came back, I went to the edge of the Drop, and I climbed down the Drop to the rocks under which the Old Ones sleep. That is the most terrible of all the Must-Nots of the Old Ones, but they didn't wake from their sleep, and they didn't strike me down. Nothing happened to me. I went into the far land, and I came back, and the Old Ones did nothing to me."

"You went into the far land," Jimlane repeated in awed tones. "Dikar! Did you see *them?*"

"I saw Them, Jimlane, an' I saw many things that made me know how very terrible it would be if they found out the Bunch lives on the Mountain. But the Old Ones did nothin' to stop me. The Old Ones sleep under the rocks, Jimlane, an' under the water that foams over the rocks, an' they cannot awaken to stop Tomball from lettin' Them who live in the far land know that the Bunch is here on the Mountain."

"But Dikar!" Billthomas broke out. "Tomball wouldn't do anythin' like that!"

"I hope not," Dikar answered slowly. "Honest Injun, I hope that he wouldn't. But I must be sure, an' I'm askin' you two to help me be sure— No wait," he said as he saw their mouths start to open. "Before you answer I want you to remember how strong Tomball is, an' how he said he would kill you, Jimlane, that time when you wanted to tell the Bunch why they were wrong in stonin' me away, an' how afraid of him you were, that time. I want you youngsters to think of that before you say that you will do this job."

"I've thought about it, Dikar." Jimlane stood very straight in the firelight. "I won't say I'm not afraid of Tomball, but afraid or not, I will watch him, an' I will do my best to stop him from doin' anythin' that will hurt the Bunch."

"Me too, Dikar," Billthomas said his voice clear and steady, his eyes steady as Dikar's own. "I am afraid of Tomball, but I will do this job the best I can."

"Good kids," Dikar said. Something had him by the throat, so that it was hard to say it, and he could not answer when the Boys wished him and Marilee a good sleep and slipped away, their naked young bodies ruddy one moment in the firelight, then merged with the noiseless dark.

"Oh Dikar," Marilee's soft voice said in his ear. "They're so young. Are you right in what you are doin'?"

"I don't know," Dikar sighed. "I don't know, Marilee." And

then he said, "It is a hard job to be Boss of the Bunch. A dreadful hard job."

HER HAND reached up to his cheek, her cool fingers touched it, lightly, "A hard job, Dikar," she said softly. "But it is night, an' just past these bushes is our little house, an' there you are not Boss of the Bunch but my mate..."

He drew her close to him, her softness close against the hardness of his body. He looked into her eyes, and then his head sank and his lips found hers.

A little later they knelt by their bed of pine boughs covered with a white blanket of rabbit fur. "Now I lay me down to sleep," they said together. "An', should I die before I wake..."

What was it like to die, Dikar wondered. He had seen death, of course, a deer killed by his arrow, a squirrel stiff and glazed-eyed under last year's leaves. What was it like to lie stiff like that, never seeing again the flaming colors of the sunrise, the shimmer of sunlight on water, never feeling again the coolness of the wind on one's skin, the warm touch of the rain? "God bless the Bunch," he said, along with Marilee. "God bless Marilee..."

Marilee rose but Dikar stayed on his knees. He heard the piping of the insects outside the little house, the peep of the nesting birds, the whisper of the trees. They were trying to tell him something, but he could not quite make out what it was.

"Poor Dikar," Marilee said. "You're so tired you've fallen asleep on your knees."

"No," Dikar said, rising, nor could he sleep, even with Marilee in his arms, their cover of rabbit-fur warm over him. Something was troubling him. Something that he must do, and he could not think what it was.

He lay wide-eyed, watching the open door of the little house grow pale with the light of the moon that was rising over the Mountain, watching the leaf shadows dance in the pale moonlight. With the moon a wind rose in the forest and the rustle of the treetops was louder, and bough-tips tapped on the roof—

The roof! That was it! Billthomas had spoken of the little gun Dikar had taken from one of them down in the far land, a black faced one, and had thrown up on the roof of the Boys' House and forgotten. Dikar had seen what that small thing could do, and Tomball had seen what it could do. Dikar must get it. Now. Tonight. Get it and hide it…

Marilee stirred in her sleep as Dikar slowly took his arms from about her. She muttered something, but she did not awaken. Dikar stole, more silent than the shadows, through the woods, reached a tree whose boughs overhung the Boys' House, swung himself up into those boughs and from them to the roof of Boys' House.

The moonlight was bright on that roof, every crack in its gray boards, every mark of them, distinct. There were faded, dried leaves on it, broken twigs…

But no gun.

CHAPTER 4

THE SOUND OF GUNFIRE

THE SUN struck brightness through Dikar's eyelids and though the night had held very little sleep for him, he was instantly awake. He flung out his arm to waken Marilee—found only the fur of the bed-covering!

He rolled over. She wasn't there beside him. She wasn't anywhere in the little house. Dikar was on his feet, his eyes wide, his heart bumping his ribs. The door of the house darkened and Marilee stood there.

"Marilee!" Dikar exclaimed. "I thought—What's the matter?" She had hold of the doorpost, as if to hold herself up by it. There was green under the bronze of her skin and her forehead was wet with sweat. "Marilee!" Dikar made the single long stride that took him to her. "What's wrong with you?"

"Wrong?" Her eyes refused to meet his. "Nothin', Dikar." She laughed, but it was not the merry tinkle that her laugh always was. "Listen, sleepyhead. The Boys are already on their way to the bathing pool." Gay shouts, the threshing of many bodies through the brush, came to him. "Go quick, or they'll be through before you have rubbed the sand from your eyes."

"Marilee." Dikar's hand was on her shoulder. "What—?" She jerked free of his hold, faced him, her lips tight and white.

"Go, you fool!" she yelled at him and thrust past him into the house, threw herself on the bed. "Let me alone."

Dikar stared at her, unbelieving. Never before had she yelled at him in anger, never before had her morning smile failed him. She lay face down, unmoving.

"Marilee," Dikar named her. "If I've done somethin' to make you angry at me, I ask your pardon, but what have I done?"

"Nothin'." He could hardly hear her. "You have done nothin'," she sobbed. "But please go, Dikar. Please leave me alone."

Dikar turned slowly away, heard his name called from outside. "Comin'," he answered red-bearded Johnstone, who called from the little house where he lived with Annjordan, "Last one in the bathing pool's a yellow belly."

They ran through the dew-sprinkled greenery, downhill to where a stream leaped from a ledge into a shining pool that foamed with the flashing limbs, the brown torsos of the Boys of the Bunch.

Dikar dived low into the icy water, swam to the opposite bank, stood up, shaking his head to clear his sight, the shining drops spattering about him. He saw Tomball, squat and shaggy under the foaming waterfall, saw Jimlane swimming nearby. Dikar dived again, swam under water to where the drooping, slender boughs of a willow dipped into the pool and made a screen behind which he came up unseen.

The Boys' House was empty when Dikar went into it by the door away from the clearing, He darted to Tomball's bed, lifted the coverings from it, pressed hands on grass-filled bag under them. There was no hard lump inside the bag. He looked under the cot—a darkening of the light straightened him, whipped him around.

Tomball stood spraddle-legged just inside the open door from the woods. His hands were stretching a bow taut, and laid across the bow was a stone-pointed hunting arrow that could kill a deer—or a Boy.

"Got you," Tomball grunted, his eyes, small and red, hating Dikar. "This is Fredalton's bonarrer. Nobody saw me leave the bathing pool just like nobody except me saw you, an' I'll be back there before they find you." The head of the arrow was pulled back to the curve of the bow's wood. Dikar's muscles tightened to dodge the arrow, but he knew he could not hope—

Whang!

TOMBALL'S ARROW was broken in two parts, was clattering to the floor! Dikar threw himself headlong down the length of the Boys' House, tripped over the bow that Tomball had flung in his path. Thrust at the floor to get up and saw another arrow quivering in the wall toward the clearing, saw Tomball dive out of the door toward the woods, got to that door only in time to see Tomball vanish in the brush.

Dikar shook his head to clear it of its stunned surprise that he was still alive, that Tomball's arrow had broken at the exact moment it was loosed at him.

"Dikar!" Billthomas, slender brown body wet-shining, face gray-white, was suddenly there in front of him. "He didn't hurt you?" There was a bow in his one hand, the other reached out to Dikar. "He didn't—?"

"No, Billthomas," Dikar said, guessing now the meaning of that second arrow. "Thanks to you." His voice was steady enough, but inside him he was shaking, knowing suddenly how close he had been to death. "That was as fine a shot as ever was made on the Mountain."

Billthomas' blue eyes shone with the praise. "It was nothin', Dikar. The sun was on Tomball's bonarrer through the other door, makin' it a good mark, an' I was only ten paces away. Any of the Boys could have hit it."

"How did you come here, just in time?"

"Carlberger ducked Jimlane," Billthomas answered. "While he was under Tomball got to shore. I saw him from the other end of the pool an' I followed, I stopped to pick up my bonar-rer where I'd hidden it near by, like you told us to last night. That let Tomball get out of sight, but I tracked him. When I got to the edge of the woods he was already in here, was pullin' tight his bow. But why're we wastin' time? I'll call the Bunch to hunt him down—"

"No!" Dikar commanded. "No, Billthomas. I will not have the Bunch know that one of them has tried to kill another. For then there will be only two things left for the Bunch to do. Either they must stone him from the clearing; an' that will make certain of his hate for the Bunch, with no hope that he will ever change; or they must kill him, which is worse. That the Bunch shall kill one of themselves coldly and with thought before, is more dreadful than that Tomball should have tried to kill me, excited an' angry."

"But, Dikar—?"

"But nothin'! This is a thing I will take care of myself, in my own way, an' it will remain a secret between you an' me. You will not call the Bunch." Dikar said sharply, his eyes commanding. "You will call Jimlane only. The two of you must track Tomball an' keep him always in sight, but you will not let him know you are around unless he does one of the things I talked about last night, or unless he tries again to hurt one of the Bunch. If that should happen, stop him, but hurt him as little as you can help, an' tell me about it. Get me?"

"I get you, Dikar."

"Then call Jimlane, an' get busy."

"Yes, Dikar." Billthomas was gone into the woods and Dikar heard the trill of a lark from where Billthomas had vanished, three times, and from far off he heard the answering three trills of a lark, and he knew that Billthomas had called Jimlane, and that there would not be a moment from now on that Tomball would not be under the eyes of the two youngsters. But Dikar's forehead was furrowed and his heart heavy within him as he turned to pluck Billthomas' arrow from the wall and the pieces of Tomball's arrow from the floor, and went out into the woods to hide them.

IT WAS queer, he thought, how he had talked to Billthomas the way he did just now, without thinking about what he was going to say beforehand. It was as if someone else had talked with his voice, someone much wiser than he was.

It was queer, too, how he knew now that what he had said was the right thing to say. How he knew now, sure as that his name was Dikar, that what he was doing was the best thing for the Bunch.

And for Tomball too. After what had happened Tomball would stay away from the Bunch, afraid of what Dikar would do if he came back. The youngsters would be watching him, but Tomball wouldn't know that. He would think he was alone on the Mountain, and he would learn what it meant to be alone, as Dikar had, and he would learn what it meant to be one of the Bunch and have a place in its life.

After a while Dikar would send Tomball word by Jimlane or Billthomas that he need not be afraid to come back, and when he did come back he would be ready to take his place in the life of the Bunch, and he would give Dikar and the Bunch no more trouble.

That was what Dikar hoped would happen.

The Boys came back, shouting and happy, from their morning swim in their bathing pool, and the Girls came back to the clearing from their pool on the other side of the clearing, and they all ate breakfast at the long table of the eating place.

Marilee came to sit beside Dikar when breakfast was all on the table. Dikar looked sharply at her, but her color was all right now, her eyes bright again. She didn't say anything about what had happened in the morning, and Dikar didn't say anything about it, only too glad to forget about it and to let her forget.

It was Steveland who first said something about Tomball and Jimlane and Billthomas not being there. Across the table so that all could hear, Dikar told him that he had sent them on a special job on the other side of the Mountain, a job that might take them three or four days, and that they would not come back till it was finished.

Before anyone could ask what the job was, Dikar started telling what everybody was to do that day, although he usually didn't do that till after breakfast.

There was a lot to do, because it was time to start getting ready for the winter.

Dikar sent some of the Bunch to hunt for deer whose meat would be dried over the fire, and whose skins the Girls would make into clothing against the cold days to come. He sent some to pick berries that would be cooked with the sugar that they'd gotten from the maple trees in the spring, and others to search for honey in hollow bee-trees, and he set some to stopping up cracks in the walls of the houses with mud.

He himself took four of the older Boys, Johnstone and Danhall and Henfield and Bengreen, up near the top of the Mountain, to where some big trees had been blown down by a storm last year, to cut them up into logs for the fire now that they were dried out and would burn well and without smoke.

When they went to the Boys' House to get their axes, Danhall said that it would be a good idea for them to take their bonar-rers along too, in case they happened to see a deer or some squirrels, and Dikar agreed. They hung their quivers of arrows on low bushes, and rested their bows against the bushes, and set to work.

It was shady and cool where they worked, and the *kerchunk-kerchunk* of their axes was a pleasant sound.

Soon Dikar had almost forgotten what had happened last night and this morning, and the day seemed no different from all the other days on the Mountain. He liked the way the flying chips shone bright yellow against the dark green of the moss and the almost black brown of the ground, and he liked the way little spots of sunlight filtered through the leaves high overhead and danced on the ground. He liked the smell of new-cut wood in his nostrils, and the smell of damp earth and of last year's leaves, and the sweet smell of the breeze that was like the scent of Marilee's breath.

IT WAS grand to feel the swell of his muscles, their smooth swell in his arms and across his back, to feel the *chunk* of his axe into a great tree-trunk, to feel the wood break apart under his strength; grandest of all to feel the touch of the other sweaty shoulders against his own as together the five would yank and haul at a hewn log.

Marilee and Annjordan, Johnstone's mate, brought lunch up to the choppers—cooked rabbit meat and dandelion greens and blackberries big as the end of Dikar's thumb. Dikar and Marilee sat a little apart from the rest, eating their lunch, washing it down with icy water brought from a nearby stream in a cup of birch bark.

"Dikar," Marilee murmured. "I have often wondered about the Drop." Her finger touched a little blue flower that grew out of the moss by her knee, but she didn't quite seem to know she touched it. "It goes all around the Mountain, an' it's so high an' steep. We were very little, Dikar, when the Old Ones brought us here. How did they climb the Drop with us?"

"They didn't." Dikar recalled his dream, recalled the memory that gave form to his dream. "The Drop didn't go all around the Mountain then. A sort of narrow hill slanted up to the top of the Drop, left by men who had been cutting away rock from the Mountain, the same men who built the houses in the clearing an' left cots here, an' these axes an' all the other tools we use. A road ran on top of that narrow hill, an' the Old Ones brought us up that road."

"What became of the hill an' the road?"

"The Old Ones hid us on the Mountain from the terrible hordes who came out of the East an' across the continent from the West an' up from the South," (Dikar was repeating words a Voice had said in his dream). "But some of them came to the foot of the Mountain, so the Old Ones brought the narrow hill down, on them and on themselves," he told Marilee what his dream had helped him to remember. "That is why there is no road to the top of the Drop, an' why the Old Ones sleep under the rocks, down there below the Drop."

"I know you went down there once, Dikar, but you never told me how you got down there, nor how you got up again."

"I plaited a rope of vines, Marilee, as long as the Drop is high. One night I tied the rope's end to a tree an' let it down where a stream leaps out an' down, so that the rope hangs behind the white curtain of the stream an' cannot be seen from below. I climbed down the rope, an' by it I climbed up again the next night, havin' seen what they have made of the far land that looks so green an' pleasant from the top of our Mountain."

"You climbed down a rope of vines!" Marilee's hand went to the flowery circlet that covered her breast. "You might have been killed, Dikar!"

Dikar nodded. "Yes, I might have been killed, an' I didn't care much whether I was or not. I'd been stoned from the Bunch, remember, an' you had cried me no fair. Have some more of these berries, Marilee. They are swell."

"No. You have them." Marilee fed them to Dikar, placing them one by one between his lips. Then they were finished. Dikar lay back, and Marilee lay by his side, quiet and drowsy, and Dikar was dreamily content.

Marilee stirred. "Dikar. Does the rope still hang behind the stream where it leaps down?"

Dikar sat up, pounding his knee with his fist. "Jeeze! It does! I did not lift it when I came back to the Mountain, an' I've forgotten it since. I must do that. Tonight I must do it, as soon as it is dark enough that I cannot be seen from below when I go to the edge of the Drop. Do not let me forget."

"I sure will not," Marilee answered. And then, with that curiosity Dikar had noticed all the Girls had so much more than the Boys, she asked, "Just where is the rope?"

DIKAR LOOKED about him, thinking how he could tell her. He knew every inch of the Mountain as well as he knew the lines on his palm. "That's funny," he laughed suddenly. "That brook, there, is the very one at whose end the rope hangs. By following it down the Mountain you would get to it. But look," he went on, rising, "the sun no longer strikes straight down through the treetops, an' much as I hate to send you away, it is time for work again."

"Yes, Dikar," Marilee sighed, reaching a hand for him to take hold of and lift her by. "Time for work." As she came up she swung close to him, and her arms went around his neck and her lips pressed against his, and they were flame on Dikar's lips, burning flame in his veins. "Oh, Dikar," Marilee sobbed. "I hate not to be with you."

"It is only for a little while," Dikar murmured. "Only till night." He held her away from him, drinking her in with his eyes. "What are you goin' to do till night, Marilee?" he asked. "I like to know what you do, all the time, because that way I can think myself with you, an' am not so lonely for you when we are apart."

"That's sweet, Dikar," Marilee smiled, touching Dikar's cheek with her fingertips. "I shall be somewhere in the woods. Bessalton wants me to hunt for a certain kind of grass that is best for sewin' with. Think of me a lot, Dikar," she said, and Annjordan called her, and she was gone.

Dikar and the rest set to work again. Marilee's lips still burned on Dikar's, and the touch of Marilee's fingertips lingered on his cheek, and he would not wipe the sweat from his face lest he wipe that touch from it too.

The *kerchunk-kerchunk* of the axes ran loud and long through the woods, and the pile of cut logs grew slowly but steadily. The beams of sunlight striking down from the leafy roof of the forest slanted more and more, and the shadows lengthened. At last Dikar rested.

"Enough for today, fellows," he said. "Tomorrow we'll—" The words caught in his throat. He'd heard a sound from far down the Mountain, a sound that should not be in the woods.

The sound came again, very far off, but Dikar knew what it was. He'd heard it down in the far land, and once, only once, on the Mountain. That time he'd made the sound himself, shooting the little gun out of the great oak that canopied the Fire Stone.

CHAPTER 5
OVER THE DROP

"WITH ME, fellows," Dikar snapped, springing to the bush where hung his bow and arrows, snatching them up. "Quick." He was off through the woods, running down toward the bank of the stream because there it was clearest of bushes and trees. The other four ran after him.

Long the time seemed, endless, that Dikar ran thus through familiar woods suddenly grown strange and fearful. Dreadful the thoughts that Dikar thought as he ran. Who had shot off a gun on the Mountain? Had that plane, last night, seen something to tell those who rode it that someone lived here? Had they climbed the Mountain, the men dressed in green that he'd seen in the far land, the men with yellow faces and black who were so brutishly cruel?

Never had Dikar run so fast. The others could not keep up with him, so fast he ran, but still he saw nothing but the flicking shadows of the woods and the glinting sun on the stream beside which he ran. The stream was rushing faster now, was hurrying to throw itself over the Drop, just ahead—

Dikar dug heels to stop himself. Something in the water—Jimlane! Jimlane lay face down in the water, very still, and the water that swirled away from the still, small body was pink and dreadful. Jimlane lay in the water, but on the bank of the stream lay Billthomas, limp as an arrowed deer, his side red and terrible with blood.

Dikar dropped to his knees beside Billthomas, and inside him Dikar was cold, cold as ice. "My fault," he heard himself groan. "I set you to watch Tomball, an' Tomball had the gun hid in the woods, an' he got it an' shot you. My fault, Billthomas."

Dikar touched Billthomas, and Billthomas moved under Dikar's hand, Billthomas' eyes opened and stared up into Dikar's face, unseeing. Then they smiled. A faint smile touched Billthomas' gray lips and they moved, but Dikar could not hear what they said.

"What?" Dikar's voice was hoarse, strange to him. "What, Billthomas?" He bent, got his ear near Billthomas' lips.

"What are you tryin' to tell me?"

"Tomball—" the faint whisper came. "Went—over Drop—Took—Marilee—with him…" The whisper faded, Billthomas' eyes closed.

"What?" Dikar yelled. "What was that about Marilee? Billthomas! Did you say Marilee-?" But he saw that Billthomas did not hear him.

Shouts, exclamations, above him told Dikar the Boys had meanwhile come up. "Jumped over the Drop!" someone exclaimed. "They must be smashed on the rocks—"

"No," something shrieked inside Dikar's head. "Not Marilee!" and he was on his feet, was twisting toward the edge of the Drop.

The stream rushed away from Jimlane's still body, rushed down to the end of the woods. Not five paces away it leaped out—up from where it leaped slanted a thick rope of plaited vines to the great trunk of the last tree of all and it was wound round and round that trunk, tight-fastened.

Tomball and Marilee had not jumped over the Drop—!

Somehow Dikar was at the edge of the Drop, careless whether from below they saw him or not. Dikar was looking down, his eyes burning.

DOWN AND down fell the white spume of the stream, down and down fell the awful wall of the Drop, gray-shadowed. Far, far below, the stream smashed itself on a great, jagged rock and joined the waters that brawled white and angry among huge rocks that might have been tumbled there by some unimaginable giants at play.

For a wide space from the foot of the Drop the ground was covered by the great rocks, and that space was made somehow fearful by the shadow of the Mountain that lay on it, but beyond it the sun still lay on a green forest that stretched away to the far land.

Dikar's staring eyes found the edge of that forest, found two figures, small as the dolls the Girls used to make out of rags when first the Bunch came to the Mountain. *Two* figures clambered over the rocks, nearing the edge of the forest, and the one behind was chunky, black-haired, and the one ahead was brown with her mantle of brown hair!

Till now Dikar had clung to a hope that he had not understood Billthomas rightly, that Billthomas had been mistaken, but now that hope was ended. A terrible rage flared up in Dikar, a rage hotter than the heart of the fire on the Fire Stone. He snatched an arrow from the quiver hung on his shoulder, fitted it to his bow.

"This was why she asked me how I climbed down the Drop," ran searing through his mind. "She planned it this mornin' with Tomball. This mornin' she stole from our bed to seek Tomball an' warn him I'd set the kids to watch him, an' they planned then to kill the youngsters as soon as they'd found out how to flee from the Mountain, together."

He had Tomball on the angle of his arrowhead. The muscles

in his arms swelled, the bow grew taut. Careful, now. Careful. The distance was great. He must not miss.

He might miss Tomball and hit Marilee.

What matter? She was as much to blame as he.

Dikar couldn't! His fingers wouldn't open on the bowstring, wouldn't loose the arrow that might bury itself in the flesh of Marilee.

But he must! Not because they fled him. Not even because they had killed Billthomas, and Jimlane. Because even if they didn't want to, the men in green would make them tell where they'd come from, make them tell about the Bunch. That thought opened Dikar's fingers.

Whang!

Dikar's arrow flew straight and fast and true—far out over the rocks it veered, was no longer a live and deadly dart, was a dead stick tumbling aimlessly down, a plaything of the wind.

Another arrow lay ready across Dikar's bow, but he did not loose it. No use. They were too far—Marilee reached the woods, and Tomball. The woods swallowed them. They were making their way through those woods to Them—

Dikar turned to voices behind him, saw Danhall and Henfield, Johnstone and Bengreen, huddled just within the edge of the woods, pale-faced, mouths agape, eyes wide and dark. "Johnstone," Dikar snapped, banging his bow over his shoulder. "Take over as Boss. Take care of Billthomas an' Jimlane. I'm goin' down."

"You dare not," Danhill gasped. "Dikar, you dare not. The Old Ones will strike you—"

"Damn the Old Ones," Dikar snarled and was in the stream, had hands on the rope. He was lowering himself over the edge of the Drop. His legs caught around the vine-rope.

THE WATER battered Dikar. The water filled Dikar's mouth and his eyes and his nose, so that he could not see nor breathe nor hear anything but the roar of the waters. The water had a hundred clubs that pounded Dikar, bruised him. Suddenly the water was only a stinging cold spray on Dikar's naked skin, and he was swinging free between the wet-black face of the Drop and the roar of the stream as it fell, and he was climbing down the rope of plaited vines.

This was as it had been that other time Dikar had climbed down this rope of plaited vines, but that time it had been night and once he had gotten through that first rush of waters it had been black-dark. Bad enough it had been to climb down into dizzy dark, but now there was light, and Dikar could see how the Drop came down from nothingness above and went straight down to nothingness below.

He could look down, endlessly down the swinging frail thread of the rope, down to where the jagged points of rock waited for him if he fell, and the stream smashed itself on the rocks as Dikar would smash if he fell.

From the rocks, so far below, there reached up hands that Dikar could not see, and they pulled at him, pulled him down to the rocks, his climbing too slow for them. Dikar wanted to let go of the rope, wild the desire was in him to let go and fall, fast and faster, down to those gray painted rocks.

Dikar was sick, sick with the terror that he would let go and with the wanting to let go. Suddenly his arms and his legs were without strength to move. He clung to the rope, unmoving, knowing that in the next moment, the very next, he would no longer have even the strength to hang on. "Dikar!" His name came through the mists that swirled around him. "Go on, Dikar. Go on." Dikar looked up to the voice, and he saw that it came not from far above, as it ought, but from the rope itself, from Danhall, hanging on the rope not far above him.

Down through the seething waters at the top of the rope, Bengreen climbed, the water streaming from him! They were following Dikar down. Danhall and Bengreen were following him where he went, in spite of their fear of the Old Ones, in spite of their fear of what might await them down below the Mountain. He was their leader, and they followed him—

Strength was back in Dikar's legs and his arms and he was climbing down again, but he kept his eyes on the wall of the Drop and did not look down. And at last his feet found rock beneath him and Danhall was beside him, and Bengreen; and then Henfield dropped off the rope.

"We wouldn't let Johnstone come," Danhall said, squeezing water from his brown beard, "because you said he should be Boss. What do we do next, Dikar?"

Dikar looked across the waste of tumbled rock to where Tomball and Marilee had been swallowed by the woods. "We go after 'em an' bring 'em back," he said through tight lips, "or we don't go back ourselves. Come on."

THEY CLIMBED across the stony space, slipping and falling. When they reached the woods, that seemed no different from their own woods, it was easy at first to follow the trail of those they followed, by the small growth they had trodden down, by twigs bent with their passage. Marilee and Tomball had gone carelessly, not knowing they would be followed.

The shadow of the Mountain lengthened with the fast-dropping sun, and it grew dim about the four who hunted a Boy and a Girl. The green faded out of the bushes about them, the brown out of the tree trunks. All color grayed in the dimness, and suddenly there were no marks by which the four could tell which ways Marilee and Tomball had passed.

They cast around, their keen eyes searching each depression in the mossy floor of the woods, the way each tiny leaf hung on the brush, but they could find no sign of where Tomball and Marilee had gone, no sign that they'd ever been farther than where a twig pressed into the last mark of Tomball's foot.

The four Boys from the Mountain came together again, and huddled close, and they became aware that the graying air was chill against their skin, and the forest seemed strangely hushed about them.

"I don't like it here," Henfield said, and it seemed right that he spoke low-toned, as though someone were near to overhear what he said, someone or some thing no one could see. "There's somethin' wrong about these woods. They're too—too quiet." He was yellow-haired as Dikar, his chin fuzzed with what would soon be a beard like Dikar's. "The birds are still, an' the insects, an' I've not seen or heard a rabbit or a squirrel, or anythin' livin'."

"I don't get it." Bengreen was the shortest of the four, his face sharp, his eyes black and deep as a forest pool at night. "I don't get it at all. It's like—like Tomball an' Marilee got this far an' then—an' then *were not.*"

"The Old Ones!" Henfield's voice was thin and piercing, louder it would be a scream. "The Old Ones have taken 'em an' they'll take us. We're lost! Dikar, we're dead an' worse than dead!"

CHAPTER 6
DEATH IN THE WOODS

A CHILL struck deep into Dikar as he heard Henfield's cry. All his life, all his life that was real to him and not a dream of Long-Ago, Dikar had believed that anyone who broke a Must-Not of the Old Ones would meet with a punishment the more awful because none knew what it was. By climbing down the Drop Marilee and Tomball had broken the most fearful of those Must-Nots.

Dikar recalled that he was the first of the Bunch to have broken that Must-Not, and that he had not been punished. "The Old Ones sleep under the rocks," he snapped, angrily because of the tremble of fear that had not yet left him. "They're not in these woods an' there is nothin' else here that could have taken Tomball an' Marilee without leavin' a sign. Stop talkin' foolishness an' use your eyes, an' you will find some sign of what took 'em, or of which way they went."

"Maybe," Danhall grunted. "Maybe *you* can, Dikar, seein' you're so smart."

"Maybe I can," Dikar answered. "Wait here, an' I'll try." He turned from them, moved to a big tree near which they were standing, ran up into its top as swiftly and easily as any squirrel. Thick boughs made steps for Dikar's feet, leaves rustled against his face, stroked his body, and then his head came out through the roof of the tree into a sunlight strangely ruddy.

The top of the forest stretched away from Dikar, a strange, bright green in that light, and solid seeming. About as far from him as from the clearing to the edge of the Drop, the forest ended and past its end the ground rose in a hill that was neither green nor stone—gray like any other ground Dikar remembered ever seeing, but a pale yellow that seemed to be striped.

Up through this yellow ground a wide brown stripe curved to the top of the hill, where, sharp-lined against the darkening sky, was a house not as long as the Boys' House but higher, its roof curiously shaped. Midway up the front of the house another roof stuck out, and the outer edge of this was post-propped like the roof of the eating place.

Just above this smaller roof, a row of windows flashed red as though there was fire within, but no smoke rose from the house, so Dikar knew this could not be.

Dikar's eyes came back to the leafy canopy of the woods. A low exclamation guttered in his throat. All that green stretch swayed a little with the wind, but, quarter way between him and the edge of the forest a tree swayed *against* the wind, and then another, just beyond, did the same.

Dikar marked the direction in which the trees moved so strangely, and dropped down to the waiting Boys. "Found 'em!" he cried. "They've taken to the treetops. They're goin' that way." Dikar threw out his arm to show.

"Come on then," Bengreen cried.

"Not in such a hurry," Dikar checked him. "They don't know we follow 'em, an' they'll be goin' slow, not sure of what is ahead.

We can take time to think, an' we must, for remember Tomball has the gun an' can kill us, one by one, before we get near enough to him to bring him down with our arrows."

"What then, Dikar?"

Dikar told them the plan that had come into his head, and, as he had ordered, they spread out wide either side of the path Tomball and Marilee traveled, wide of each other because that way there was less chance of making noise to warn Tomball. Then they moved in the direction those they hunted moved, swift and soundless as when they hunted a deer downwind.

NOW THAT Dikar was alone he needed no longer to pretend to be unafraid. These woods were fear-filled, as Danhall had sensed, but not for the reason Danhall had named. The Old Ones did not prowl them, nor were there any other strange beings in them that could make a Boy vanish.

The dread that lay heavy here was the dread that lay over all this far land, of Them who were more cruel than any beast, of their fists and whips and guns and the fearful things they did to the people who once had lived peacefully in this land.

There was no longer an endless, rolling thunder in the sky, such as Dikar remembered from his dream of the Long-Ago, but in the sky was a dark, dark cloud, unseen but very real, that laid over all the land, over the forests and the fields and the cities, a night of the soul that had lasted long, too long.

Only on the Mountain had there been any light, this long time, any hope of a tomorrow. Dikar was thinking of his dream, as he ran naked and silent through the woods, was thinking of the Voice he had heard in his dream, the Voice that had spoken to the mothers who, with their very littlest children and the very oldest of the men, were the last ones left in the last city untaken by the hordes, the city there no longer had been any hope of saving from them.

"*This is the dusk of our day,*" the Voice had said, "*of the America we lived for, and die for. If there is to be any hope of a tomorrow, it must rest with these little children in an attempt to save whom you are about to sacrifice yourselves. If they perish, America shall have perished. If by some chance they survive, then, in some tomorrow we cannot foresee, America will live again and democracy, liberty, freedom, shall reconquer the green and pleasant fields that tonight lie devastated."*

The little children of whom that Voice had spoken, all of them who survived the flight from the city, had grown now to be the Bunch on the Mountain. And now, when almost they were ready for their task of bringing that tomorrow to these once green and pleasant fields, two of them swung through the treetops to betray them to their enemies, and destroy them.

It was of this that Dikar thought as he ran through the woods. Had Tomball been only his own enemy, only one who had taken his mate from him, if Marilee had been only the mate who was false to him, Dikar would have sent Danhall and Henfield and Bengreen back to the Mountain and pursued them alone. But it was the enemies of the Bunch he hunted, the enemies of an America, love for which, though he had never known it, was part of Dikar's blood, part of his breath, part of his soul.

And so Dikar came to the edge of the forest and fell to his hands and knees and crawled a little way out into the high, yellow grasses that striped with yellow the hill beyond the forest, and lay there waiting.

Somewhere in these grasses, Dikar knew, along the front of the woods, lay the three others, their eyes on the tops of the trees, on the green brush that met the grasses, arrows fitted to their bows, as his was. For this was his plan.

When Tomball and Marilee came to the edge of the woods, and came out into the open, the nearest Boy would shoot them down at once, before they were seen, before Tomball had a chance to use his gun. That they would come into the open, Dikar did not question. Had not Tomball tried, last night, to show the flame of the fire stick to the plane? Tomball was not afraid of Them. Tomball had come down to the far land to look for Them.

If only it did not get too dark to see Tomball, and Marilee, before they came out of the woods. The sun no longer lay on the grasses here. It just touched the roof of the house, there on top of the hill, soon would leave that too.

THE SUN no longer lay on the grasses, here where Dikar hid, but the hot smell of the sun was in his nostrils, and the ground was still warm with it. The ground was warmer than the ground on the Mountain ever got, it was warm as the body of Marilee when Marilee lay against Dikar's body, and the scent of the grasses was like the scent of Marilee's breath.

A lump rose in Dikar's throat. He was waiting here for Marilee, waiting to send an arrow into her slim, brown body. As so many times he had waited hidden in the forest to kill a deer, he was waiting to kill Marilee.

In that very instant that her lips lay on his, burning, Marilee had been thinking how she would find Tomball, how she would tell him of the rope that hung over the edge of the Drop! With her arms about Dikar, she had planned how to help Tomball kill Jimlane and Billthomas!

If ever anyone deserved to be killed, it was Marilee!

The ache in Dikar's breast was not an ache but a terrible, tearing pain—his muscles tightened. His head lifted, his lips tight-pressed within his beard, his nostrils flaring, ears and eyes straining.

Dikar started to ease, tensed again. No, that rustle in the treetops was not made by the wind. It came nearer. Nearer. Something brown, moving, showed among the leaves. Vanished. An arm it had been, of this Dikar was sure, though he could not be sure whether it was Marilee's or Tomball's. They had come straight to him. He it was who must kill Tomball. Who must kill Marilee.

The pain within Dikar was as if someone had plunged an arrow into his vitals, was twisting it—

Dikar saw a form, crawling out on a thick bough. It was screened by the leaves at first, then Dikar saw black hair, a thick-lipped face. Tomball! Peering out of the tree with narrowed eyes. Dikar leaped erect, his bow taut—

Whang!

A feather quivered where Tomball's eye had been. Tomball, sprawling, black-shaggy, tumbled out of the tree, thudded into the brush beneath. A scream, a Girl's scream, came out of the tree and Dikar had another arrow laid across his bow, was tautening his bowstring once more. Shadowy in the treetop he could see Marilee. Marilee's voice came out from among the leaves. "Dikar!"

Marilee was out now, where Dikar could see her plain. Erect on the bough where Tomball had been, she held to an upper bough with one hand, stretched the other out to Dikar.

She was crying his name again. Her long hair was caught back among the leaves out of which she'd come, and Dikar could see her satin body, her lovely body he had held in his arms. His eyes fastened on the flowery circlet over Marilee's left breast. He would shoot her there—

"Dikar! What are you doing, Dikar? You're not going to—" Marilee's cry was checked by the arrow that was in her side, caught by its head in her flesh. She swayed, started to fall. Dikar's shot had gone wrong!

Dikar hadn't shot at all. *His* arrow was still across his tautened bow! Marilee fell! She caught the tree's lowermost bough with blind hands, hung from them, red streaking her side from where the arrow was caught in it. Someone else had shot her with that arrow. One of the other Boys. Marilee's left hand dropped from the bough by which she hung. The right hand let go and she fell—

INTO DIKAR'S arms, somehow he was under the tree in time to catch her. Her weight crashed him down into the brush, but he fell sitting, with Marilee in his arms.

"Dikar." Her lips were white, her nostrils flaring. "You killed Tomball." There was pain in her brown eyes, but they were shining. "I'm glad. He was awful. I saw him shoot Jimlane and

Billthomas, an' then he turned the gun on me—said he'd shoot me if I didn't go with him. He had the gun an' Jimlane's bonarrer, an' he'd found the rope long ago. First I was going to let him—kill me—but then I went with him, hoping to get a chance to take the gun away from him an' shoot him before— before—he told Them—"

Marilee's voice, strong at first, faded away. Her head rolled sidewise to Dikar's shoulder, lay there. She lay limp in Dikar's arms, as so often she'd lain asleep. But she wasn't asleep now. She was—

"Dikar!" Danhall was standing above them. "I was too far away to hear what she was saying." Dikar hadn't heard anyone come up, but Danhall and the other two were there. "I shot her. I couldn't hear what she was sayin' to you, thought you were holdin' your arrow because you couldn't get a clear aim at her. I could, so I shot her. Can you forgive me, Dikar? Can you—?"

"Forgive you, Danhall?" The words fell like stones from Dikar's lips. "You didn't know—Sure, I forgive you for killin' Marilee."

"Killin' her!" Bengreen exclaimed. "Bunk! She's not killed. Look at the way she's bleedin'. I've killed too many deer not to know bleedin' stops when one's dead. She's alive, you nuts, but she won't be alive long if you keep on sittin' there, holdin' her like a ninny an' lettin' her bleed."

"Not dead," Dikar whispered, staring down at the redness that welled out of Marilee's side and ran down over his thighs. "She's not—"

He could think again, could move again. He lifted Marilee across his arms, laid her gently down on a bed of soft moss near the foot of the tree out of which Danhall had shot her, knelt again.

"Find me some of those leaves that stop bleedin'," he threw over his shoulder. "Quick." He saw now that the arrow had gone deep in Marilee's side, but its point had hit bone and so it had not gone in far enough to kill her, not even far enough for its barbs to be held except by a little skin. Dikar pulled the arrow out, flung it away. Blood spurted and he put his hands down on the wound, pressed.

"*Lift han's up, you fella!*" a new voice ordered, hoarse and terrible. "Hurry befoh you get one big lot lead in you."

Dikar's hands were red with Marilee's blood, but the bleeding had stopped and if he lifted them it would start again. He turned his head to say so, saw a great long gun pointing from out in the light, saw the black hands that held the gun, and the man against whose shoulder the hands held the gun.

The man stood straddle-legged out in the yellow field. He was dressed in dark green, and the little round things that held the green together were yellow bright in the fading light. His black face was flat-nosed and shiny, animal like. His thick, purplish lips snarled like those of a wildcat, just before it pounces on its prey.

CHAPTER 7
REFUGE

THE BRUSH rustled, a little way from Dikar, where Bengreen and Danhall and Henfield had been looking for the leaves Dikar needed. "Come out you fella," the black man ordered. His big eyes, that had too much white in them, moved back and forth a little and his long gun moved back and forth. "Come out fom dere."

Dikar's heart bumped his ribs. Neither eyes nor gun were moving quite to where he was. The black man hadn't seen him! The black man was out there in the light but Dikar, bent down behind the tall brush that marked off the field and the woods, was in the deep shadow of the woods and so the man with the gun hadn't seen Dikar at all.

Arms above his head, Bengreen came out in the field, and Henfield and Danhall came out beside him. "Stop dere," the man said, and the look on his black face, gaping at them, was funny. "Wat kind fella you are?" the black gasped. "W'ere your clo'es?"

"What clothes?" Bengreen asked, grinning. "This ain't winter, is it?" Dikar looked down at his hands. They were red with Marilee's blood but she wasn't bleeding any more. If he took his hands away she would start bleeding again, and she would die.

"You one fella tink you smart, huh?" Dikar heard the black man's hoarse voice, but Dikar was remembering what he had seen men like him do to white women, that dreadful day when he had been in this far land before. Better for Marilee to die than that. "But Jubal smarter," he heard. "Jubal know you 'scape from one fella jail camp an' take all clo'es off so if you get killed nobody know wat guards you pay to let you 'scape. See? No use try fool Jubal. You tell Jubal were you come from, so Jubal get rewahd, an' Jubal make fings easier foh you."

Dikar took his hands away from the wound in Marilee's side. "A good sleep to you, Marilee," he whispered. "A good night. I'll be with you soon."

"W'ere you come from?" Jubal asked again, slow and hoarse, and there was something in his voice that made Dikar shiver. A gust of wind brought the smell of Jubal to Dikar, and that was worse than his voice.

Dikar pulled an arrow from his quiver, looked around for his bow. "If we told you,"—the grin was still in Bengreen's voice—"you would know as much as we do." Dikar remembered that his bow was out there in the field, dropped there when he jumped to catch Marilee. The arrow was no good without the bow.

"W'at you gonna know after Jubal blow you to little pieces wit' dis gun? Don't fink Jubal, no do it. T'ree more dead 'Merican make no diff'rence, Jubal kill plenty already."

"Go ahead. Blow us to pieces an' see if we care. I dare you, an' double—" Dikar didn't hear the rest of what Bengreen was saying because Dikar had slithered silent as a snake, behind the great trunk of the tree. And now he was erect, was leaping high to the tree's lowermost bough, was lying motionless along that bough while all about him was the rustle of leaves, loud and terrifying.

"W'at dat," he heard Jubal's shout. "W'at dat in de tree?" All of Dikar, inside him, pulled together, waiting for the thunder of Jubal's gun, waiting for Jubal's lead to tear through him, but he managed to make a sound through his rounded mouth, the *"hoooo-hooo"* of an owl.

"Nothin' but an owl, Jubal," Danball laughed. "Ain't you ashamed, bein' scared by an owl?"

DIKAR SLID along the bough, slowly, very slowly, very carefully, and now the tree's leaves made no more sound than as if the wind were blowing through them.

"Jubal no scared," the black's voice came up to him. "Jubal not scared of not'in', but you better be big fella scared of Jubal. You tell were you come from, befoh Jubal count five or Jubal shoot. One on end, with yella hair, first. All right. One—"

Dikar could see them now, through the leaves, the three Boys from the Mountain standing in a line, their arms over their beads, brown and naked except for their little aprons, Jubal, spraddle-legged, black and huge, his eyes small now, and red, his long gun butted against his green shoulder and pointing straight at Henfield.

"Two—"

The Boys were under the tip of the tree boughs, but Jubal was farther out in the field, seven paces at least. Dikar slid further out along the swaying bough.

"Three—"

Dikar was almost to the end of the bough, and it was bending with his weight. If Jubal looked up now, he would see Dikar, couldn't help but see him.

"Four—"

Dikar, gathering his legs under him, saw cords stand out on the back of the black hand whose finger was curled around the little thing on the gun that, pulled, would shoot it off. Jubal was going to say five now, and then—

"No," Henfield screamed. "Don't shoot. Don't shoot me. I'll tell. We're from—"

Dikar leaped, the whip of the bough added to the lash of his muscles sending him out, far out over the heads of the Boys. He hurtled down, straight down on top of Jubal, pounding the black down. Thunder deafened Dikar but his hand slashed down, the arrow clenched in it, lifted and slashed down again on the heaving, screaming thing beneath him, and warm wetness spurted over Dikar's hand and that which was beneath him heaved no longer.

Dikar was on his feet, and the Boys were around him, jabbering words he could not get. Dikar saw Henfield's face, eyes still wide, mouth still agape. Dikar's hand lashed out, slapped, open-palmed, across Henfield's cheek.

"You yellow-belly," Dikar heard himself say. "You lousy yellow-belly," and then he was striding, stiff-legged, back to Marilee, was once more kneeling beside her.

Marilee lay on the green moss, terribly still and terribly white except where the blood was scarlet on her side and browning at the edges. Browning! The blood flowed no more out of Marilee's wound. She'd stopped bleeding—

But Dikar saw the pale nostrils flutter, and he breathed again. Her wound, he saw, had closed of itself. That was why she'd stopped bleeding. The wound wasn't bad, Dikar saw now. Many of the Bunch had been hurt lots worse and none had died...

"Here's your bow, Dikar," Bengreen said, bending to him, "An' Jubal's gun." Dikar looked up.

"You keep the gun," he said, "an' take the Boys back to the Mountain. Go in the tops of the trees, that way you'll leave no trail. It will be night very soon now, an' you have a good chance to get back without their bein' able to follow you."

"To follow us!" Bengreen exclaimed. "What about you? What about Marilee?"

"Marilee can't be carried through the treetops," Dikar sat back on his haunches, "without openin' her wound, an' so she will surely bleed to death on the way. If we make somethin' on which to carry her along the ground, we will make so many signs that we would lead them straight to the Mountain. So Marilee must stay here. I will stay with her, but I promise you that if they come, they will not find either of us alive. Now go, Boys. The quicker you start, the better your chances. Go."

Bengreen shook his head. "No, Dikar. We do not go without you an' Marilee. But you are right about leavin' a trail to the Mountain if we carry her, so we must stay here with you. I must stay. I should say I have no right to speak for the others."

"You speak also for me, Bengreen," Danhall said. "I do not go back to the Bunch without you an' Dikar and Marilee."

"*I* speak for myself." Henfield stood straight in the forest shadows that had grown so dark that he, too, seemed a shadow. "Dikar! You slapped my face. You called me a yellow-belly. Did you have a gun pointin' at you? Did you bear a voice count, 'One, two, three, four,' very slow, an' know that when it counted 'five,' you would die?"

"No, Henfield."

"Then what right did you have to slap my face an' call me a yellow-belly?"

"I suppose I had no right, Henfield. I suppose I was no fair."

"You had no right, Dikar, but you *were* right to call me that. I was a yellow-belly, but I am not, an' never will be again. I looked death in the face, an' I did not die, an' I never again will be afraid to die. Dikar, will you let me stay with you an' Bengreen an' Danhall an' Marilee? Because I want to. I want to very much."

DIKAR LIFTED to his feet, put his arm around Henfield's shoulder, and smiled. "You are no yellow-belly," he said, very quietly. "But I will not let you stay, an' I will not let Bengreen or Danhall stay. The Bunch needs you three, an' you can do nothin' by stayin' here. I am still your Boss, Boys, an' I order you to go, an' it is for the good of the Bunch that I order you—" Dikar whirled to a rustle in the brush, saw that a formless shape blotched the fading yellow of the field beyond, saw that Bengreen and Danhall had their bows lifted, arrows across them.

"Don't shoot them things off at me," the shape said, its voice thin as a Girl's but higher-pitched and very tired sounding. "Not that I got much to live for, but I'm a friend, and I came to help you."

"Don't shoot, Boys," Dikar said, and moved nearer, peering. He made out that it was a woman who stood waiting for him, her dress gray and shapeless about her thin, bent frame, the skin of her face stretched tight over the bones beneath, her hands like birds' claws, her hair brown as Marilee's, but drab and lifeless. "You are white," he said. "You are not one of them." In one of her hands was something Dikar could not make out.

"No," the woman laughed, and the sound of her laugh sent a chill through Dikar. "No. I'm not one of them. My name's Martha Dawson and I was born in that house on the hill, and my father was born there, and his father before him. But who and what I am doesn't matter, and it's better for me not to know who you are. I can see that you must have escaped from one of their concentration camps, and I came down to warn you to get away quick, before the patrol comes along to change the guard here, and finds you."

"I can't go away," Dikar said. "My Marilee is hurt too bad to be taken away."

"Your who?" Martha Dawson looked in the direction Dikar had motioned. "Oh. The Girl who fell out of the tree. I heard her scream and I looked out of the window and saw you catch her." She was bending over Marilee. "She ishurt bad, isn't she? She must have been cut by a stone when she fell. Oh, the poor thing."

The woman went down on her knees, putting what she carried down on the ground. "So pretty too, and her hair's long. I never seen—Why, she has no clothes on, only this queer grass skirt. You all must have been hiding in the woods a long time. Yes, I can see that you were. You look too well fed to have been living on the scraps they give us. Your wife has lost an awful lot of blood. She is your wife, isn't she?"

"My—" Dikar checked himself. He'd remembered what "wife" meant. It was the same as mate. "Yes. She is my wife."

"I thought so when you called her 'my Marilee.' Well, don't you worry about her. I saw the way you fought the soldier and I thought one of you might be hurt, so I brought some stuff along. I'll just put a plaster on this cut to hold it together, and then you can carry her up to the house and I'll fix her up right."

"Carry her—!" The way Martha Dawson's hands were working at Marilee's side, Dikar knew that she could heal her, but—"But won't They find her there? Won't that get you into trouble with Them?"

"I've had trouble enough. A little more won't hurt. Besides, I don't think They'll find her, or you neither, unless they search a lot harder than they have already—Oh!" She rocked back on her heels, her eyes widening. "But they will. They'll find that soldier dead in the field and they'll know I couldn't have killed him but they'll be sure I know who did it."

"We can hide Jubal in the woods."

She shook her head.

"No. That won't do. They'll see the blood all around here, and they'll find him, never fear, them blacks is like Indians. Oh goodness. I don't know what to do."

"I do," Dikar exclaimed. "Look, Martha Dawson. One of us wanted to give us away to them an' we had to kill him." By the calm way the woman had acted when she saw how bad hurt Marilee was he knew he could tell her that without her getting excited. "We'll fix things so it will look like he shot Jubal with an arrow, an' that Jubal killed him with his gun before he died."

"Good!" The woman nodded. "That will do it. But you better carry your wife up the hill while your friends are fixing things.

We'll go up by the road, the way we come down, so as not to leave more tracks than can be helped."

DIKAR TOLD the others what to do and then he picked Marilee up in his arms, and went to the road, Martha Dawson beside him, went up the road toward where the house was a pale glimmer in the deep dusk that now had come down over the hill and the fields just as they reached the house, Dikar heard a shot, and he knew that Tomball had no face any longer, knew that Bengreen was laying the long gun back in Jubal's dead hands, and that Danhall and Henfield were wiping out as much as they could of the marks that would show there had been more there than just Jubal and Tomball.

Martha Dawson opened a door for Dikar, and he went into darkness that smelled a little like the eating place on the Mountain. The door closed behind him, and he felt a hand on his arm.

"Bring her upstairs," the woman said. "This way."

Dikar didn't know what she meant, but he went the way her hand guided him. His toes struck wood, and he half stumbled. "Come on," the woman said, tugging at his arm.

"But there's somethin' in the way here. I can't go any further."

"Something? Oh dear Lord! Don't you know what stairs are?"

"Stairs?"

"Wait. I'll strike a match." Dikar stood stock-still, listening to the sound of her going away from him. He didn't like this place. He was afraid of it. It was too closed in. He could hardly breathe. The woman was coming back, and there was a strange, scratching sound and then there was a little flame growing on the end of a tiny piece of wood in her hand, and her other hand was cupped over it, and she was looking at Dikar as if she'd never seen a Boy before.

"Don't know what stairs are," she said again. "Well, I never—! Look. There they are in front of you." Dikar looked and he saw a kind of hill built out of wood. "Hurry and take her up, before someone comes."

Dikar climbed up what Martha Dawson called stairs, and came to a level place, and they went along the level place, and came to more stairs that he climbed. At the top of these stairs they came into a big room whose roof was high in the middle but slanted down low towards the sides, so that there were hardly any walls at all except in one place where the wall was made higher to make space for a little window.

Dikar stood still, Marilee nestled in his arms, and looked around him. By the light of another match Martha Dawson held he saw that the room was full of tables and little benches, and boxes, and a lot of things Dikar had never seen before, all old-looking and dirty and piled every which way on top of one another, right up to the roof. So full was the room that Dikar couldn't see where he was to put Marilee.

"Wait," the woman said and went past Dikar to a box that stood on end in the middle of the pile's front, a black box almost as big as she was. She knocked on this in a funny way.

The box moved—not the box but the side that was all Dikar could see of it. The side swung out on one up-and-down edge, like a door, and inside the box was a tall man with a thin white face and gray hair. The man was stooped over, and his eyes, deep-sunk in his face, glittered in the matchlight like the eyes of animals glitter in the night-blackened woods.

The man saw Dikar. His lips pulled away from his teeth and his hand came up, and in his hand was a little gun that aimed right at Dikar.

CHAPTER 8
SEARCH

"IT'S ALL right, John," Martha Dawson said. "They're all right. They escaped from a concentration camp, and this young man's wife is bad hurt and I've promised to hide her here with you."

The man John peered past Martha Dawson, looking more closely at Dikar. "From a camp?" His voice was deep, much deeper than Dikar thought could come from so thin a chest, and it was a very tired voice. The woman moved so that the match light from inside her cupped hand fell on Dikar. "Aye, I see now. I could only see a black shape in the dark, and I thought that I had been betrayed, and that they had forced you to show them where I was."

"Never!" Martha Dawson cried out, and then. "Who would betray you, John? Who would tell them you are here?"

John looked at her, and Dikar saw that there were deep lines in his face, lines of pain, and that his lips were gray. "I've just had bad news, Martha. They raided zee-seven this morning, so suddenly there was no chance to blow it up, and they took Ed Stone alive. But we're keeping our friends standing. Bring her in here, my friend," he said to Dikar, moving back into his box. "Bring her in."

John's voice came out of blackness inside the box, but something in that voice told Dikar he need not be afraid of him, nor of anything in the blackness, and he went into the box carrying Marilee. Martha Dawson's match went out, and Dikar stopped short, the blackness thumbing his eyes.

Martha Dawson pushed against Dikar's back, and he got moving again, and the other side of the box wasn't there, as he'd expected, but he went right on into a feel of bigger space. He heard sound of door-closing behind him, felt a hand on his arm stopping him, and then there was light.

The light came from a shining thing that hung by a wire over Dikar's head, and Dikar saw that he'd gone right through the box into a room hidden behind the pile.

"Lay her there," John said, pointing to a bed that stood against one side of the room. "It's clean and comfortable, I assure you."

Dikar put Marilee down on the bed, and Martha Dawson was beside the bed. Her hand took hold of Marilee's wrist and she seemed to be listening for something, and then she smiled and said, "Her pulse is strong." She put her hand on Marilee's forehead, and said, "She has no fever at all."

Dikar didn't know what the words meant, but he knew that Martha Dawson meant that Marilee would be all right, and breath hissed from between his teeth. "Martha," John said. "You'd better go down and make some hot water to wash her with, and bring it up with the iodine and bandages. You ought to have light on down there anyway, or our sweet guardian might start wondering what you're up to."

Martha (the man called her that, Dikar noticed, instead of the longer Martha Dawson) looked queerly at John. "Our guardian won't notice anything," she said. "He's dead. This young man killed him."

"Ah," John nodded. "That means trouble, of course. Well, we can only hope and pray as we've done all along. Go on, my dear."

He moved, and there was darkness again. Dikar heard the boxdoor open and shut. The light came back, and Dikar was peering around the room, so much in it strange to him.

There was the bed on which Marilee lay and a little table in the middle of the room, and a little bench with a back. The wall of the room in which was the door was covered with things Dikar vaguely recalled were named "books." The roof slanted down to the wall opposite this, and this was low except for a narrow space where it was built higher to make space for a window, but the window was covered over with a gay-colored, thick rug so that Dikar couldn't see them.

BUT IT was at the fourth wall at which Dikar stared longest. A narrow table along the full width of this. Under the table were a lot of small black boxes, and on top of it was a jumble of wires and black boards standing up and lying down, and round things marked with little white lines, and a lot of shining things like what hung from the ceiling and made light in the room. In the middle of the wall above the table was something that Dikar recognized.

It was from a thing like it that the Voice in Dikar's dream

had come, the Voice that had spoken about the dusk that had come to America, and the tomorrow that might never be. Dikar remembered the name of this thing, and said it aloud.

"A radio," he said.

"Yes," John said. "And now you know that you're in one of the stations of the Secret Net." His hands went wide. "The oldest of them, my friend. Five years I've operated it from here, five long years since I escaped from a concentration camp and in all the five years I have not seen the sun. In those five years I have had from that loud speaker"—he pointed to the thing on the wall that Dikar had recognized—"news of the unearthing of hundreds of our stations, news of the death of hundreds of our co-workers. Time and time again that speaker has brought me word that we were almost ready to rise against the invaders, and time and time again it has brought me word that they had found our leaders and hung them, and that all the work was to be done over again.

"Yes," John said. "This is the oldest of the stations, now that at last Ed Stone's gone, and I am the luckiest of the agents of the Secret Net, but tonight, my friend, I somehow have a feeling that my luck has run out. Perhaps that is only because I am tired and hungry, for Martha dares not bring me food until dark. They do not, I know, suspect that I am here, but they know I am alive, somewhere, and always they keep a sentry, out there in the woods, watching my wife and waiting for me to contact her." He smiled, and his smile was bitter. "That is why they have permitted her so long to live on here, unmolested. But I must hear your story. I thought that the prison camps were now too well guarded for anyone to escape from them. How did you and your wife manage it? What camp do you come from?"

Dikar shook his head. "We come from no camp. I don't even know what you mean by that word, camp."

"You—you don't—! You're American, aren't you?"

"Yes," Dikar said. "We are American." He knew, without just knowing how, that he could talk to this man freely and that it was important that he talk to him. "We come from the Mountain, off there beyond those woods."

And then Dikar went on to tell John about the Bunch, and about how they came to live on the Mountain, and about their life there.

JOHN LISTENED without interrupting, except to ask a low-toned question or two, when Dikar stopped, and soon after Dikar started talking, Martha came in and listened too, while she tended Marilee. Dikar told about his dream, and how he had come down into this far land and seen what went on here, and how he had gone back to the Mountain.

"I knew then that somehow, sometime, I must lead the Bunch down off the Mountain and try to take back this land for America," he came near the end of his story. "But I could not think how we few could do anything against the black and yellow men when you who are so many could do nothin' against them. Perhaps you can tell me, John?"

"Perhaps I can," John said, his eyes shining. "I must think. But you did come down again to us, Dikar." (Dikar had told them his name.) "And without any plans. Why did you do that?"

Dikar told him about Tomball, and what Tomball had done, and how Tomball died.

"There you are," John turned to Martha. "There's the innate depravity of human nature for you. Here are these youngsters who were isolated from the world when the oldest of them was only eight, who grew up together in such an ideal communion as man has not known since Eden, and yet a renegade turns up among them who would sacrifice them all because his personal ambitions were thwarted. Doesn't that make you despair, my dear?"

"No!" Martha answered, her hands still busy with Marilee. "No, John. Because if Dikar's story has in it one black-souled renegade, it also has in it forty who have worked for one another and lived for one another, sweetly and unselfishly, from childhood to young man—and womanhood. Because it has in it courage and loyalty and self-sacrifice and love that was not taught out of books. Despair, John? No. Dikar's story gives me new hope, new courage."

John moved to Martha, where she knelt by Marilee's bedside, and laid his hand on her head. "I'm wrong, Martha. You are wiser than I. Far wiser—" Just then Marilee stirred, and her eyes opened.

"Dikar," she whispered. Then, fright in her voice: *"Dikar!"*

Dikar leaped to her. "It's all right, Marilee. Everything is all right. We've found fr—"

"Hush," John broke in. "Quiet. Listen." At once the room was throbbing with silence.

Into that silence, well-muffled, came the sound of men's voices, shouts. "The patrol's here," John said low-voiced. "They're looking for the sentry you killed. You'd better get downstairs quick, Martha. They might come to ask you about him."

Martha was on her feet, her face set, her hands trembling. John's arm went around her, and he was holding her close to him. He was saying something Dikar could not quite make out, and then they were apart and Martha was going toward the door, straight, trembling no longer. The light went out, and the door opened and closed.

"Let's take a look outside," Dikar heard John say, and he heard him moving in the darkness. Then there was pale light in the darkness, starlight breaking the blackness of a wall, John's hand blotching it as it held aside that which hung over the window.

Dikar darted across the floor and was pressed against John, looking out.

Just below was the smaller roof Dikar had seen from the woods, and below that, yellow light lay on the ground. Down at the bottom of the hill, bright lights danced in the yellow grass and on the brush and trees at the edge of the woods. Black against these lights were the forms of men, and it was from these men that the shouting came.

"Look," John whispered, "there in the wheat." Dikar saw the black shape of his finger pointing, and looked in the direction the finger pointed.

WHERE THE finger pointed, in the middle of the field, was one man who did not move. The arm held a light, and the light was on his face, and Dikar could see that the face was round and yellow. The mouth of that face was a straight, thin line and the eyes were slanted slits in the yellow skin, and there was a look on the face that made Dikar afraid.

"That's Captain Li Logo," John said. "He's provost for this district. He's shrewd as a fox and cruel as a tiger. It's hard luck that he had to come along with the patrol, on this night of all nights."

Dikar felt Marilee press against him from behind. "Go back to bed, sweet," he said. "You'll hurt yourself more."

"I'm all right, Dikar," Marilee whispered. "I feel fine. And I want to see too."

A louder shout came through the window. "They found the body," John said quietly but, pressed against him, Dikar could feel that now he was trembling.

The lights moved together, clustering at one place just at the edge of the woods. Captain Logo went down to where the lights clustered, and the babble of shouts from there stopped, and all Dikar could hear was a single high-pitched voice.

"I'll open the window," John said, "if you'll let me get at it." Dikar and Marilee moved back a little.

"Are you sure you're feelin' all right?" Dikar whispered under cover of a scraping noise in front of them.

"Sure. The woman gave me something to drink, before I quite woke up, and it's made me all warm inside, and strong again."

Cold wind came in on them, and the sounds from outside were louder, the sound of that single high-pitched voice, but Dikar could not understand what it said. Then there was another shout, hoarse like Jubal's, and a light showed within the edge of the woods, and Captain Logo went in there.

"They've found Tomball," Dikar said. "We'll soon know if we've fooled them."

Logo's high voice stopped the shouting again. The other shapes were separating. They were running back and forth in what John had called wheat, their lights shining on the yellow grass, and on their black faces. They were all dressed in green, like Jubal, and had queer round things on their heads, and they all had long guns like Jubal's.

"There are seven of them," Marilee said. "I counted."

One of the lights stopped, suddenly, and the one that carried it bent low, and straightened again, and as a shout came from him Dikar saw what the light shone on.

"Jeeze!" he grunted. "It's my bow. I forgot all about it. There was one by Tomball, so now they know there was at least one more of us."

CAPTAIN LOGO came to the black who had found Dikar's bow, and he looked at it, and then he put his hand to his mouth, and there was shrill sound from him. The blacks all came running to him, and clustered about him a minute, and then they were all running up the hill toward the house, their long guns in their hands, slanted across the front of them, their lights out.

"That's torn it," John said, low-toned. "They're coming to search the house, and they're certain to find this hideout. My premonition was right. My luck has run out. Well," he said, pushing back from the window. "There's only one thing left to do."

"What?" Dikar asked.

"To let them get inside," came the answer in John's tired voice, "and then push a button on this radio table, a button that will blow the house and everyone in it to pieces. If you kids are afraid to die, you can get out by this window and surrender, but I wouldn't advise it. No," he sighed. "I would not advise you to surrender to them."

"Wait," Dikar said. "Maybe—" He was still looking out and down. They had reached the house, and had stopped in front of it, and Li Logo was saying something to the black men he bossed, was waving his arms around. "Maybe something will happen to save us yet. Maybe they'll go away without searching the house."

"Not Logo," John answered. "Not when he's on the scent of something. But I'll wait as long as I dare."

Down below, the black men were separating. One moved a little away from the house and stood in the field, his gun in his two hands, looking watchfully around him. Two went one way, one another, and disappeared around the corners of the house.

"They're going to watch," Marilee whispered, "on all sides to see that nobody gets away."

An owl hooted, somewhere in the dark. The three blacks left went with Logo under the little roof that stuck out from the front of the house, and there was the sound of knocking from down there. The sound of knocking was in the room! Dikar whirled around.

"It's all right," John said. "I've just turned on the speaker system—something that lets me hear everything that happens downstairs—" He checked as another voice came into the room. It was Martha's voice.

"What shall I do, John?" she asked, very quietly.

"Let them in, dear, as we always planned," John answered her, just as quietly. "And—Martha. I'll meet you—on the Other Side."

"On the Other Side, John dear," Martha's voice came through the knocking.

There was the sound of footsteps going across the floor. There was a rattle, and the sound of knocking stopped, and Dikar heard a door open.

"Good evening, Missee Dawson," he heard Captain Logo's voice, very gentle, very smooth. "So sorry I must bother you, but I wish to come in with my men. You have no objections, of course."

"Of course I have objections, but they won't do me any good, will they?"

"Sorry, no. So very sorry." Feet trampled, many feet. Then, "Well, Missee Dawson. Where is he?"

" 'He'? I don't understand."

"You understand quite well. One of my men was murdered, down there in your field, some time today. He got one of the assassins, but there was another. That other is your husband, come home at last. I want him."

"Go ahead and look for him, if you think he's here. Search the house."

"I do not wish to bother. You will call him to surrender."

"I will not."

"I think you will, Missee Dawson," and then there was a scream in Dikar's ears, a scream loud and shrill and very dreadful. "So sorry," Captain Logo hissed. "So very sorry."

CHAPTER 9
TOMORROW WILL COME

DIKAR HEARD that from the sill of the window on which he was crouched. Marilee's hand was pulling John's hand away from the button on the radio table. "Shut the talkin' thing off." Dikar heard her whisper, as he'd told her to, and while she was telling John the rest of what Dikar had told her to, Dikar dropped to the little roof below. He crouched out there, looking down to where, quite suddenly, quite silently, the black who watched the front of the house had crumpled into the wheat.

"*Hooo—*" the hoot of an owl came from his lips, and "*Hoooo—*" came an answer from near the still, black heap in the wheat. What little sound Dikar made jumping from the roof to the ground was covered by Martha's screams inside the house. The yellow light from the house's windows glimmered on the naked brown skin of Henfield, lifting up out of the wheat to meet Dikar.

"There were four outside," Dikar whispered.

"We got 'em all," the answer came. "I took two an' Bengreen an' Danhall each took one." Two other shadowy forms rose out of the wheat beside them. "What next, Dikar?"

Dikar hooted twice, then whispered his plan. "Give me your bonarrer, Danhall," he finished. "I'm a better shot than you." He took them, turned to the open door of the house, where Martha's screams had stopped.

The door was wide and Dikar could see everybody in the room inside. One of the blacks had hold of Martha. The top part of her clothes were torn and a knife in Li Logo's hand was red-tipped, and now Martha's flesh was bleeding, but Martha and Logo and the blacks were looking at the stairs that came down out of the roof of the room, at the gray-haired man who stood halfway down the stairs, hands behind his back, tall and straight and proud.

One of the blacks held Martha and the other two pointed their long guns at John, but it was Logo who spoke to John, what he said coming clear and distinct to Dikar. "Ah, John Dawson," Captain Logo said in that soft, thin voice of his. "I thought your wife's screams would bring you out of your hole."

Once more Dikar hooted, and in the same instant he loosed the arrow, and the twang of his bow was joined by the twang of two other bows in his ears. Inside the house the three blacks crumpled to the floor, an arrow in each of their backs, and John's hand came out from behind his back and the little gun in it flashed fire, and Captain Li Logo was down on top of one of his blacks, but his head was lifted, his eyes looking hate at John.

"So sorry," John Dawson said. "So very sorry, Captain Li Logo," and his little gun flashed fire again, and Li Logo's head fell down, and he was as dead as the men he had bossed for the last time.

THE COOL, green-smelling dark of the woods closed around

the five from the Mountain, and around John Dawson and Martha. The Bunch would have wondered, could they have seen, what strange, heavy loads they were that the Boys and John carried, and they would have wondered at the light without fire that came to life in the hand of Marilee as she followed behind Martha and the men, smoothing out such signs of their passage through the woods as she could.

"Eight rifles, nine revolvers, and all the stuff necessary to rebuild my wireless," John chuckled. "Quite a beginning for what we'll need to bring *tomorrow* to America, as you put it. But you did a good job with your bows and arrows, you four."

The pallid, gaunt man seemed now to have found a new vitality; he walked with the step of a young man, and the memory of horror no longer lived in his eyes.

"We did only our best," Dikar muttered, looking back uneasily. "Martha said their blacks are good trackers. Is that right, John?"

Thunder blotted out the start of John Dawson's answer, a great clap of thunder from where they'd just come, and back there the sky was lit with red light. And then the sky was black again, and the thunder had ended, and John was chuckling.

"Yes. Dikar," he said. "Their blacks are good trackers, but I doubt very much that they will be tracking us. Now you know why I had you carry all the corpses into the house. It was already mined, as you know, and I set a time-fuse before we left, and all that anyone will ever find back there will be a big, charred hole in the ground and a mass of fragments too small to be identified. It isn't the first station of the Secret Net that has been blown up during a raid, and not the first in which everyone, prisoners and raiders, have perished. That is what they will think happened there, and they will not bother to look for Martha and me, nor will they ever know you and your friends were there."

"Ah," Dikar said, and felt eased. There was yet a long way to go to the Mountain, and there was still all these people and all these things to be gotten to the top of the Drop, and the load on his shoulders was heavy, but when he thought of what they would do with the load, of all the plans John and he would make, the load and his heart were light as the feathers of a bird.

THE SUN struck brightness through Dikar's eyelids and woke him, and though the night had held very little sleep, he was instantly awake. He flung out his arm to waken Marilee found nothingness—remembered that he had given his place in the bed in his little house to Martha Dawson, was back again, for this night, in the Boys' House.

Dikar leaped from his cot, and all around him the flashing brown bodies of the Boys of the Bunch leaped from theirs, and there were shouts of welcome to him, but Dikar ran out of the house and through the woods toward his little house, and Marilee. He went quietly when he neared the little house, and stood in the doorway peering in, and then his heart bumped his ribs as he saw that only Martha was inside on the bed.

"Where's Marilee?" Dikar demanded. "Where's my Marilee?"

Martha smiled at him. "Come in," she said. "Come in, son, I want to give you a little piece of advice."

Dikar went in, wondering, and squatted on the floor by the bed. Martha's fleshless hand reached out and took his, and she said, very softly, "Listen son. Don't bother your Marilee mornings. And be very gentle with her, very tender."

"I am," he said. "I try always to be."

"I know," Martha answered. "But try harder now. Don't mind it if she is irritable with you, and unreasonable, and angry over trifles."

"What do you mean?" Dikar cried. "What are you talkin' about?"

He had drawn taut now, staring at her and fear had come suddenly into his eyes.

"Go ask her," Martha said. "She is the one to tell you what I mean, though I had to tell her, myself, this morning. You children," she said, and there was a wetness in her eyes. "You precious infants. Go, Dikar, I hear her outside."

Dikar rose and he went out again, and Marilee was coming toward him out of the bushes, and her face was greenish as it had been the morning before, but her eyes were shining. "Dikar!" she cried, lifting her arms wide to him, and Dikar ran to her. "Oh, Dikar. I have something to tell you."

And then Dikar was holding Marilee close, close to him, and she was whispering something in his ears, and his heart leaped within him and in his veins his blood ran laughing and glad as the streams that laugh down the Mountain.

But after a while Dikar sobered, and his face was grave, his voice solemn. "Now indeed, Marilee," Dikar said, "I must work hard for the day when I shall lead the Bunch down from the Mountain to an America retaken for freedom and liberty. For you an' I, Marilee, were the children of a dark yesterday, but ours must be the child of a bright an' shinin' tomorrow."

BRIGHT FLAG
OF TOMORROW

CHAPTER 1
THE MEANING OF FEAR

THE SUN, an hour risen, flooded the Mountain with brightness. The morning wind whispered softly through the forest
that cloaked the mountain with a robe of living green. Within
the cool underbrush-shadows of the forest scuttered the small
woods creatures; the chipmunks, the rabbits, the field mice. The
forest walled the clearing with the dark brown pillars of its
boles, with the shining green of its foliage, and out of the clearing rose a unison of young voices.

"We pledge allegiance to our Flag..." the voices chanted in
unison.

Before the Fire Stone at one end of the clearing, Dikar stood,
straight and tall and proud. The sun dusted with gold his bronzed
limbs, his muscle-banded torso. It made golden his silken beard,
his shock of yellow hair. There was strength in his broadly
sculptured face, solemnity and thoughtfulness in his high brow
In his blue eyes was a light that did not come from the sun.

Braced against Dikar's taut belly was the lower end of a
straight, white pole that a week ago had been a birch sapling
in the woods. Dikar's great hands grasped the pole, holding it
slanting only slightly forward, the muscles swelled under the
smooth, brown skin of Dikar's arms. Above Dikar's shining
head the flag hung from the pole. The folds of the flag lifted a
little in the morning wind, settled down, and lifted again.

Red-striped the flag was, and white-striped, and in one corner
of the flag was a white-starred square of blue deep as the cloud-

less sky at dusk. The sun's light lay on the flag, but the brightness and the glory of the flag seemed to come from the stuff itself of which the girls had sewn it.

"And to the country for which it stands…"

High and clear and youthful, the voices of the bunch chanted the words Johndawson had taught them. Row on row the boys and the girls of the Bunch stood in the grass of the clearing, facing Dikar and the flag, their right arms upraised.

To the right of the Bunch was the long, low, weather-grayed wall of the Boys' House, to their left that of the Girls' House. Behind them was the post-propped roof of the Eating Place and beyond that the mountain lifted high and green and shining into the shining blue of the morning sky.

The Girls made the forward rows, their slim forms robed in the lustrous mantles of their hair. Rounded shoulders, sun-browned flanks, peeped through those black and blond and russet robes. Waists were clasped by thigh-length skirts plaited from reeds, deepening breasts were hidden by circlets woven from leaves for the unmated, of gayly-hued flowers for the wed.

Behind the Girls were the Boys, a few full-bearded like Dikar, some hairless as yet, their faces rashed with pimples, the faces of most fuzzed with the sparse beginnings of beards. All the boys were naked save for small aprons of twigs split and deftly intertwined, all were clean-limbed, narrow-hipped, their hollow bellies and deep chests plated with flat, lithe muscles.

In the eyes of boys and girls alike, was the same brightness that glowed in the wind-lifted stuff of the flag.

"One nation, indivisible...."

ONE NATION. On this shining morning it was a nation enslaved. From the circling base of the mountain, far and far to where the sky and ground met and unthinkably far beyond that meeting, yellow-faced men, black-faced men, were masters of the land for which the starry flag stood. Ravening, brutish hordes. They had come out of the East and out of the West and up from the South in a long-ago time of fear that Dikar recalled only dimly and most of the Bunch not at all. They had come with a rolling of thunder, and a death-hail that rained from sea and sky, and though the people that dwelt in the land had fought

Arrows sped downward as the naked boys plunged to the attack; and above it all rose the yellow men's cries of terror.

them, desperately, frantically, when their thunders rolled to silence and their death hail no longer shook the earth they had made themselves masters of the land, and of those of the people that still lived in the land.

"With liberty and justice for all."

No liberty was there in all the land, no justice. Only the whips and the guns of the green-clad men who were its masters, only their barbed-wire fenced prison camps and their hangman's nooses, their driving and their cruelty.

In all the vast land there was liberty and justice only here on the Mountain to which, in the time of fear, the Old Ones had brought the little children who now were grown to be the Boys and the Girls of the Bunch, and had hidden them here from the green-clad hordes.

High, twice and three times as high as the tallest tree in the woods, a drop circled the base of the Mountain.

The face of the drop was sheer rock that gave neither hand nor foothold to an unaided climber, and circling the base of the drop was a wide space of tumbled stones. While the death-thunder still rolled in the flaming sky, the Old Ones had brought the little children to the Mountain and had blasted away the one narrow, slanting hill atop which ran the road by which they had reached the Mountain.

The Old Ones themselves had been crushed under the falling stones of the narrow hill, but they had left with the children Musts and Must-nots that the children obeyed, and because they faithfully obeyed the Musts and Must-nots of the Old Ones, and because the woods screened them from the far land below, and from the planes in the sky above, the children had grown tall and strong on the mountain.

They who were masters of the land knew nothing of the children on the mountain. And the children had known nothing of the far land below and nothing of Those who were masters of the far land until Dikar had ventured down the drop and into the far land, and had learned the terror that stalked it, and had brought back from the far land two, Marthadawson and Johndawson, who had taught him more.

And because of what he had learned, and because of a dream he had dreamed all the time he had lived on the mountain, a dream that was not a dream but a memory of the long-ago time of fear, Dikar had added to the pledge Johndawson had taught the Bunch, another pledge, that the Bunch now were chanting.

"We pledge ourselves, our strength, our lives," the clear, young voices of the Bunch proclaimed, *"to drive the invader from the land and make our country free again."*

The chorus ended, but for a moment longer the brown arms remained outstretched to the flag, and there was a lump in Dikar's throat, in his eyes a stinging of unaccustomed tears.

THE ARMS fell. Dikar dropped the butt of the pole to the ground, catching on his arm the folds of the flag that they might not trail the ground, and as he did so, Marilee, Dikar's brown-haired, gray-eyed mate, came lithe and silent from the front row of girls.

Dikar rolled the flag smoothly about its staff and slanted the staff down so that Marilee might draw over it the long bag of black cloth she had sewed for that purpose, and tie its mouth about the peeled, white wood of the staff.

The Bunch broke up into chattering groups that moved off to the jobs Dikar, Boss of the Bunch and of the Boys, and Bessalton, black-haired Boss of the Girls, had given out at breakfast. But Dikar went into the woods beyond the great oak whose spreading, leafy top canopied the fire from the eyes in the sky, and Marilee went with him.

It was cool and shadowy in the woods as Dikar and Marilee went towards a new little house that the Bunch had built there, away from the clearing.

"Dikar," Marilee said, "do you think we ever will?" Her eyes were grave in her elfin face, her tanned body was slim and supple within its ankle-length mantle of lustrous brown hair, though in that body Marilee carried her child, and Dikar's.

"Do I think we ever will what?" Dikar asked, smiling tenderly.

"Ever free America from the Asafrics?" That was the name by which Johndawson called the masters of America, explaining to Dikar and Marilee that it was a shortening of the long words, Asiatic-African Confederation, that was the real name of the green-clad hordes. "We are so few, Dikar, and they are so many," Marilee worried. "What can we do against them?"

Dikar's eyes were shadowed. "I don't know, Marilee." The brush rustled about their bare legs, and the forest seemed to darken with a kind of dread. "I don't know," Dikar repeated, after they had gone a space in silence. "But we can try. We've got to try." His white teeth flashed in a wide grin and his voice was young again, boyishly confident. "We'll make a good try, too. You just wait and see."

"I know you'll try, Dikar." They were coming to the little log house in the woods. "And I want you to try."

The house was like those in which the mated pairs lived, in the woods behind the Eating Place, but it was larger than the rest and up from its roof rose a strange network of wires that glinted red-yellow where the forest foliage had been cut away to give them space.

"But I'm afraid," Marilee whispered. Dikar stopped to lift down the flag from his shoulder, so that it might go through the doorway of the house.

"Not for me am I afraid, but for you. I've been afraid for you ever since I saw them, down in the far land, ever since I saw their long guns and shining knives, and their cruel eyes."

Dikar held still, his face troubled. "But, Marilee—"

"Marilee," a new voice said from inside the little house. "You've been afraid for your man two weeks." Marthadawson came into the doorway. "I've been afraid for mine for so many years that I have forgotten what it is not to be afraid."

CHAPTER 2
THE SILENCE A-TREMBLE

HER SKIN was tightly drawn over the bones of her face, strangely pale by contrast to Marilee's. Her unbound hair was brown as Marilee's, but without luster, and it neither fell unbound nor was braided as the girls braid theirs while working, but was piled, straggly and thin, on top of her head. Her scrawny frame was clothed in a gray and shapeless dress, her feet in broken, shabby shoes.

"Long ago, Marilee," Marthadawson said and put a hand on Marilee's shoulder, "my John went off to fight the Asafrics, and that was when I began to be afraid for him." Her voice was a tired shadow of a voice. "All the time the fighting kept on I was afraid that he would be killed. And then the fighting ended, and news came through of what they were doing to our men who had not been killed, and I was afraid that John had not been killed."

Marthadawson stopped talking for a moment, the woods were very still, and Marthadawson's eyes remembered agony.

"One night," she began again, telling what her eyes remembered, "there was a scratching at my door. I opened it and a thing fell in that I thought was the scarecrow from the cornfield. Then I saw that it was John.

"Before I dared do anything for him," Marthadawson's low, tired voice went on, "I had to carry him up two flights of stairs to the attic to hide him. He had been a big man when he went away to fight, and I am not strong, but what there was left of him I could carry easily.

"When I had brought him back to life, I wanted him to flee with me to the woods, as many had done, to live there like hunted animals or to die, but to live and die free. But he told me he had been chosen as an agent of the Secret Net that works always, blind and in the dark, against the invaders, and we did not flee.

"That was five years ago, Marilee. For five years I hid John in the attic, and for every minute of those five years, every second, I was afraid, afraid as you cannot be who do not know what they do to the agents of the Secret Net whom they catch. For five years, my dear, I lived with fear, but never once did I reproach John for the work he had chosen, or ask him to give it up.

"Reproach him? Ask him to give it up?" Marthadawson straightened, and her head was high and proud. "I would have cut out my tongue first. I would have killed myself with my own hand."

Marthadawson's voice had risen to a fierce, ringing note.

"Oh, Martha!" The name was a sob in Marilee's throat, and Marilee's arms were around the older woman, Marilee's face buried in the other's flat breast. "I'm so ashamed. I—"

"Now, honey," Marthadawson crooned, stroking the girl's back. "Now, my dear. There is nothing for you to be ashamed of in being afraid for your man. Only you must learn not to let him know that you are afraid. And you'll learn that lesson fast enough, for it is the hard and bitter lesson the first woman learned when the first man went into peril, and it is the lesson every woman has learned ever since."

"NO!" MARILEE'S hands pushed her away from Martha. "No!" Marilee cried again, her gray eyes flashing, red mouth rebellious. "When he goes into danger I go by his side, and you and no one here has the right to tell me that I shall not go with my mate, to share his peril, to share whatever comes to him."

"What's going on here?" a cheery voice said, and Dikar turned to the man who came around the end of the house. "What are you three talking about with such long faces?"

Johndawson was tall, taller than Dikar. His hair was gray and his cheeks sunken, and his eyes were deep-sunken in hollow sockets, but there was quiet courage in them and a flame of new hope.

He was stripped to the waist. The cage of his ribs pressed through pale skin that was netted with old scars.

"Where have you been, John?" Marthadawson asked. "I couldn't see you, after the pledge, so I came right back here." They did not touch each other, those two, but Dikar sensed the love between them, a love too deep for touch or for words or kisses.

"Just walking in the woods." John's thin nostrils flared as he pulled in a long breath. The way he did that, the way his scarred chest swelled and swelled, made Dikar aware in a new way of the familiar forest smells, of the green smell of the woods and the tangy smell of the pines, the stinging smell of some crushed leaf and the warm, deep life-smell of the dark loam underneath it all.

"Feeling free space about me, Martha, and the free wind on my skin. Feeling the free spring of the earth under my feet." His long-fingered hand made a little gesture. "After five years— But I'm keeping you standing with that heavy flagstaff in your hands, Dikar. Come inside, son, and put it away. I've got something to show you two."

"You've got it finished, John?" Dikar exclaimed.

Johndawson nodded, his thin mouth smiling clumsily, as though it was just learning how to smile again. "I think I have, Dikar. I haven't had a chance to test it yet. But come along."

The dimness and the smell of the forest was inside the little house, and the clean, sharp smell of new-hewn wood, of the pine boughs that, piled butt-ends down, needles up and covered with blankets of white rabbit-fur, made the bed at one end of the room.

There were in the house two stools—half-logs footed with short lengths axed from saplings, the gray, moss-blotched bark left on them; and a small table similarly fashioned. Into the wall above the bed, wooden pegs had been driven to hold the few clothes John and Martha had been able to bring with them from the far land. All this save for the clothes, was the same as it was in the houses of the mated, but there were things in this house that were different and new and strange to the mountain.

Into the wall opposite the doorway, for instance, had been driven two longer pegs, high up, across which Dikar placed the flag. Beneath these ranged still more pegs, row on row, and on these rested eight long things of shining wood and dull-gleaming metal, things that were silent now and harmless-seeming but that could speak with a loud, frightful voice, the voice of death.

Long guns, these were, or *rifles,* as Johndawson called them, and the Asafrics to whom they belonged lay dead down in the far land, in the ruins of the house where Johndawson hid from them for five terrible years.

From one peg each, beside the rifles, hung nine little guns, *automatics,* that also once belonged to the Asafrics, and on a shelf beneath the eight rifles and the nine automatics were piled belts that held in many little pockets the *cartridges* that all the weapons needed to give them the voice of death.

Nor were these things all.

"Come here," Johndawson called from the other end of the house. "In two minutes it will be time to make the test." He was seated on a third stool, and his voice was not loud, but there was a quiver of excitement in it, and in his gaunt neck the cords stood out, rigid.

DIKAR WENT, with Marilee close beside him. Martha stood on the other side of Johndawson, her hand on his shoulder.

In front of them was a long shelf that ran along the endwall of the house, from one sidewall to the other. Under the shelf were little black boxes—and Dikar recalled how heavy these boxes had been when he had helped to carry them through the woods from the house of Johndawson to the top of the high, steep drop that circled the mountain.

On the top of the shelf was a jumble of wires, and small black boards standing up and lying down, and round things marked with little white lines, and a row of pear-shaped things that you could look through and see a lot of tiny wires inside of. These, Johndawson had told Dikar, were called *bulbs*.

Against the wall above all this hung the almost flat disk that Dikar had remembered, when he first saw it in the attic of Johndawson's house, was called a *radio*. And from one end of the shelf, and from the radio, wires ran up to the roof, and through the roof to the maze of wires glinting red-yellow against the green of the foliage that had been cut away to make room for it.

Right in front of Johndawson lay a little round thing with a white face. There were black marks around the white face, and two thin black lines that were joined at the center of the face. The little round thing was a *watch*. It made a ticking noise, and the thin black lines moved, very slowly, and Johndawson was looking at them, and a tiny muscle twitched in his cheek as he looked.

Johndawson pulled breath in between his teeth, the breath hissing, and touched something on the shelf. Little lights sprang to life in the bulbs, little yellow lights.

"One minute now," he said, "and we shall know if we can hear and be heard."

"Suppose the Asafrics hear you," Dikar said, because he had to say something, "instead of the ones you want to talk to. Won't they know what you say? Won't they be able to find out that you are talking from the mountain here?"

"No, Dikar. When the Secret Net was first set up, they did both those things, and because they did a great many of our agents died, but we found a way to scramble our signals so that they are meaningless until unscrambled in a way only we know, and we learned how to mask the sources of our signals so that they cannot be traced. The Asafric Intelligence will know a new station is talking, but they will not know what it says nor where it—time!" he broke off. "It's time now." He reached out to one of the round black things with white lines, moved it a little. His face was masklike, but where his shoulder pressed into Dikar's side, Dikar could feel it quiver.

There was no sound in the dim room. There was no sound except the ticking of the watch and the rustle of leaves outside, and the soft breathing of the four who listened.

There was no expression at all on Johndawson's face. But on the edge of the shelf his left hand was fisting, very slowly, and very slightly it was quivering.

The silence in the room was quivering....

CHAPTER 3
TIDINGS OF WRATH

A SOUND broke the hush, a high-pitched whine that came from the disk on the wall. Marilee shrank against Dikar, her eyes wide and startled.

The whine broke, started again. It was no longer a straight, thin thread of sound in the silence. It flickered, like a loose bowstring plucked by uneven fingers. It rose and fell, and Dikar knew that it was a voice that talked to Johndawson, though Dikar could not understand what the voice said.

"Zee-prime is calling for the roll of the stations in the district," Johndawson murmured. The whine broke, started again. No, this was another, only a little different in tone. "That's Zee-One," Johndawson said. "I'm glad Hen Parker is still okay. He's a good man. And there's Zee-Two." Dikar noticed the difference in the sound from the radio. "Zee-three," Johndawson said, "and—" He cut off. The whine had stopped. There was a gasping sound in Johndawson's throat.

"Zee-four doesn't answer the roll," Martha whispered. "Something's happened to Tomparker. And we thought Tom was safest of all, in the cellar of that bombed silk mill in Patterson."

"None of the Net is safe," Johndawson said, bitterly. "As long as there are crawling, black-hearted whites to spy on us and betray us. But—" His hand darted forward to a black, hinged rod on the shelf as the wall-disk spoke again. "There's Zee-five reporting all clear. I'm next. *Now!*"

His fingers, clutching the end of the hinged rod, tightened— were working it up and down, up and down, very fast. "Zee-six," Johndawson said aloud what his fingers were saying. "Reporting—" And then he broke off, and he was staring up at the round disk on the wall. The whine was coming from the disk, and Johndawson's lips were gray.

"They don't hear me," he whispered. "I can hear them, but they don't hear me."

"Never mind, John," Martha whispered, touching his cheek. "You'll fix it—"

"Hush," he hissed. "I want to hear who answers. There was a blank for me and one for Zee-seven. I got the news that Edstone was raided, you remember, Martha, just before Dikar and Marilee showed up. Zee-eight's reporting. Zee-nine—I'm glad Hankorbett is still working. His unit's done fine work up there in Rochester. They even blew up a munition factory last month."

"There was near a hundred of our people killed in that explosion," Martha said.

"And they're better off than slaving under the whips of the blacks," John answered grimly.

The whining sounds went on and on. The sound wasn't just a high-pitched noise to Dikar any longer. It was a voice coming out of the sky, coming out of the far land. It was the voices of men who, skulking in cellars, in attics, in caves, harried and hunted by the masters of the land, betrayed even by groveling traitors among their own, still hoped to bring freedom to the land.

The radio whined into silence. "That was Zee-twenty-three." Johndawson sighed. "Zekrandall in Bangor. He's the last."

"Twenty-three," Dikar said. "Even allowing for those who didn't answer, that's a lot."

"You've only heard the roll call of District Zee," John answered. "The seaboard states from Delaware to Maine. Other districts of the Net cover the whole country. Zee-prime is the leader of this district. None of us knows who he is or where his station is located. We—"

"What's happened to the radio, John?" Marilee broke in. "It isn't saying anything."

"THAT'S BECAUSE Zee-prime is on another wave-length, answering a roll-call of the district primes, called by National Prime," the gray-haired man replied, smiling. "Even the primes don't know anything about him, although I have an idea he's somewhere in the Rockies. Yes, Dikar, the Secret Net has a fairly good organization, but it hasn't been able to accomplish much in the six years that it has been functioning.

"We rescued many from the prison camps in the early days, but that was quickly stopped. Since then we've managed to send some warnings of raids, to accomplish some sabotage, to keep up the courage of our people a little bit, and that's about all.

"We have no arms, no means of transportation. All our old leaders are dead or imprisoned, and as fast as new ones arise they are captured and join the others in the concentration camps or the grave. Sporadic revolts break out, it is true, here and there, but they are quickly put down, and mercilessly punished. When we started we had some hope, we haven't got much left."

The whine of the radio began again. "Zee-prime is back." Johndawson told them what the flickering whine was saying. "He's rebroadcasting to the District Net the daily bulletin of news being sent out from National Prime."

The trees rustled outside, and from far away came the faint sound of laughter, and the dull sound of chunking axes where the boys cut down trees for next year's fires. "The Ministry of Mines has announced that the production of coal from the

Pennsylvania fields must be increased by twenty-five percent," Johndawson said. "Hours of labor there are lengthened from twelve hours a day to sixteen, and the miners will not be permitted to come to the surface at all, except on Sundays… Due to the industrial demand for power, the use of electricity for lighting white homes is further restricted to one hour at night. Windows must not be shaded in any way, so that the Asafric local patrols may observe any infraction of this order. Punishment for such infraction will be administered on the spot by the patrol leaders. You know what that means, Martha."

"Whips," Marthadawson whispered, "for the men. For the women—" She broke off, but Dikar read horror in her eyes.

"The new wheat crop is a bumper one," Johndawson droned on. "Therefore Viceroy Hashamoto has decreed that beginning next Monday, twenty percent of wheat flour may be added to the potato-bread rationed to whites, instead of ten. But, beginning next Monday also, whites will be permitted meat only one day a week."

"Why such saving in food?" Dikar asked. "You have told us how rich America is in those things."

"Rich, yes," Johndawson replied. "But not so rich as to supply the teeming millions in the homelands of the Asafric Confederation and the whites of our country too. They drain America. They bleed her white… Good Lord." He was abruptly intent on what the radio was telling him.

"What, John?" Marthadawson asked.

"There's been a riot in the concentration camp at San Antonio. The prisoners killed their guards with their bare hands. Before they could get through the barbed wire, planes bombed them to pulp. One white escaped—reached Tee-eleven. The refugee was raving mad after he'd told his story. His screams would have betrayed Tee-eleven, so the agent—shot and buried him…"

"How awful!" Marilee gasped. "He must be a devil."

"No," John said, a white line about his mouth. "He had to do it. Life is cheap in America today, Marilee— Here's news that will show you how cheap life is. In Minnesota an Asafric troop train was wrecked, night before last. The wreckers escaped, but Hashamoto has ordered that every tenth white man in the county where this happened be publicly flogged to death as a warning that sabotage must stop."

A LITTLE moan came from the girl. Her hand crept into Dikar's. It was icy cold, and Dikar was cold all over. Though the sun still struck through the forest roof, its leaf-filtered light dancing in through the windows and the doorway of the little house, it seemed to Dikar that a chill wind moaned in the sky.

"Hello!" Johndawson exclaimed. "Martha!" There was excitement in his voice. "Normanfenton is alive. Wait!" His lifted hand checked Marthadawson. "All this time he's been in Dannemora Prison. Now the Asafrics are moving him to Newyork."

"Oh, John," Martha breathed.

Johndawson was listening so intently that he forgot to repeat aloud what the radio was saying. "Who is Normanfenton?" Dikar whispered to Marthadawson.

"He led the Adirondack Uprising last year," she answered, keeping her voice low. "He had gathered a thousand mountain men and more were flocking to him, but they were trapped in Ausable Chasm and annihilated. Or so we thought. Fenton is a great man, a great leader. He might have saved America if they had not caught—"

"They're not taking him down by plane," John interrupted. "Martha! Do you know what those devils are doing? They're bringing Fenton through the state, chained in an open truck, so that everyone can know what happens to leaders of revolts against them." His eyes burned with rage. "And then they're going to hang him from the peak of the skeleton of the Empire State Building. Damn them! Oh, damn—"

"Isn't there going to be an attempt to rescue him?" Dikar demanded.

"Rescue? How can he be rescued? He'll be heavily guarded.

If there was time perhaps something might be done, but there isn't. The caravan has already left Dannemora. It's swinging around to go through Watertown, then back through Syracuse and Utica. Fenton will be exposed in his chains in Utica all night, then taken to Albany and shown there till noon. At noon they'll start bringing him down river towards Newyork, through Kingston—"

"On this side of the river, John?" Marthadawson seemed excited. "They'll pass near here—"

Johndawson nodded, still listening. "Yes. They'll reach Newburg late in the afternoon, will display Normanfenton there till dark, then they'll rush him—"

"Along the Storm King Highway—"

"No. They're still having trouble with landslides there, even though it's so long since they bombed West Point. No. They're going inland from Newburg, on old Route Thirty-two. That will bring them nearer still—"

"Nearer!" Dikar interrupted. "How near, Johndawson?"

"Even nearer than my house was to here. But—"

"And when? Can you tell me when?"

"Not yet, except that it will be after dark, but the Net is sending reports on their progress, reports of the effect of all this on our people, and tomorrow—"Johndawson broke off, a strange look on his face. "Why, Dikar? Why do you want to know all this?"

Dikar smiled, but there was no smile in his eyes. "Because, Johndawson," he said slowly. "Because I an' the Bunch might have somethin' to say about their hangin' Normanfenton."

CHAPTER 4
THE STRENGTH OF A MAN

"YOU MIGHT—WHAT do you mean?" A sudden light flared in Johndawson's face. "What do you mean, Dikar?"

"I'm wonderin' if we can't take Normanfenton away from the Asafrics and bring him here to the Mountain, like we did you, an' hide him—"

"If you could." Johndawson came up to his feet, and his face was shining again. "If only you could. It would show our people that their conquerors are not invincible. It would give them new heart— But we're talking nonsense." He made a despairing gesture.

"When you rescued us there was only Li Logo and a half dozen Blacks, and they expected no opposition. There will be hundreds of heavily armed Asafrics guarding Fenton, and they will be on the alert against any attempt to take him from them." The light was out of his eyes and his voice was flat. "Skip it, son. It can't be done."

"No, Johndawson, I will not skip it till I have thought about it some more. Many times all of the Bunch have told me something could not be done, but when I thought about it, I found a way to do it."

"But, Dikar," Marthadawson said. "Even if by some miracle you could take Fenton away from them, the Asafrics would search every inch of the countryside, on the ground and from the air, and never rest till they found him or his dead body. They would surely search this Mountain, and that would be the end of your Bunch, the end of everything for you."

"You see, Dikar," John said, drooping and tired-looking. "It's a hare-brained idea. There's no use thinking about it."

The smile was no longer on Dikar's lips, and there was defeat in his eyes. "Well," he conceded. "Perhaps you are right—"

"No, Dikar!" This was Marilee. "They're not right." She stood tall beside him, her hand trembling on his arm, its soft touch thrilling him, as always. "They're terribly, terribly wrong."

"But, Marilee," Dikar argued, unhappily, "even if we do take Normanfenton, that will be the end of safety for the Bunch."

"Sure," she answered him. "Sure it will be the end of safety for us. But if we ever do anythin' except make beautiful pledges to the Flag an' talk about what we're going to do for the Flag and the Country for which it stands, there will be no more safety for us. Today or tomorrow or a year from now, the choice will always be the same, hide here on the Mountain in safety, or go down off the Mountain an' say goodbye to safety. You've got to choose sometime, Dikar, an' it might as well be now."

"But, Marilee—"

"You've *got* to choose now, Dikar," Marilee went on, not stopping to hear what he would say. "Because once you choose safety instead of duty, the next time it will be so much harder to choose different, an' each time it will be harder, an' pretty soon you will not be able to choose anythin' but safety."

"That's youth talking," Johndawson put in. "First, let me train your Boys in the use of rifles and pistols. Let me fix my radio so I can talk to the Secret Net as well as listen. Let me consult with Zee-Prime and National Prime, confer with them how best to act, decide on just how to go about the matter. Then we can wait for another opportunity—"

"*Wait!*" Marilee flung at him, her eyes, her voice, scornful. "You've been waiting for five years, Johndawson, plannin', conferrin', decidin' on just how to do things—an doin' nothin'! an' all the time your enemies have been gettin' stronger, your friends weaker. No! I don't want Dikar to wait an' wait an' wait, an' do nothin'. I want him to decide now, once for all. Dikar!" She turned to him. "You've got to decide now. Don't you see that you've got to?"

DIKAR LOOKED at her, and he looked at Johndawson, and he could not decide. "I don't know which of you is right," he

mumbled. "Marilee, I don't know. The safety of the Bunch—"
A threshing sound broke him off, a threshing sound in the
brush outside the House. He swung to the doorway and a thin,
high voice was crying, "Dikar! Dikar!" from the brush, and then
a brown form broke out of the brush.

It was Halross, and he was in the doorway, was holding on
to the side of the doorway with desperate hands, as if his legs
no longer had strength to hold him up.

"Dikar," Halross gasped, his cheeks twitching, his lips without
color. "Oh, Dikar—"

"Steady, youngster," Dikar said, one long stride taking him
to the panting youngster. "What's up?"

"Johnstone." Halross's eyes clung to Dikar's, and there was
a little more of sense in them, of reason. "Chopping. A tree fell
on him. He's—he's—" He shuddered.

"Killed?"

"No. But it's crushing him an—an we can't get him out. We
can't…" the Boy's voice rose to a scream, cut off, as Dikar plunged
past him.

Dikar was running through the woods, the brush whipping
his legs, the brambles tearing at him. Effortlessly he climbed
the steep slope, till ahead there was a babble of voices and he
thrust through a leafy screen into a small clearing and saw the
fallen tree, twice as thick through as his own body, and the still
form that lay under it.

"Here's Dikar," a Girl's voice said. "Here's Dikar, dear. Dikar
will get you out."

Dikar saw Johnstone's red-thatched head on the ground, and
Johnstone's red beard, and the tight-drawn lines of pain in the
pale mask of Johnstone's face. The great tree-trunk lay across
his chest, and its pointed, yellow butt was on the ground beside
the stump from which it had been hewn. Beyond Johnstone,
on the other side, the trunk was balanced on the rounded top
of a rock. Dikar saw that if it moved on the rock, the least bit
to either side, it would settle and crush the life out of Johnstone.

"We're afraid to touch it, Dikar," Bengreen said in his ear.

"I see," Dikar said, slowly. "I see." What he saw was that the bark of the trunk was pressing hard into Johnstone's chest, and that the slope of the ground lifted from Johnstone to the rock, so that there was only one place, halfway between, where it was clear of the ground by a space just high enough for a Boy to crawl under, if he dared.

"If we only had a block and fall," Johndawson said. "We could get a straight lift up."

Dikar didn't know what a *block and fall* was, but he knew that a straight lift up was the only thing that could save Johnstone. There was nowhere the Boys could stand above the tree-trunk to pull it straight up, but—Dikar was going to the place where the great trunk was clear of the ground by just a little more than the breadth of a Boy's body. Of Dikar's body. He was getting down on his knees there, facing the trunk. He was lying flat, face down.

"Good heavens!" he heard Johndawson exclaim. "What is he going to do?"

DIKAR ROLLED his head and said, "Danhall. Bengreen. Stand by Johnstone to pull him out, but don't touch him till he's free." Marilee's lips were tight and thin, but there was a smile in Marilee's watching eyes.

Inch by slow and careful inch Dikar pushed himself forward on the ground. There was sun on the back of Dikar's head and now there was shadow, and he knew that it was the shadow of the great trunk above him.

He squirmed forward, the ground rubbing his chest, his belly, the ground soft and cool against the palms of his hands. Now there was sun again on the ground and on the back of Dikar's head, and there was a tiny purple flower just where his eyes looked down, and on one of the petals of the flower there was a bug so small that Dikar could not have seen it if his eyes had not been so close to it. And Dikar stopped.

He turned his head so that he could see the tree-trunk, and

it was gray-brown and huge over his back, and it seemed as big as the Boys' House.

Dikar pulled his hands back, back along the ground until they were flat on the ground either side of his chest and close to his chest. He pulled his knees, little by little, forward under him. That lifted Dikar's back, slowly, lifted it till he could faintly feel the touch of the tree-bark on the skin across the small of his back, lifted it till the touch of the tree-bark was firm and hard and rough against the small of his back.

Dikar pulled in a long, deep breath, and the green smell of the woods was in that breath and the warmth of the sun, and the life-smell of the black forest earth.

And there was strength in that breath, strength that ran tingling in Dikar's veins, that seeped into his muscles as the warm summer rains seep into the ground.

Dikar closed his throat on that breath, and the strength swelled in his muscles, pushing his hands and knees down hard against the earth. And Dikar's back was lifting. The weight of the trunk was the weight of the world.

Dikar lifted, lifted slowly, his arms straightening, his arms quivering with the weight upon them, his thighs quivering. The weight was too much, he could not lift it any more, could not hold it—

Somewhere there was shouting. Somewhere there were words, shouted, but dull in Dikar's ears. "All right. All right, Dikar. He's— We've got him out."

And Dikar started to let the tree trunk down. Slowly. He had to let it down as slowly, as carefully, as he had lifted it. He had to let it straight down, so that it would come down exactly on top of the rounded top of the rock, so that it would rest there exactly as it had rested before he lifted it.

Or it would roll on the round top of the rock, the great weight of the trunk would roll and come down, lower, lower, cradled on Dikar's back, till Dikar lay flat on the ground and the trunk lay on top of him, pinning him down.

Down. It was harder to let that weight slowly down than it had been to lift it. Down. Surely it must be down to the rock now.

SUDDENLY THE terrible weight of the tree was a little less on Dikar's back, and the weight was quivering a little. Now there was only the touch of the bark on Dikar's back. Now there was only the pain where the bark had gouged his back and Dikar was lying flat on the ground, and the purple flower was against his nose.

Dikar's breath went out with a great *whoosh,* and blew the little bug off the flower.

Dikar pushed himself back and back, slowly, carefully, and the shadow of the tree trunk was on his head, and then the sun was on the back of his head again.

Dikar lay on the ground panting and blind, and about him there was a wild hurraying, but Dikar heard only Marilee's voice, "Dikar. Oh, Dikar." He felt only Marilee's soft hands on his back, taking away the pain and the hurt.

Dikar heard Johndawson's voice. "That was a brave thing to do, son. But it was a foolish thing, too. One slip and you both would have been killed. You should have thought of that before you tried it."

"I did think of that," Dikar answered Johndawson. "But I couldn't let that stop me. I had no right to think about danger to me when one of the Bunch was in danger an' I could help him. I—" Dikar stopped. He rolled, and sat up, and his eyes were wide.

"Marilee!" he exclaimed. "I see now—I see— That's the answer."

"What's the answer?" Marilee asked, squatting on her brown thighs. "What do you mean, Dikar?" she asked. But Dikar saw in her eyes that she knew.

"Just like I had no right to think about danger to myself when Johnstone needed me," Dikar told her, "the same way I have no right to think of danger to the Bunch when our country needs the Bunch."

CHAPTER 5
WHERE DANGER CREEPS

JOHNSTONE WOULD be laid up for some time, but he was not hurt bad. Dikar himself was sore all over, but Marilee had bound to his back certain leaves that would heal the wounds there quickly.

"The soreness is nothing," Dikar said to Johndawson. The four of them were back in Johndawson's little House. "It will be gone by night. I will be ready to go down to the far land as soon as it is dark."

"As soon as it's dark!" Marilee echoed. "But Dikar! It's tomorrow night They will be bringin' Normanfenton near here, not tonight. Why should you lead the Bunch down there tonight?"

Dikar turned his grave smile to her. "I'm not leadin' the Bunch down there tonight. Tonight I go alone."

"Alone!" The exclamation came from all three.

"Yes," Dikar smiled. "Alone. Marilee was right in sayin' that we must not wait to act, but so were you, Johndawson, in sayin' we must not act without plan. So I must go tonight to where Normanfenton will pass tomorrow an' see for myself how we must do to take him from the Asafrics, an' what chance there is that we can do so, or if there is any chance at all. I must see if there is any chance that, havin' rescued him, we can bring him back here to the Mountain without givin' away the secret of the Mountain to our enemies."

"Oh Dikar!" Marilee wailed. "You haven't changed. You're still thinkin' first of the Bunch."

"I'm thinkin' of the Bunch, my dear, not first, but as part of the job the Bunch must do. If the Bunch is destroyed, it can do nothin, an' all our fine words, all the years of our struggle to live here on the Mountain, all that the Old Ones did, long-ago, to save the Bunch, will be useless an' wasted."

"That's good sense, Dikar," Johndawson approved. "I'll go with you tonight, and—"

"No," Dikar said. "I go alone." He said it quietly, but there was in his voice, in his eyes turned on the gray-haired man, a something that the Boys and Girls of the Bunch had long known meant that what the Boss ordered to be done must be done, without talk or argument. "You cannot move as fast as me, nor, like me, without leavin' any trace that you have passed. You will tell me where to go, but you will not come with me."

Johndawson nodded. "All right, Dikar. I'll make a map for you."

"A map?"

"A picture by means of which I can more easily tell you where to go. Wait a minute." Johndawson rose from his stool and went to the doorway, and came back with a pointed stick he'd picked up from the ground outside. He squatted down and scratched round marks in the hard-packed earth that was the floor of the House. "Suppose you were high up in the sky, looking down. The Mountain would look like this, wouldn't it?"

"Yes," Dikar agreed, getting up from his stool and squatting down beside Johndawson.

"Now suppose," the latter went on, "that this is the direction of the rising sun." He pointed with his stick. "The name of which is East. Way over here would be the Hudson River." He scratched four long wavy lines in the dirt. "And about here," making a little cross between the wavy lines that were a picture of the River and the round picture of the Mountain, "would be the House where Martha and I used to live."

"I see," Dikar said. "If I wanted to tell someone how to go from the Mountain to that house, all I would have to do is show them on this picture, and they would know to go toward the rising sun. To go East."

"Good boy!" Johndawson exclaimed. "You learn fast. Now let's learn the names of the other directions before we go on. If this is East, toward the rising sun, this, toward where it sets, is West. Then this way is North, and the other South."

"East. West." Dikar's hand pointed. "North. South. Right?"

"Right. And in between is North-East, North-West, South-East, South-West. You see?" Dikar nodded, his lips forming the words Johndawson had said. "Now, Dikar. From the top of the Mountain you have seen that there are woods all around the Mountain, like this." Johndawson's stick roughened the dirt around the Mountain-mark to show where he meant.

"Before the invasion, this region was known as a Park, as the Palisades Interstate Park, and no one was allowed to cut down the trees in it or live in it. It was kept as a wild playland, and it has grown even wilder since the Asafrics came, so thick and wild, so full of ravines and caves, that men and women who have escaped from the camps have been known to live in these woods for years, though the Black trackers hunt them continually."

"Here, Dikar," Johndawson went on, "about twenty miles North and a little East of here," he made a big mark next to the wavy lines that were a picture of the River, "is Newburg. As I said before, the caravan will swing inshore from there, following a road that runs this way...."

The stick scratched a line that wandered along southwest from Newburg. "Through these little towns of Vailsgate and Highlandmills and Centralvalley and Harriman." He made little circles as he said the names. "And that road goes through the edge of the woods, right here, about four miles due west of the Mountain. If there's any place at all where a rescue might be effected, this is it."

"A road through the woods," Dikar pondered, low-toned. "An' not far, not too far, from the Mountain. Yes," he whispered. "Yes. I must see that. I must see that tonight...."

NIGHT BRINGS no hush to the forest that cloaks the Mountain, brings rather new sounds, new life. Night brings a furtive, teeming, awakeness to the creatures of the forest, but the Boys and the Girls of the Bunch have said their Now-I-lay-me's and are asleep.

Every night it is the turn of two of the Bunch to stay awake, watching the Fire whose flames leap from the Fire Stone in the Clearing; feeding the Fire, or to putting it out at the first faint buzz that gives warning of a nearing plane, for the Bunch, too, is hunted.

This night two others of the Bunch stand awake in a little House of the Mated.

The form of the one, half-seen in the dark, is tall and stalwart, the form of the other slender and supple, warm and throbbing in the embracing arms of the first. "Why?" Marilee whispers to Dikar. "Why must you go alone? Why can't you take some of the Bunch with you, Bengreen maybe, an' Danhall?"

"Only one is needed for the job that is to be done tonight," Dikar answers, low-toned.

"But two or three could put up a better fight," Marilee urges, "if there is a fight. The more who go, the safer all will be."

"Safer in the goin', perhaps, an' in fightin', if fightin' there is. But goin' or comin' back, two would leave more trace than one, an' three more than two, to lead the Black trackers to the Mountain. No, I must go down to the far land alone."

"An' you must come back, my Dikar," she insisted. "You must come back to me."

"I shall do my best to come back," Dikar murmured, his lips close to her ear, tingling with the cool touch. "But if I do not come back, you must remember that the Bunch will go on without me."

Dikar felt the slender form of Marilee quiver, hard against him. He heard the beginning of a sob in her throat. The rest was smothered by the hot, sweet tightness of his lips on Marilee's lips.

Dikar whirled to a sudden sound behind him, his great hands

fisting, the muscles tightening across the back of his shoulders. A dark form blotched the pale glimmer of the doorway—

"Dikar," a whisper breathed from the doorway. "Marilee! Are you wake?"

"Annjordan!" Marilee exclaimed. "You—Johnstone is bad sick! He's worse hurt than we—"

"Hush," Annjordan hissed, gliding into the House. "No one must hear us. No one must know I've come to you. My mate's all right, Marilee, thanks to the brave thing Dikar did, an' that's why I have to tell you—" She broke off.

Annjordan was a shadow in the darkness. Her voice was a shadow. Dikar could not understand how by sight or hearing Marilee had made out who it was. "What are you talkin' about?" he demanded.

"I promised to keep it a secret. I swore cross my heart not to tell you and Marilee about it. But I must. Even if the Old Ones strike me dead, I must tell you, after the thing you did for my Johnstone."

"Who did you promise not to tell me somethin'?" Suddenly Dikar's heart was heavy. Was it beginnin' again? Secrets kept from him, whisperings behind his back? He had thought all that sort of thing had ended with the death of Tomball, whom he had had to kill with his bonarrer so that the Bunch might live. "An' what is it you have promised not to tell me an' Marilee?"

"The pledge—" Annjordan's whisper stopped, started over again. "Dikar. When we make the pledge in the mornin', we Girls, the mated Girls an' most of the un-mated, do not make it." Breath hissed from between her teeth, as though a long time she had held it, had held something within her that had fought to get out like held breath.

"Not make the pledge," Dikar repeated, puzzled. "But Annjordan, I hear you make it, each mornin' after brekfes. I see their hands outstretched to the Flag."

"You see our right hands outstretched." Annjordan seemed

to speak more easily, now that she'd begun to speak. "But you do not see our left hands, hidden within our long hair—"

"No."

"Hidden, an' their first two fingers crossed."

"Crossed!" Marilee gasped. "Crossed fingers denyin' the pledge your lips say!"

Dikar's mouth was dry. He licked his lips. "Who got you Girls to do this, Annjordan? Who got you to do this thing, an' to keep it secret from me?"

IN THE darkness the form of Annjordan was stiff, and Dikar sensed that her eyes were on him, but she sobbed only, did not answer. It was Marilee who answered for her.

"Bessalton, Dikar. Annjordan! It is Bessalton, isn't it?"

"Yes."

"Bessalton!" Dikar groaned. "But Bessalton's Boss of the Girls an' my right hand. She's—"

"Your enemy, Dikar," Marilee cut in.

"You're crazy, Marilee! Why should—"

"Why? My blind, blind Dikar. Why? Look Dikar. Bessalton loved Tomball an' wanted him for her mate, but Tomball wanted me, an' so Bessalton hated me. Then I mated with you, an' she thought she had her chance at Tomball, but he fought you an' you killed him, killed the Boy she loved, an' so she hates you an' is your enemy."

"But she's Boss of the Girls. Her duty—"

"She tries to do her duty to the Girls an' the Bunch in spite of her hate for you, but because of her hate for you, she cannot help but be certain that what is close to your heart is wrong, an' so—"

"I see," Dikar interrupted. "I get it. But— Look here, Annjordan. I thank you for tellin' me of this, but there is nothin' I can do about it tonight, so now you better go back to your Johnstone an' to sleep. A good sleep to you, Annjordan, an' good dreams."

"A good sleep to you both," Annjordan whispered. "Good dreams to you both." She slipped away, blotched the pale doorway like a shadow, was gone.

"Now there's no use your goin' down to the far land, Dikar," Marilee murmured, a sort of relief in her tone. "The Girls can stop the Boys from followin' you down to the far land, and so—"

"The Girls can stop 'em from followin' me, but the Girls will not. Tomorrow mornin' I call a Council—Tonight I go down to the far land." There was a tightness in Dikar's throat that would hardly let him talk. "Tomorrow mornin' I will have this out with the Bunch. It is late now. I must get goin'—"

Marilee's kiss warm on his lips, Dikar went through the woods like a drifting shadow. He made less noise than the rabbits that played in the brush, less noise than the rippling stream to which he came and by whose side he went down the dark slope of the Mountain, through the dark woods. Dikar came at last to where the stream leaped out over the brink of the Drop, and down, down into the dark depths to smash itself on the stones beneath which the Old Ones slept.

Dikar bent and felt with his hands for the rope of interwoven vines that was fastened to a tree here where the stream leaped out, and slanted down into the stream and hung behind its curtain.

Each time before that he had ventured down, Dikar had met with deadly peril and had escaped it, but he felt in his bones, in his chilled blood, that this third time he was to meet with dangers to which those others would be as nothing.

Down there in the far land Dikar had learned the meaning of fear. Fear rode his shoulders now, weighted him, as he swung himself down over the edge of the Drop, swung himself down through the battering roar of the stream, climbed hand over hand down the rope of vines, down and down and down into the depths.

This was the third time Dikar broke the most terrible of the

Must-nots of the Old Ones. Was this the time that the Old Ones would choose to punish him for breaking their Must-nots?

CHAPTER 6
THE BLACK PIT

THE BRUSH through which Dikar moved was exactly the same as the Mountain's brush. The smells, even, were the same. But there was a difference between this forest of the far land and the forest of the Mountain. The difference tightened Dikar's skin on his body, bristled the hairs at the back of his neck.

A hush lay heavy in these woods, a brooding and fear-filled hush. No shrill chorus of insects came to Dikar's ears, no scutterings of small woods creatures, no twitterings of nesting birds disturbed in their sleep, no hoot of a hunting owl.

And this made Dikar afraid.

He stopped, suddenly. He shrank against a huge tree trunk, the black shadow enfolding him, and peered back.

There were shapes there, tongueless and threatening. There were eyes watching him, a myriad of pale eyes.

Dikar knew the shapes were only the shadows of trees, the shadowed bulk of bushes. He knew the eyes were only speckles of moonlight. He could see nothing to fear. Hear nothing. Nothing moved—

It seemed to Dikar that something *had* been moving, behind him, and had stopped in the instant he stopped. It seemed to him that something was watching him now, invisible in the fear-filled dark.

Invisible, perhaps, in dark or light!

A long time Dikar peered into the night, and nothing moved, and there was no sound in the thick and brooding hush.

After a while Dikar started off again, flitting noiseless through the forest. He must watch where he placed his feet, he must watch that he bent no leaf, left no trace that might be followed by the Black trackers of the Asafrics, back-tracking him to the Mountain. All Dikar's thought, every tingling nerve of him, was taken by this need, and he forgot to be afraid.

He came to a stream rippling between low, grassy banks. It was wider than any on the Mountain, its waters running across his course as fast as the Mountain streams run when they near the Drop and start hurrying to throw themselves over the Drop, but it was no more than thigh-deep to Dikar, and he waded across it easily.

Afterward Dikar was to learn that the stream had a name, the Ramapo River.

And now there was sound ahead of Dikar, a rumble like thunder far ahead of him, but Dikar knew it was not thunder, for it was low down, not in the sky, and it seemed to move, now to one side, growing, now straight ahead, now to the other side, dying away.

Dikar stopped, fright throbbing in his chest. He listened to the fading of the strange sound, and his brow knitted.

His nostrils flared to a new smell that drifted through the woods, a stinging smell Dikar could not remember at all, a smell that yet seemed queerly familiar like something out of a forgotten dream.

A dream? The smell belonged to Dikar's dream, in that dream of the long-ago that came to Dikar again and again and was not a dream but memory of the long-ago Time of Fear. The smell was strong in a part of that dream, in the part where Dick Carr, the little boy Dikar once was, rode in a truck crowded with the children the Bunch once were, and the Old Ones drove the truck. The smell did not belong to the children or the Old Ones. It belonged to the truck.

Was it a truck that had made the noise like thunder, there ahead from where the smell came? It must be. But, Dikar recalled, trucks go only on roads, so there must be a road not far ahead, the road Johndawson drew in his picture, the road for which Dikar looked.

He was near the road, and near the road the danger that some Black might come across his track was the greatest. Dikar knew how to fix that. He went up the trunk of the tree near which he had stopped, hearing the thunder. He went toward the road in the tops of the trees, running confident along swaying boughs as a squirrel might, swinging across the spaces between boughs in free, soaring leaps.

And he came to the road.

DIKAR LAY along the bough of a tree that hung over the road, and looked down upon it. It was very wide and in the moonlight it glimmered like the pale night-things of the woods. It curved out of the dark woods and passed under Dikar's bough, and went on into the dark woods again.

On the other side of the road were woods again, their boughs overhanging the road like the boughs of the woods on this side did. Dikar shifted a little—shrank down close to his bough.

He had heard, far to one side, a low rumble begin, like that which he had heard before. The rumble grew louder fast, came nearer fast, and there was light on the road, a bright and glaring light, and the light streamed from two, great blazing eyes that hurtled toward Dikar, roaring.

The roaring battered at Dikar, and for terror of the roaring Dikar could not move, and the light was all about Dikar, the tree suddenly green in the light, Dikar's hands, clutching the bough suddenly brown and cord-ridged in the light. The deafening thunder was beneath Dikar. A monstrous huge thing was hurtling by, right under Dikar.

There was no light about Dikar any longer. The light was going fast, fast along the road away from Dikar, and the monstrous thing from whose eyes the light came. The thunder was dying.

Shaken, gasping, Dikar clung to his bough. The truck-smell was strong in his nostrils, truck-smell and man-smell. The man-smell was like the smell of the Bunch, and it was different. It was the smell of Li Logo's Blacks, from whom Dikar had saved Johndawson and Marthadawson. It was the smell of the Asafrics.

There had been Asafrics in that monstrous huge truck. Johndawson had said the Asafrics would bring Normanfenton along this road in a truck. Would rush him towards Newyork. Dikar's heart sank. The trucks went too fast. They came and were gone before a Boy could move. It was no use. The Bunch could do nothing with anything that went so fast.

Too bad. This place, otherwise, was a good place for a rescue. The woods thick to the very edge of the road. The tree-boughs overhanging the road…

If only the truck carrying Normanfenton could be made to go slow.…

Dikar went through the treetops along the road, in the direction Normanfenton would come. He knew that direction from the picture Johndawson drew on the floor. Just beyond the curve a little stream brawled in the woods across the road. It vanished at the other edge of the road, but just below the tree where Dikar had paused, he could hear its swift rush. He peered downward, made out that the little stream came out again from under the road, had carved a deep gully for itself in its hurry to join the wider stream that he'd crossed.

Dikar's brows knitted. The road dipped here, and where the stream poured under it was the lowest part of the dip. The ground on the other side of the road was higher than that on this side.

Maybe this could be turned to use—

Dikar started to think about it, but it struck him that he'd been away from the Mountain a long time, and he'd gone far, and it was far back to the Mountain. He should be starting back, and besides, Johndawson might help think how the truck carrying Normanfenton might be stopped. Dikar started away from the road.

For a while he stayed in the tree tops, but he could move faster on the ground, so when he had dropped down again to the ground to cross the wide stream that ran across his course, he stayed on the ground. He went silently through the silent woods, not forgetting to watch where he put his feet, to watch how his body brushed the bush leaves, not forgetting to be careful not to leave a trace of his passing. Suddenly he was standing stiff, not breathing. His widened eyes were staring into the darkness. His nostrils were flaring.

He'd seen, or thought he had seen, a flicker of yellow light far off in the blackness. He could not see it now. He could hear nothing. But—yes—he could smell something.

Dikar smelled, very faintly, a tang of smoke threading the smells of the woods. Fainter, there was another smell that should not be in the night-air of these woods. A man-smell. Or was it man-smell?

Dikar was puzzled by this smell. It was not like that of the Bunch. It was not like that of the Asafrics. There was man in it, but there was animal in it too, more animal than man.

This was some kind of animal different from any on the Mountain.

What about the smoke-smell then? Smoke meant fire. No animal Dikar knew made fire. Men then? Beast-Men?

Dikar was afraid. Very terribly he was afraid of the Beast-Men whose smell was fear. Dikar wanted to run. He wanted to run away from that dreadful smell, from the creatures whose smell it was.

Whatever kind of men, or if men at all, they were between the Mountain and the road. If Dikar led the Bunch to the road, tomorrow night, he would have to lead the Bunch past them. If they were men, they would be a danger to the Bunch. Or even if they were animals, strange animals who made fire, who covered their fire—

DIKAR STARTED off. He started going toward where he'd seen the light, toward where the smell of fear came from. Dikar was

Boss of the Bunch. If there was danger here for the Bunch he must know it. If the danger took him, if he never went back to the Mountain, the Bunch would know there was danger here and would not come down here from the Mountain.

Dikar drifted like a shadow through the shadows of the woods, and the smell of fear grew stronger and ever stronger in his nostrils.

A black thing rose before Dikar, and Dikar stopped. The smell was strong here, so strong that he could swear whatever it came from was here, right here in front of him, but there was nothing here from which the smell could come.

There was nothing around Dikar except the black columns of the trees through which he'd come. He was in a little open space, brush-crowded, and the brush was more plainly moonlit here because of the break in the tree-ranks' roof made by the little open space.

The thing that rose in front of Dikar was moon-lighted. It was a sort of earth-bank, high as Dikar's chest. Leafy, vinelike trailers dripped over its top to cover its face.

Queer. The strange smell seemed to come out of the leaf-covered earth-bank itself.

Dikar peered at it, trying to make out how the Beast-Man smell could be coming from it. A muscle twitched in his cheek. Though the brush leaves at his feet were crisp and green, the leaves of the trailers that dripped down over the earth-bank's edge were a little wilted. Dikar moved closer—

Earth gave way under his feet and threw him forward! He fell into the face of the earth-bank—*right through it!* Through leaves, through something soft and awful. He was falling down into a space behind the seeming earth-bank, was blinded by reddish light, and there were shrieks all about him, and animal-like yowls, and a high, shrill wildcat scream!

Dikar hit hard on hard ground, rolled desperately, saw yellow fangs agape in a black-haired muzzle. He thrust at the ground to lift himself, was born down by a hairy body that hurled itself upon him. Other bodies came down upon him, hairy, rasping. He was smothered under a squealing mass, pinned down. He heaved, trying to throw them off him, trying to get free space to fight, to make some try to fight for his life, but the weight of the bodies held him down—

Dikar lay gasping for breath under that stinking mass, and somewhere there was a shrill scream, "Kill! Kill him!"

CHAPTER 7
WITHIN THE CAVE

A VOICE muffled by the body that lay over Dikar's head shouted hoarsely. "Shut up, Mom! Shut that damyelpin!" The scream cut off. The voice went on, lower but short-breathed like Dikar's when something happened and he had to give orders quickly. "Pull them quilts together, someone! You, Ruth. Might as well have a beacon to tell where we are, the way the firelight's shinin' out. Chuck!" The voice was afraid. "Slip out the back way an' see if there's any more around. Walt an' me kin handle this bozo." Yes, there was fear in the voice.

The weight on Dikar lightened, but his legs were still held down, and he still could not see because of the body across his head. Fingers, rough, hurting, grabbed his arms.

"Marge," the voice said, still low, still afraid. "Gimme them ropes from the corner."

Dikar could hear a low, whimpering sound now. He could hear the crackle of a fire. The smoke-smell was sharp, even through the Beast-Man smell of the body that held his head down.

"Here, Nat," a woman's voice said.

Dikar felt something tightening around his wrists, drawing them together, cutting in. Around his ankles, too.

"That'll hold you," the voice said, and the body rolled off Dikar's head.

The Beast-Man was big, bigger than Dikar, bigger even than Tomball, who had been the biggest Boy of the Bunch. Feet spread apart on the dirt floor near Dikar's head were tied up in bunches of dirty rags. Spread legs were like tree trunks. Pants like Johndawson's covered them, but the pants were all torn, so that hairy flesh showed through.

Above the pants more rags fluttered about a deep chest matted with black, springy hair. The head of the Beast-Man seemed to be set neckless on huge shoulders so great was his black beard. Worst of all were the eyes that peered out of the hairy mask, the little red eyes that peered down at Dikar, hating him.

"Hashamoto must be bringin' over some new kind of savage to hunt us down," rumbled from out of that animal-face. "This guy ain't neither yellow nor black, an' look, Marge, he's naked as the day he was born."

"He's nice built though, Nat," a Girl said, coming up. "An' awful good-lookin' with that gold hair an' beard." She wasn't much older than Marilee, Dikar thought. Within the rags she wore her body seemed slender as Marilee's, but she moved heavily, as if there was some unseen weight on her. Her eyes were dull, her reddish hair tangled and dirt-matted like Nat's. "I could go for him."

"Oh, yeah?" Nat said tonelessly. "You could go for him, huh?" His arm swept up almost carelessly. The back of his hand hit Marge's mouth and she crumpled to the floor.

"Try goin' for that," Nat said, and for a minute there was no other sound except the little whimperings Dikar had been hearing.

Marge lay where she'd fallen, rubbing her mouth and looking up at Nat with no anger in her dull eyes. The fire from which the light came danced on the earthen floor near her, and wavered over little, blackened bones on the floor. The roof of this den curved low down where the shadows were, and the little whimpering noises came out of the shadows.

The whimpers came from a hunched, rag-covered Shape that haunched in the shadows. The Shape had an old, old face, a gray face wrinkled like the underside of the pale things that grow overnight in the woods. The eyes that looked out of that face were tiny as the eyes of a chipmunk, and as tiny.

"YOU SHOULDN'T have done that to Marge." As Dikar's head rolled to look who said that, he saw that the curved roof of the den was of earth, and that thin, threadlike rootlets came down through the earth. "It isn't nice—"

"You keep out of this, Walt," Marge yelled. "I'm Nat's wife, an'—"

"Shut up," Nat growled. "I'll handle this."

Walt was smaller than Nat, and thinner. His hair was brownish and there wasn't so much on his chest or his face. His eyes were not as small or as red-hating as Nat's.

"I was only trying to say—"

"I've got all the say here," Nat rumbled. "Do I have to learn you that all over again—?"

"All right." Walt's shoulders shrugged. "You've got the say." His voice was flat, dead-sounding, as if he didn't care about anything any more. "What's your say about our visitor?" His hand jerked at Dikar.

"I'm waitin' to hear what Chuck finds out. If there's more of 'em prowlin' 'round—"

"There are no more," Dikar told him. "I'm the only—"

"Oh, you talk English, do you?" Nat leered down at him, his yellow fangs showing between thick, cracked lips. "An' good English at that. But don't expect me to swallow anythin' you give me."

"Swallow!" Dikar's belly muscles pulled him up to a sitting position. "You want to eat—"

"Eat!" the gray-faced shape in the shadows squealed. "Eat!"

She went down on all fours, started to crawl out. "He's brought us somethin' to eat—"

"Get back, Mom," Marge said to her. "There's nothin' to eat."

"Nothin'," Mom whimpered, stopping. "Nothin' to eat." She clawed up one of the little bones from the floor, started to mumble it with toothless gums.

"Look," Walt said, and turned to Dikar. "What Nat meant was that you can hardly expect us to believe that you ventured alone into these woods."

Dikar's eyes widened. "But why should I lie to you?"

"Why?" a new, thin voice came from near where Dikar had fallen in. "That's funny!" The Girl stood by a big, raggy-looking thing, the soft thing Dikar had fallen through. She was about Marge's height but her hair was yellow and her face rounder. "That's the funniest thing I've heard in a long time," she said, and started to laugh.

The way she laughed made Dikar feel creepy. She laughed with her mouth only, with her eyes she was afraid. They were all afraid, these Beast-Folk. They were afraid of Dikar, tied up though he was, but they had been afraid before Dikar fell in here.

They lived in this big hole and fear lived here with them.

Dikar was afraid of these Beast-Folk because *they* were afraid.

"Stop it," Walt was saying to the Girl who laughed. "Stop it, Ruth. It isn't as funny as you think. It isn't funny at all." She stopped laughing and Walt looked at Dikar. He looked puzzled. "Who are you?" he asked. "Where do you come from?"

"My name's Dikar. I come from—" Dikar stopped short. He'd almost said he came from the Mountain.

"Go on," Nat grunted. "You come from—"

"The woods," Dikar said. That wasn't a lie, it just wasn't all of the truth. "I live in the woods, over near the River."

"You're one of us, then," Walt said. "You're—"

"He's as much one of us as Hashamoto himself," Nat growled.

"I know everybody that lives in these here woods. I know every tree an' bush, an' I knew pretty near every rabbit an' squirrel till they were all killed off by the guys that's hidin' out. I know what you are." His foot banged into Dikar's side. "You're an Asafric dog. You were sent to track us down, an' you have tracked us down, but it ain't goin' to do them what sent you any good. You ain't goin' back to West Point to tell 'em where we are." His knife slid out of his belt-rope and caught the fire light. It was long and very sharp. "You ain't goin' to tell nobody nothin'." The fire glimmered redly on the knife. Nat reached down and his free hand closed on Dikar's shoulder.

"No," Walt said. "You can't do that, Nat. It would be murder."

"MURDER?" NAT'S thick lips pulled away from his yellow fangs, and the redness in his little eyes was flame. "Sure. An' what's what They're doin' to our people, all over the country?"

"They didn't—"

"Yeah, I know. They didn't shoot little Georgie or kill him with a whip. He just starved to death. I suppose that ain't murder?"

"Yes," Walt whispered. "Yes. But killing a man in cold blood—"

"We should let this ape go, huh? We should let him go back to West Point an' bring Them to round us up—?"

"Maybe even that."

"Yeah. You'd like to die. So would I. I'd like to die fightin' them black soldiers of Theirs, just so long as I took a couple with me. You 'n' me, Walt, we kin fight if the blacks come after us, an' die fightin', but Ruth won't die. Marge won't die. They won't kill *them*."

"Okay," someone said in the shadows beyond Mom, and then another hairy-faced Beast-Man crawled past her. "It's me. Chuck." He stood up.

"Well?" Nat grunted.

"There ain't nobody nor nothin' stirrin' within miles of here," Chuck said, clawing dirt out of his beard. "So you kin go right ahead with slicin' this yellar-haired bastard's throat. I heard what you said as I crawled through the tunnel an' I agree."

"Look," Dikar said. "Look. You don't want to kill me. I'm not an Asafric and I don't come from 'em. I swear, cross my heart, I don't. I'm white, an' I hate 'em as much as you do."

"You lie," Nat growled.

"Look," Dikar said desperately. "You said yourself an Asafric wouldn't come into these woods all alone. I live in these woods. I've lived in 'em ever since the Asafrics came to America. I—"

"Maybe he ain't lyin'." Marge was on her feet again. "Maybe he's tellin' the truth, Nat." She put her thin-fingered hand on Nat's arm. "I kind of believe him. I kind of feel, in here," she pressed her other hand against her flat breast, "that he's tellin' the truth, an' that it would be a sin if you killed him."

"Hell," Nat grunted. "You'd believe any man as pretty-lookin' as this."

"I'm inclined to believe him too," Walt urged. "He seems too simple, too naïve, to be one of Them, and he's certainly neither black nor yellow. I think you'd be making a mistake if you killed him."

"Mebbe," Nat hesitated, "Mebbe you're right." He scratched his head with the point of his knife. "I dunno but—"

"You're a fool, Walt." Ruth came away from the wall, her face tight, black flame in her eyes. "You're a pack of fools." She was standing above Dikar and she was pointing down at him. "You've only got to look at him to see he's lying."

"What do you mean, Ruth?" Walt demanded. "What do *you* see when you look at him?"

"I see someone that's well-fed, that's never known a hungry day." Walt's eyes opened wide. "He says he lives in the woods, and you know how all the creatures of the woods have been hunted out or frightened away. Do you know anybody in these woods who's not skin and bones like us starved rats? Do you—?"

"By all that's holy," Walt exclaimed. "You're right. You're

altogether right, Ruth, and I'm a soft-headed fool. What are you waiting for, Nat?"

"I'm not." Nat's arm stiffened suddenly, throwing Dikar back on the ground. The big Beast-Man was down on his knees beside Dikar. His knife swept up, caught red brightness of the fire and already seemed to drip blood—

Dikar rolled, using all the strength of his muscles to roll him away from that dreadful knife—Chuck dropped, smashing his knees into Dikar's belly, smashing the wind out of him. Chuck's hands grabbed Dikar's head, forcing it around, forcing it back to tighten his neck for the knife. The knife was coming down—

"Nat!" Mom squealed. "Chuck!" Heads jerked to her. She was scrabbling out of the shadows. *Not Mom!* Some brown-coated animal— It rose—

"Gawd," Marge gurgled. "It's a girl."

Everybody was suddenly as still as if they'd turned to stone. The Girl stood slim and tall, the red firelight playing on her slim brown body, making red lights in her long hair, stroking the taut arms that stretched a bow, that held a stone-headed arrow straight across the bow.

"The first one that moves," Marilee said, "I will kill."

CHAPTER 8
PERIL IS THE PLEDGE

THERE WAS a gasping silence, with the crackling of the fire the only sound. Marilee had all the Beast-Folk in front of her, and her bow moved just a little, back and forth, back and forth, so that it seemed to cover all at once. Dikar could read in her eyes that if any moved the arrow would fly, and he knew they all could read that in Marilee's eyes.

Back and forth, back and forth, the arrow moved. A laugh shattered the throbbing silence, a high, wild laugh from the reddish-haired Marge.

"Injuns!" she spluttered through her laugh. "Save us, they're red Injuns. The Injuns have come back—"

"Injuns," Chuck choked out. "No wonder I couldn't see nor hear her!"

The corners of Marilee's mouth quirked. "I could hear you. You made more noise tramplin' around the woods than two fightin' deer. I kept behind you all the time an' followed you here, an' listened, back there in the long hole, to what was goin' on in here." There was amusement in her voice, but there was pity too. "But I'm not an Injun, nor is Dikar. We're Americans, white Americans, just like you."

"You're not Indians, no." Ruth said, thin-lipped, her eyes burning. "You're not Americans red or white. You can kill us, but you can't fool us—"

"Because we're well-fed, an' you starvin'? I heard. But if Dikar had told you— Why didn't you tell 'em the truth, Dikar? Why didn't you tell 'em where you come from?"

"I didn't dare, Marilee. The secret of the Mountain—"

"Should be kept secret from our enemies, not our friends, you great silly. It's a good thing I worried about you, comin' down here alone, an' decided to follow you—"

"To follow! Then it was you—"

"Yes, Dikar," Marilee's eyes were laughing at him. "It was me followin' you all the way. You heard me once, didn't you? When you stopped an' looked back—"

"What's all this about a secret Mountain?" Marge broke in. "What—?"

"Not a secret Mountain," Marilee answered her. "But the secret of the Mountain. That the Bunch live on it, have lived there since we were children. The Mountain that is ringed around with high, straight rock—"

"Quarry Mountain!" Walt exclaimed. "But nobody lives on that. Nobody could get up there since the Asafrics bombed away the road to the stone workings, years ago."

"The Asafrics didn't bomb the road away," Marilee told him.

"The Old Ones did that, and we were already on the Mountain. The Old Ones took us away from the City when we were little children, an' hid us—"

"By jingo," Nat grunted. "There is an old story about children bein' taken away from Newyork in trucks, just before it was blown up. But the trucks were all machine-gunned—"

"Not all," Dikar put in. "One escaped…."

HE TOLD about how they'd grown up on the Mountain, how they lived there. The six Beast-Folk listened, mouths agape, and belief came into their eyes. Marilee's bow lowered, and at a sign from Nat, Chuck and Walt worked open the ropes that tied Dikar. As the ropes came off Dikar there were a thousand stinging prickles in his arms and his legs, and he stopped talking.

"Go on," Nat grunted. "Go on talkin'."

"But I hurt," Dikar complained.

"Go on," Ruth said, coming down to her knees beside Dikar and starting to rub his arms with her hard hands. Marge looked at Nat, Nat nodded, and Marge started to rub Dikar's legs.

"Why did you come down off your Mountain?" Walt asked. "You might have run into one of Their patrols and that would have been the end of you. Why did you take the chance?"

Dikar told them why. He told them that he'd come down to find out some way to rescue Normanfenton.

Nat exploded. "You're nuts even thinkin' of that. You wouldn't have a chance—"

"We would," Dikar answered him, "if we could slow up their trucks, some way."

"Yeah? How?"

Dikar told how he'd thought out it could be done. "But we can't do it unless the trucks go slow," he ended, getting up on his legs out of which Marge had rubbed the stinging pains. "An' I can't figure how to do that."

"Look!" Walt grabbed Dikar's arm. "Look, Dikar." The deadness was out of his voice. It was excited, and his eyes were excited. "You can stop worrying about that. We'll slow them up. Look, Nat!" He wheeled to the big man. "You know where that brook from Lake Mombasha, west of thirty-two, runs under the highway through a culvert?"

"I know," Dikar exclaimed. "I saw it. It—"

"—runs through a deep, narrow gully, this side of the road, on its way to the Ramapo—"

"Gotcha!" Nat barked, slapping his thigh. "Gotcha, Walt! That'll slow 'em, all right. Tell him, Walt. Tell Dikar what you mean."

There were shining eyes in that cave as Walt talked, and when at last Dikar and Marilee were slipping again through the forest night, Dikar's heart was light within him.

"We'll do it," he whispered to Marilee. "Nothin' can stop us now. With their help—"

"With *their* help," Marilee breathed. "The poor, starvin' people. How they brightened with the first hint that there was somethin' they could do against the invaders! How eager they were at once, to help! But they could have thought it all out themselves."

"They've lost the habit of thinkin' for themselves," Dikar responded. "They've lost hope. An' that's the biggest thing we can do for them, for the people of this country. Give 'em hope again...."

DAWN WAS already breaking as Dikar and Marilee gained their own woods. Johndawson, his eyes red with sleeplessness, his face lined with worry, came toward them. "You're back!" he cried. "I'd about given up hope."

"We're back," Dikar answered him, "an' with great news. Look, Johndawson." He told him what they'd seen, what they planned.

"Your scheme's insane," Johndawson said when Dikar was through. "Mad as a lunatic's dream. But just because it's mad, it might work."

"It's got to work," Dikar replied. "It's going to work. But come on. We've much to do before tonight. First thing, I've got to call a Council right after brekfes—"

"After we make the pledge, you mean," Marilee corrected.

"No," Dikar said. "After brekfes. There will be no pledge after brekfes this mornin'. An' maybe there will be no pledge at all."

"No pledge!" she exclaimed. "But, Dikar—"

"Have you forgotten what Annjordan told us? I'll have a pledge without crossed fingers, Marilee, or I'll have no pledge at all."

"What's this, Dikar?" Johndawson demanded. "What's this all about?"

…The bright morning sun struck down into the Clearing, and a babble of voices rose out of the Clearing, a babble of excited, curious voices.

"Why no pledge this mornin'?" Steveland asked of Halross. "Why has Dikar called a Council this mornin'?" Ruthnisson asked of Billthomas. "Why does Dikar look so stern, this mornin'?" Carlberger asked of Alicekane. But neither Halross nor Billthomas nor Alicekane could answer the questions asked of them.

No one asked questions of Bessalton, Boss of the Girls as she went to take her seat on one of the two bench rocks that stood either side of the Fire Stone, under the great oak. Her slender height cloaked in the black mantle of her hair, her dark face was sultry, her red mouth bitter, and there was something about her that seemed to set her apart from the rest of the Bunch.

Dikar, watching Bessalton from within the forest green, whispered to Marilee. "She guesses what's comin', an' is ready for it. Except you, she is the finest Girl of the Bunch, an' I'm heavy at heart that it is she I must fight this mornin'."

Marilee laid her hand on his arm. "Be kind to her, Dikar. Be as kind as you can."

"As kind as I can, Marilee. I promise."

The forest green rustled as Dikar came from it and moved to the waiting bench-rock that stood at the right of the Fire, the Boss's seat.

Dikar stood for a moment, his face grave. For a moment he wondered if he was right in what he was about to do. But the moment passed, and he sank into the seat that was his by right because he was Boss, and the Clearing waited for him to speak.

"BOYS AND Girls of the Bunch," Dikar began. "This is no ordinary Council I have called. For the first time, we shall not be bound by the Musts and Must-nots of the Old Ones, but be talkin' whether or not we shall break the most fearful Must-not of the Old Ones."

He paused, and the pause was filled by a curious, hissing sound, the sound of forty breaths indrawn.

"And yet," Dikar began again, "we shall still be guided by the Old Ones. Their Musts and Must-nots were laid down for our safety. Now we are no longer little children. We have changed, and the world has changed from what we an' the world were in that long-ago. We have outgrown the Musts an' Must-nots the Old Ones made for the children we were, an' so, this mornin', we think of what the Old Ones would say we must an' must-not do now."

Bessalton stirred at that and Dikar turned to her, gravely smiling.

"I want to ask you somthin'," she said, her eyes veiled. "Dikar, the Old Ones sleep under the stones below the Drop. They cannot speak to us. How are we to know what they would say if they could speak? Or"—suddenly her eyes, her voice, were mocking—"or are you goin to tell us that they *have* spoken to you in a dream?"

"Yes, Bessalton." Dikar smiled. "I am goin' to tell you they have spoken to me, an' in a dream."

Bessalton flung her hands wide. "Oh," she cried. "If you've called a Council to tell us your dreams—I have dreams too, but even though I'm Boss of the Girls, I don't call Councils to hear them. I tell them to the other Girls, when we've got nothin' better to talk about."

A Girl laughed, and another took up her laugh, and then the whole Bunch was laughing.

THE LAUGHTER beat at Dikar, but he sat quite still, quite expressionless. After a while, the laughter died down and the Bunch quieted.

"In a dream, Bessalton," Dikar said then, quite as if he had not been interrupted, "that is not really a dream but a memory of the long-ago, when the Old Ones brought us here and just before. Maybe you have the memory too, Bessalton. You should have, because you are in that dream-memory of mine. Can you remember, Bessalton?" Dikar's eyes took hold of her eyes. "Try, Bessalton. Can you remember that night?"

She wasn't trying to remember. She was trying to tear her eyes from Dikar's, but she couldn't.

"In that dream of mine, Bessalton, you are in a long, dim cave," Dikar's voice was even, low-seeming, but so clear that every ear in the Clearing heard it. "An' in that dream you are afraid. You are afraid of the thunder that smashes at the cave, of the thunder of death that rains on the City over your head. You are afraid of the way the whole earth shakes. You are clingin' to your mother, not cryin', just shudderin' as each new blast of dreadful thunder pounds you. Your arms are around your mother's neck, and one of her arms is tight around you. What is it your mother murmurs to you, Bessalton?"

Bessalton pulled a trembling hand across her forehead. " 'No, poppet,' Muddy is sayin. 'No, Bess-love. Don't be afraid.' But it isn't what she says that helps, it's feelin' her tight against me, feelin' her hand on my hair."

"Then you remember how the thunders stopped," Dikar talked on, "an' how the Voice came, the tired Voice from the radio there in that cave. Do you remember what it said, Bessalton?"

"I—I almost do, Dikar. Almost—I can't quite—"

"I remember, Bessalton, because I hear it again and again, in my dreams. It speaks not to us children but to the mothers in the cave. It tells them that there is no hope left, that the hordes have conquered all America save our City, an' that our City is about to fall. An' it tells how there is still one gap left in the lines that circle the City, how if the mothers will fight to keep that gap open, we children may be taken out of the City through that gap, and be saved.

" 'This is the dusk of our day,' the Voice goes on, Bessalton, 'of our America. If there is to be any hope of a tomorrow, it must rest in your little children. If they perish, America shall have perished. If they survive, then in some tomorrow we cannot foresee, America will live again....' Do you remember the Voice, Bessalton?"

Her eyes were wide, staring, and there was agony in them. "I remember the Voice, Dikar."

"You remember the Voice now, Bessalton," Dikar cried, his eyes releasing Bessalton's, himself turning to the Bunch, "an' now you all remember the Voice, Boys an' Girls of the Bunch. The Voice you remember is the Voice of the Old Ones. It is the Voice that sent our mothers out to die that we might live, that sent the Old Ones to give their lives that we might survive. Our mothers died, the Old Ones died, not for us, Boys an' Girls, but for the country for which the Flag stands, for the hope of a Tomorrow.

"An' that Tomorrow has come, Bunch. That Tomorrow is Today!"

THERE WAS no laughter now. There was no sound at all from the brown-limbed, straight-backed Boys and Girls. Dikar was talking again. In low, even tones he was telling the Bunch of the things he had seen in the far land, of the barbed-wire fenced prison camps, of the dried bodies hanging from poles where roads cross, and the whips of the Asafrics flogging white men and women to labor.

And then Dikar told of the Secret Net. He told of how leader after leader had been trapped by the Asafrics, and he told of the leader Normanfenton who had fought so bravely in the mountains to the North, and had been taken by the Asafrics, and would be hanged tomorrow.

"We can save Normanfenton," Dikar ended. "An our savin' him will give his people new hope, new strength, our savin' him may be the savin' of America. But to save him we must break the oldest an' most fearful of the Must-nots of the Old Ones. We must go down off the Mountain; we must become no longer Boys an' Girls of the Bunch, but Men an' Women of America.

"Once we do this one thing, my Bunch, there will be no turnin' back. We will not be able to find again the safety the Old Ones gave us here on the Mountain. We will live with danger an' with fear, an' if we all do not die, some of us surely must. Because of this I may not order you to follow me to the rescue of Fenton, I can only ask you to. The choice is yours."

Dikar's voice stopped, and there was a stillness in the Clearing, but in the brightening eyes of the Bunch, he read what their decision was. He had won. "Wait!"

It was Bessalton, who had risen and was standing before the Bunch. "Wait," she cried, "my brothers an' sisters of the Bunch, before you make the decision for which Dikar calls. You have listened to his story of the long-ago Time of Fear an' remembered it, as I have remembered. You have listened to his story of what the people in the far land suffer an' you have been filled with horror an' with pity, as I have been filled with horror an' with pity. You feel that you want to help 'em.

"But have you thought, as I am thinkin' now, of our life here on the Mountain, of how we work together? Have you thought how the Mountain gives us all we need, how we need nothin' that the far land can give us? Have you thought that we are the Bunch, that we have made our own life for ourselves, that the people of the far land are strangers to us?

"We are the Bunch," she cried. "Here we have liberty and justice for all. We may be struck with horror at what is happenin' to the people of the far land, we may feel pity for 'em, but what happens to 'em will make neither a worse nor a better life for us."

Dikar read the changing faces of the Bunch. He read that some already had swung to Bessalton, and some were in doubt, and some were still loyal to him…. Not to *him!*

Suddenly Dikar knew that the fight was not between himself and Bessalton, but between a way of thought that had spoken through him, and a way of thought that was speaking through Bessalton.

THE FOREST took her voice and swallowed it, and the rustling silence moved into the Clearing.

And out of the forest shadows came a man who once had been tall but now was bent, a man with the marks of whips on his gaunt body, with a gray, wrinkled face and gray hair. Johndawson stopped before them, and almost it was as if one of the Old Ones had come back from his sleep under the stones at the foot of the Drop.

"May I say something to the Bunch, Dikar and Bessalton? May I say something to help the Bunch decide?"

"No," Bessalton answered swiftly. "No. This is a Council of the Bunch an' no stranger has a right to speak."

A muscle knotted in Dikar's cheek. "What right have you to say no, when one asks to speak at the Council?" Dikar turned to the Bunch. "What say you?" he cried. "Will you hear Johndawson?"

There was a murmur in the Clearing, but no voice spoke aloud in answer. "I call for a show of hands," Dikar cried. "Those who do not want to hear Johndawson raise hands."

Hands rose, high-held. Many hands.

"Down," Dikar cried. "Now those who want Johndawson to speak, raise hands."

Hands rose, high-held. Many hands. "Down," Dikar said,

and turned to Bessalton. "What say you, Bessalton? What has the Bunch decided?"

She looked at him with somber eyes. "They have decided to hear Johndawson," she said.

"You may speak," Dikar told Johndawson.

The old man faced the Bunch. "I have listened to what Dikar and Bessalton have said," he began. "This is no new problem you face. This is no new decision. Long ago, the people of the world beyond the seas suffered as the people of America suffer now, and in America there were those who wanted to go to their aid, and there were those who said, 'They are strangers to us. We need nothing from them. What happens to them will make neither a worse life nor a better for us. Why should we fight for strangers? Why should we die for them?'

"Aye, long ago we Americans had this decision to make, and we Americans decided, as Bessalton wants you to decide, that America was our land, that what happened to the strangers of other lands was no concern of ours. We decided so, and we stayed within the seas that encircled us, and we pitied the people of other lands, but we did not risk our safety to help them.

"We *thought* we did not risk our safety, but we thought wrong. For, Boys and Girls of the Mountain, when the peoples of the other lands had been enslaved, their conquerors came across the seas and invaded America. We fought them, we fought desperately, but we fought alone and we fought in vain.

"Now I do not say that if we had chosen otherwise, if we had chosen to help the people of other lands fight against the invaders, that we should have won. But I do say that we *might* have won had we fought with the other peoples of the world. Our strength might have tipped the scales for liberty.

"We know now, to our sorrow, that the choice we thought we had was really no choice at all. We know now that when we decided to leave the stranger peoples to fight alone, we decided that we, too, would have to fight alone, and doomed ourselves to certain defeat."

Johndawson stopped to pull in a long breath, and the hiss of his breath was the only sound in the Clearing. Then his weary voice was heard again. "I have only one thing more to say to you. You argue now about a choice you think you have, but you have no choice at all. You may stay here on your Mountain, encircled by your Drop, and think you are safe. But tomorrow, or next week, or next year, the masters of America will discover that you are here, and they will come up the Drop, they will come down out of the sky, and make themselves masters of you. You cannot divorce your fate from the fate of the rest of America."

Johndawson's hand made a motion as if it gave something back to the Bunch that it had held while he spoke, and he turned, and shambled wearily across the end of the Clearing and into the leafy shadows out of which he had come.

It was Bessalton who spoke first. "I was wrong. Bunch, I was wrong. The Mountain is not our home. America is our home. All America. I vote that we fight for it."

A great throbbing cry came from the throats of the Bunch. "We fight for America, Dikar! Lead us." And then suddenly the Bunch were on their feet, and they were standing straight and proud in the Clearing, and their right arms were lifting—

"We pledge allegiance to our Flag." Bessalton's voice rang out, and the voices of the Bunch joined it. *"And to the Country for which it stands, one nation indivisible, with liberty and justice for all. We pledge ourselves, our strength, our lives, to drive the invader from the land and make our country free again."*

There were no crossed fingers anywhere in the Bunch. There was no denying of that pledge.

CHAPTER 9

DEATH IN THE FOREST

DIKAR CLIMBED over the last great stone of those that tumble about the base of the Drop and reached the black edge of the far land's forest. He shook from himself the water that had not yet dried since he'd come through the stream that screened the vine-rope.

Shadows drifted among the tumbled, huge rocks across which he'd come. Beyond, the Mountain loomed, the pale high glimmer of the rock-faced, steep Drop, the darker vastness that lifted high, high from the edge of the Drop into a star-sprinkled but moonless sky.

This was the other side of the Mountain from that which Dikar had come last might. Five white streaks sliced down the paleness of the Drop. Behind them, Dikar knew, hung the five thick ropes of vine that the Girls had woven, working busily all day. He smiled, thinking how Bessalton had driven the Girls to that work.

Bessalton had wanted to come with them tonight, but Dikar had forbidden it. He had forbidden Marilee too, or any of the Girls. There would be no use in their coming. There were deep bonarrers enough only for the Boys. The lighter bonarrers, used in hunting birds and rabbits and squirrels, would be of no use for the hunting the Bunch were going to do tonight.

The shadows among the rocks clambered nearer. Dikar could now see they were Boys. The shadows reached the black border of the forest. Vanished. Dikar made the sound of an owl hoot. Hoots answered from the woods either side of him. There was no nearby sound at all, no rustle of leaves, but there were shadows beside Dikar. The woods around Dikar were full of silent shadows and each shadow was a Boy, a quiver of arrows slung over his shoulder, a long bow in his hand, a knife stuck in the waist-string of his little apron.

"Danhall," Dikar said low-toned. "You four here?"

"Here, Dikar," a low voice came out of the darkness.

"Henfield?"

"All here."

Fredalton, Bengreen, Johnstone softly answered their names. These five older Boys led groups of four others each. It had been Johndawson's idea to split the Boys up this way, into what he called *squads*.

"Gather 'round me," Dikar ordered.

The shadows moved. They huddled close around Dikar. "Now listen," Dikar said. "This is the last time I'm goin' to talk to you. It's the last time anybody must talk at all.

"We've gone over an' over what we're goin' to do, an' how, but I want to go over the signals again, because it's most needful that everybody knows what they mean.

"Now," Dikar said. "The first one's the owl hoot, that we've just used. That means to come together. Then there's cricket-chirp. If I or one of the squad-leaders want to know where you are, we chirp an' each Boy answers in order. The next one, the tree-toad peep, is very important. The instant anyone hears or sees anything at all that looks like danger he peeps once, an' everybody freezes where they are while I find out what the danger is, an' what to do about it. Two peeps means all right, start movin' again.

"If someone gets in some kind of trouble that doesn't really mean danger, like getting caught in brambles, or something like that, he'll give the bull-frog croak. Everybody will stop when he hears that, so we don't lose each other, an' the nearest squad-leader will go to help the Boy who's given the signal.

"Last of all, there's the signal to attack, the wildcat shriek." A thrill scampered down Dikar's spine when he said that and he heard quickly stifled gasps as the others thought of what would happen after he gave that shriek. "Everybody got those straight?" he asked, trying to keep his voice steady.

"Yes," whispered out of the forest dark.

"Good," Dikar said. "Now only one thing more. You've all hunted in the woods for many years. You all know how to move through the forest without makin' a sound, without leavin' a trace. But you've got to remember tonight that the least misstep, the least little carelessness, will mean not just losing a deer but your life maybe. You've got to remember that it may mean not losing only your own life, but the lives of everyone of us. If you'll remember that, every minute, every second, we've got a chance to come back to the Mountain. If you don't, we've got no chance at all.

"And that's all, except—except that I wish you all good luck. All right! Spread out now, the way we decided."

THE HUDDLE of bodies melted away into the darkness, left and right. The darkness took them. The weird hush of the far land forest settled about him, and Dikar was alone in these strange woods. Not quite. By turning his head to the left he could just make out a still shadow that was not a tree but Danhall. He knew that beyond Danhall, just within sight of him, was little Steveland, and beyond Steveland, Halross and beyond Halross the other two Boys of Danhall's squad, and then Fredalton, and the four Boys of his squad. To the right of Dikar was Henfield, beyond him, the four of his squad, each Boy just within sight of the Boy to the left and right of him, and then Bengreen and his squad, and Johnstone and his.

Dikar gave the shrill chirp of a cricket. Chirps answered him as the crickets answer one another in the night-woods, the chirping running away from him first to the right, then to the left, and when they'd ended he'd counted twenty.

"Peep-peep," Dikar gave the signal to start, and he was moving, and he knew that in a long line either side of him twenty Boys of the Bunch were moving through the forest, but, save for the drifting shadows that were Danhall and Henfield, either side of Dikar, there was no sight of any movement, and no sound of any movement at all.

The mouldering leaves of the forest floor were cold and damp against the soles of Dikar's feet. The smells of the forest were in his nostrils. He was as much a part of the forest as the trees and the brush and the night.

Always, when Dikar prowled the woods, he had felt that a sort of life flowed through the woods and the things of the woods, the trees and the brush and the creatures, and he had felt that life flow into him and through him. He felt that life flow in his veins now, and he felt something else—a tingling excitement that came of the hunting in this night forest, of the knowledge that he was hunting and hunted, that hunter and hunted were the greatest game of all, Man.

Dikar carried death in the quiver that hung from his shoulder, carried a death-knife in his waist-string. Death waited for Dikar in the forest, waited for the twenty and one naked Boys who drifted through it, silent, flitting shadows.

A little wind stirred in the forest. Dikar's nostrils widened to a taint on the wind. *"Peep!"* Dikar heard, and froze, motionless at the trunk of a tree, more motionless than the boughs of the tree that the little wind stirred.

"Peep."

The tiny peeps of a tree-toad, the tiny sounds that meant danger was sighted, came from the right. Dikar went that way, darting soundless from tree-trunk shadow to shadow, stirring the night less than the little wind stirred it, and as he went the taint on the wind grew stronger.

He smiled abruptly, and moved more easily, though still with the greatest of care. A bush bulked black ahead of him, and blacker against the bush was the crouched figure of Carlberger. Dikar touched Carlberger lightly on the shoulder.

The Boy looked up, his pimpled face pale in the dimness. One hand laid a finger against his lips, signaling silence, the other pointed past the bush.

Dikar nodded and went around the bush, crouching low, and he saw what it was that Carlberger meant. He saw a man standing by a tree, some five paces ahead, peering intently about.

The man jumped when Dikar's voice said, close behind him, "Chuck." He whirled, his knife flashing to his hand. "Oh it's you," he gurgled. "Gawd! I didn't hear—"

"How is it you're here, Chuck?" Dikar whispered. "I didn't expect to meet any of you till we got to the Ramapo."

Chuck's thick lips twitched in his hairy face. "You ain't goin' to get to the Ramapo. Nat sent me to see if I could find you an' stop you before you got near it. It's all up, Dikar. We're licked."

"Why? What's happened?"

"The Asafrics have outguessed us. They ain't takin' no chance on an ambush. They've got sentries, Blacks, posted in the woods all along the road, both sides. There's a soldier every thirty yards, an' you can't get past that line because the minute one of them sights anythin' wrong he'll fire his gun, an' that'll bring all the rest of 'em on the run."

Dikar felt the muscles in his face harden. "Every thirty yards," he muttered. "How far is thirty yards?"

" 'Bout three times as far as to that big ash over there."

"Hmmm. An' they're in the woods, you say."

"Yup."

"Then each Black can't see the next one."

"I guess not. But they can hear them. Them Blacks can hear the snap of a twig for a mile, let alone a gun-blast— Say! What you got in mind—?"

"Come with me." Dikar slipped back to the bush behind which Carlberger hid. "You're in Johnstone's squad," he murmured. "Get him an' the rest of your squad, an' meet me here. Pass the word to the rest that they're to wait here till they hear somethin' up ahead. If it's a loud bang, they're to go back to the Mountain, quick as they can. If it's the scream of a loon, they're to come ahead, the way we've planned, till they meet one of us. Henfield's to be leader till we're together again. Get it?"

"I get it, Dikar," Carlberger whispered, and melted away into shadows.

"Gosh all godfrey," Chuck muttered. "I thought I was good in the woods but I never seen the like of the way you fellers kin sneak aroun'—"

"Listen, Chuck," Dikar interrupted. "Where's Nat and Walt?"

"In the woods this side of the Ramapo, but as near the creek from Lake Mombasha as they dare git. They're waitin' for me to get back an' tell 'em you've give up."

"Well, you get back there an' tell 'em it ain't time to give up yet. You wait there an' listen. If you hear a gun go off, you'll know what to do. If you hear a loon-scream, then you're to go ahead the way we planned. Understand?"

"Yeah. But—"

"Get goin'," Dikar snapped. "Hurry!"

Chuck went off. He's pretty good too, Dikar thought, but he makes a lot more noise than any of us would. Then Johnstone sifted out of the dark, and the four Boys of his squad, an' Dikar was whispering to them what he had in mind.

"It's takin' a terrible chance," he finished. "If there's the least slip-up we're as good as dead. You don't have to do it if you don't want to. You don't have to try it."

"Let's go," Johnstone whispered. "What are we waiting for?"

DIKAR CROUCHED in the brush, eyes narrowed. Just ahead of him stood a huge black man in the uniform of the Asafrics. The black man held his rifle slanted across his shoulder and he kept looking around him. Dikar could see his eyes, strangely white in the blackness of his face as he looked around, and he could hear his breathing.

Dikar's right hand was clutched around the handle of his knife. In the fingers of his left hand there was a little pebble. Dikar's left hand threw the pebble past the Black. It made a little rustling sound, and the Black spun to it.

Dikar's left hand grabbed the gun, jerked it away. His right slid his knife cleanly through cloth and flesh, left the knife where it was and flashed to the mouth of the Black, clamping over the gurgle that was starting to come from that mouth, muffling it. The Black's body sagged against Dikar, and Dikar's left arm went around it, holding it, letting it gently down to the ground.

The black body lay on the ground, very still.

Dikar was sick. The dim forest whirled around him, and then it was still and a shadow was drifting out of the dimness. "All right," Carlberger whispered. "All right, Dikar. I got mine." And then there was another shadow there, and another, and all five of those whom Dikar had taken with him were there, and all five had said that they'd gotten a Black the way Dikar had gotten the one that lay so still at his feet.

Six of the sentries would give no alarm tonight, or ever. There was a gap of over two hundred yards in the line of sentries the Asafrics had posted to guard the road against an ambush.

Dikar's blood was suddenly hot and rushing in his veins. His lungs filled with air.

High and shrill with mad triumph, the cry of a loon screamed through the weird forest silence of the far land.

CHAPTER 10
FINGERS UNCROSSED

THE ROAD from Newburg glimmered pallid in the starlight. It came out of the woods to the North and sloped gently down to where a stream rushed under it and then lifted gently again to be lost in the dark shadows of the woods on the South.

Halfway up the slope to the North of the creek, the arm-thick, far-spreading lower boughs of three great oaks overhung the road. The foliage of those oaks was very thick, and the starlight could not reach through it. It could not reach the strange, silent fruit that clustered on the arm-thick boughs of those oaks and weighted them so that the light wind that swayed the boughs of the other trees could not sway these.

There was a rumbling of thunder in the North.

The strange fruit of the middle oak stirred, ever so slightly.

"Quiet," Dikar hissed. "Quiet," and the stirring stopped.

Dikar lay along the lowermost bough of the middle oak. He peered down the road to the bottom of the dip, and his eyes widened. A darkness was coming up over the edge of the road there. It was spreading across the road. A tiny red spark glinted on the darkness. Another.

The yellow sparks were the reflection of stars in water. The darkness that was reaching from both edges of the road, that already was joining in the middle of the road, was water. Water of the creek that rushed down the hill otherside the road and under the road, hurrying to the Ramapo.

Hurrying no longer. *Under* the road no longer. Nat and Walt and Chuck, as they had planned last night, had tumbled great boulders into the gully through which the stream ran. The boulders had blocked the gully, and the stream was rising. It was rising above the level of the road, was backing up and filling the road.

The rolling thunder to the North was a little louder, a little nearer.

It wasn't thunder. It was the noise of trucks. Of the truck that carried Normanfenton and of others. Dikar could tell by the noise that there was more than one truck. How many more?

The yellow-spangled darkness down there, that was water, was spreading sidewise swiftly, was deepening swiftly. But the rolling thunder that was the rumble of nearing trucks was also growing louder, nearer, swiftly. Would there be enough water in the road to slow the trucks, to stop them, before the trucks got here?

Dikar's heart pounded within his chest. He was afraid of what would happen when the thunder got here. His throat was dry, and the palms of his hands that held his bow, that held his first arrow, were wet with sweat.

Something moved in the black woods on the other side of the road, down there where the water was spreading in the road. The something came out into the road and it was a man, a black-faced man in the green clothes of the Asafrics.

The Black went to the edge of the Water, peered down at it. There was a twang in the tree next to Dikar's, a flash in the air. The Black pitched forward, splashed into the water. The water covered him, hid him. It was deep enough! But—

Light! A shaft of white light slanted up from the top of the rise, to the right of Dikar, to the North! Thunder! The thunder of the trucks was loud in Dikar's ears, was battering at him. Smells! The smell of the trucks, the smell of the Asafrics, stank in Dikar's nostrils.

THE LIGHT swept down, and the road was bright as day, and a huge, black mass was roaring over the top of the rise, was roaring down the slope. Another. And another. The first truck was roaring past the oak to Dikar's left. Someone shouted from it. It was slowing.

It was slowing, and Dikar could see that it was filled with Asafrics, black-faced and yellow-faced, that it bristled with their guns. The second truck slowed behind it. There were Asafrics in this, but not so many.

In the center of the second truck, bathed by the light from the third, squatted a white man, ragged, chains festooning him, clamped to his wrists, his ankles.

The trucks had slowed, were stopping right beneath the trees whose boughs were laden with the Boys of the Bunch. The third truck was filled with Asafrics, bristled with guns—

A yowling, furious shriek rose on the air, right over the middle truck. A wildcat's shriek, and it came from Dikar's throat, and then the air was filled with the terrible, blood-chilling shrieks of wildcats, from twenty-one throats.

The air was filled with the twang of bowstrings, with arrows that showered down out of the trees, that spanged into flesh, into the flesh of Asafrics. Wild, blood-chilling, were the wildcat shrieks in the treetops, blood-chilling the sudden rain of death that showered out of the tree-tops, that struck down the Asafrics, too terrified by that sudden caterwauling of death, by that sudden rain of death, to move, too terrified to use their guns, to do anything but yowl their terror.

Dikar dropped from his bough into that middle truck. His knife was in his hand and it sank and rose, sank and rose, slicing flesh, stabbing flesh. From the middle tree, from the other two trees, bronzed and naked and caterwauling Boys dropped into the trucks, knives flashing, knives slashing—

Somewhere a shrill voice screamed an order, somewhere gun-crash was beginning, but Dikar had whirled to the white man who had squatted, chained, in the center of the middle truck. Dikar's arms were around Normanfenton and he was lifting Normanfenton in his arms, was carrying him to the end of the truck.

A black face rose in front of Dikar, a gun was leveled at him. A knife flashed, and the black face was gone, and Dikar was dropping over the end of the truck, was lifting Normanfenton down to him.

Crash and crash and crash, the night rocked to the crash of the guns. Red fire streaked the night, death-jets streaked the night. Dikar was in the woods, Normanfenton thrown over his shoulder, and death was whistling all about Dikar, was clipping leaves from the trees, chipping bark from the trees, and from Dikar's mouth was coming the owl-hoot, and owl hoots were all around Dikar.

"Great work!" grunted the man who was slung over Dikar's shoulder. "Great work man, but I'm afraid it's no good. There was a tank following behind— *Listen!*"

A noise shook the woods, a deafening noise, and the woods fountained flame, ahead of Dikar. And there was the noise again, and again the fountain of flame, and this time the flame lit Bengreen redly, and then Bengreen was pulped mass on the woods floor, and the merciful dark shut down over him.

"The Blacks don't dare follow you," Normanfenton gasped, "but their guns—"

"The treetops," Dikar called to the shadows that were leaping through the woods all around him. "Quick!"

The shadows leaped upward into the shadowy treetops, and Dikar whirled to a tree; but he knew he couldn't climb it with Normanfenton across his shoulder.

The terrible gun-noise shook the woods again, and fiery death fountained. "Hand him up," a voice said, above Dikar. Dikar looked up, and Johnstone was reaching down out of the tree, and beside him Fredalton, and suddenly the weight of Normanfenton was gone from Dikar's shoulder.

And then Dikar could climb.

CRASH AND crash, and the fountaining of death flames in the woods, and Dikar was up in the treetop, crouching on a bough with Johnstone and Fredalton, the three holding the chained Normanfenton between them, and suddenly there was no more of that terrible crashing.

But back from where they had come there were shouts, and a threshing of brush. "The officers are rallying what you've left of the men," Normanfenton gasped, "and are ordering them to scatter through the woods, to track me down. That's why the tank guns have stopped firing."

Dikar saw that Fredalton's side was red-dripping, that Johnstone's left arm hung awkward and loose. But there was no time to do anything about these things now, because of the threshing in the brush.

"Peep!"

Somewhere in the dark there was the peep that meant danger. *Twang!* From that same place the twang of a bowstring, and a thud.

"That's one Asafric that won't look for us any more," Johnstone grinned through the white agony of his face.

"Peep," again, and twang again, and again a thud.

"Good Boys," Dikar breathed. "Most of the Boys have kept their bows an' are cuttin 'em down. The Asafrics ain't goin' to stand much of that."

"Hush," Fredalton hissed, and Dikar hushed, and right below them there was a threshing, and a dark form moved noisily below their tree. Dikar could make out a squat, dark form, and a pale face, and he knew that this must be one of the yellow leaders of the Asafrics. He crouched, very still. The three here had no bows, and they had Normanfenton with them—

A chain clanked! The yellow man below wheeled, peered up into the tree. "Ah," his thin voice said. "Got you!" His arm rose, and there was a little gun in it. The little gun pointed right into the tree, right at Dikar—

A dark something leaped out of the darkness and there was a flashy thud, and the yellow man was down. A voice grunted below: "You won't do no more shootin'—"

"Nat!" Dikar called softly. "Nat!" The man below straightened. "Come up here in the tree before they find you."

"The devil I will," Nat grunted. "I'm lookin' for Fenton. I got the keys to his chains."

"Glory!" Normanfenton exclaimed.

Dikar reached out a brown hand in imperious gesture.

"He's here. He's with us," Dikar called down. "Come up here!"

"Great jumpin' Jupiter!" There was the scrape of clothes against bark, and then Nat's hairy face showed in the dimness, and Nat was straddled across the thick limb. "Here," the fellow said, "Here's the keys. I caved in the head of the captain with a rock, an' I got them off him." He was reaching something across to Dikar.

"What are those?" Dikar asked, staring at them. "What do you do with them?"

Dikar stared at him solemnly, his deep young chest rising

and falling quickly, his long fingers curled at his sides into loose
fists.

"Holy—!" Nat grunted. "I forgot that you— All right, I guess
I can hitch back here an' reach."

He did something to Normanfenton's chains and one of
them came loose. "Well," Nat mumbled. "You rescued him, like
you said you would, but what are you goin' to do with him now?"

"Take him back to the Mountain with us, of course."

"An' have Them trail you there?"

"They won't trail us."

"But they'll hunt this country, trackers an' planes, till they
find him or know he's dead. They'll finecomb that Mountain
of yours—"

"Wait!" Dikar exclaimed. "Wait. I've got an idea. Can you
put those chains on someone, like you're takin' 'em off?"

"Sure."

"Then— Look here, Nat. There's poor Bengreen down there."
A sob caught in Dikar's throat, but he forced his voice past it.
"He's so smashed up nobody can tell who he is, but maybe he
can do one last thing for the Bunch. I know he'd want to.
Suppose—suppose we put those chains on what's left of him,
an' these clothes that Normanfenton's wearin. He's about the
same size. Then, when the Asafrics find him—"

"They'll think he's Fenton," Nat exclaimed. "An' stop huntin'
for him. An' They'll figger the bunch that hopped 'em was some
of our own people, hidin' in these woods down here, so They
won't worry about lookin' over Quarry Mountain…."

Dikar nodded emphatically, and Nat fell swiftly to work.

DIKAR CROUCHED at the edge of the far woods. Out there,
the tumbled stones that ring the Mountain glimmered wan in
the starlight. Beyond them rose the pale, steep face of the Drop,
and from the top of the Drop the black Mountain rose, height
on height, to the gold-dusted sky. Dikar was tired, dreadful

tired. Pain throbbed in his every muscle, his every nerve, but he wasn't thinking of that. He was thinking of Bengreen—

He must not. He must think that here was the Mountain, and that he'd brought the Bunch back to the Mountain. He'd brought Normanfenton safely back to the Mountain.

How many others had he brought back with him?

Dikar chirped like a cricket. Chirps answered him, running away to the left and the right in the woods-hush. He counted them.

Seventeen.

Three, then, of the Boys had been left behind in the far woods. Bengreen was one of the…. Who the two other were Dikar must find out. He must hoot the Bunch together and call the—

"Peep!"

Dikar stiffened, jerked around to where that tree-toad peep of danger had come from. A blackness moved in the black brush, came out where he could see—

A slender brown form, bare arms lifting to him!

"Marilee!" Dikar said. "Marilee! What—?" She was clasped in his arms, she was trembling against him, and her lips were on his, were drinking thirstily of his.

"Oh, Dikar," Marilee sobbed. "Dikar."

"Marilee," Dikar whispered. "What are you doin' down here?" Another form moved into the pale light, and it was Bessalton, her black hair cloaking her, her face no longer sullen but happy. Smiling. "What are the two of you doin down here, Marilee?"

"I couldn't wait. *We* couldn't wait, doin nothin', while you Boys were out there in the dark, fightin'. So we came down the Drop an' went into the woods an' found the women of the Beast-Folk, Ruth an' Marge, an' brought them back here to our Mountain. But we didn't bring Mom, Dikar, because Mom, poor old thing, Mom died last night— But Dikar! You're hurt. You're—"

"I *was* hurt, my sweet," Dikar murmured, "an' tired an' heavy at heart. But I'm not any of these things any more, for I have you once more in my arms."

They got Normanfenton and the Beast-Folk to the top of the Drop, to the Mountain, though they had to make slings of the rope-vines to do it, and pulled them up the face of the Drop. Those of the Bunch who were not bad hurt stayed down till dawn brought light enough for them to make certain no traces were left in the far woods near the Mountain of their passage, and then these, too, climbed to the top of the Drop, and the adventure was over.

What that adventure of Dikar and the Bunch was to mean to America Dikar could not yet know. But this he knew, that at last the first step had been taken, the first try made toward the attainment of that hope for a brighter Tomorrow that a Voice had uttered in a despair-filled bomb shelter while death rained on a doomed City. This Dikar knew, that at last the first rift had been made in the dark cloud that overarched the once green and pleasant land for which stood the starry Flag the Girls had made, that the first thin beam of sunlight had fallen on that land....

The light *would* dawn once more.

And Dikar knew that never again would there be crossed fingers when the Bunch made their pledge to the Flag.

THUNDER TOMORROW

PROLOG

DICK CARR was four years old when the hordes of the Asiatic-African Confederation, having swarmed in triumph over Europe, began to attack our own country, from the south and west.

Of all this, and of the long and desperate defense that followed, Dick Carr had, of course, no comprehension, and hence when he became the almost legendary person we know as Dikar, he could not remember clearly that terrible past. But Dikar has vague dream-memories, of being always hungry, of being always afraid, of the thunder always in the sky, getting nearer and nearer.

The sharpest of his memories is of a siren howling like an enormous devil in the sky while he runs through the street, holding on to his mother's hand so the other running women and kids won't separate them. They get to a dim cave that once was a subway station, and they all crouch there in the almost-dark, while the earth shakes with great thunders.

In the station is a little girl, brown-eyed, brown-haired and pretty. When Dick shyly asks her name she runs the two names together, making one of them "Marilee." And from Dick's two names she makes "Dikar."

The thunders stop at last, and from the radio in the change booth a Voice announces that America has been vanquished. Yet there is, the Voice says, one last hope.

"A small, but determined force may be able to keep open a

certain gap in the enemy lines, to the north, long enough for us to take your little children out through it. We have some arms and ammunition available, but no one to use them except you mothers who hear me.

"It is a bitter thing I ask you to do," the Voice goes on. "I should not ask it except for this one thing. If there is to be any hope of a tomorrow, it must rest in your little sons and daughters. If they perish, America shall have perished indeed. If through your sacrifice they survive, then in some tomorrow we cannot foresee, America will live again and democracy, liberty, freedom shall reconquer the green and pleasant fields that tonight lie devastated."

The Voice stops, and the mothers go out of the station, faster and faster, and there are tears in their eyes but their faces are shining....

Later that same night Dikar is in a truck moving through a dark that is terrible with rolling and imminent thunder. On the driver's seat are two old people, Tom and Helen. The truck is jammed full with kids and in Dikar's arms sleeps Marilee.

They ride for a long time and come at last to a mountain. All around the mountain the rock has been quarried away so that cliffs rise to a great height, unclimbable except where a narrow ramp slants up to a clearing. Here the men who worked the quarry once lived in two long, many-windowed houses.

HELEN TEACHES the girls how to cook and to sew, and Tom teaches the boys how to make bonarrers and hunt with them, how to catch fish and make fire. The old ones make a lot of rules for living on the Mountain, a lot of Musts and Must-nots, and they say that because Dikar is the oldest he shall be Boss of the Bunch. And though the Bunch do not know it, Tom has planted dynamite at the bottom of the narrow hill that slants up to the Mountain.

One day a band of Asafric soldiers approaches the Mountain, and Tom and Helen rush down to meet them. Then, when the tumult of a great explosion dies away, Dikar sees only tumbled stones down there, nothing moving. The soldiers are under the stones, and under the stones are the Old Ones.

There is no longer any way to climb the Mountain without help from above, and the Asafrics never find out the Bunch live on the Mountain.

Now the Boys have grown tall, clean-limbed and slim-hipped; and they prowl the Mountain naked save for small aprons of split twigs deftly intertwined. The Girls are clad only in thigh-length reed skirts, their deepening breasts covered by circlets of leaves. Laughing-eyed and lovely the Girls have grown, but to Dikar the loveliest of all is brown-haired Marilee, whom he has taken as his mate.

Their life on the Mountain is a good one, and to all except Dikar the Mountain is their whole world. But Dikar wonders much about the Far Land that lies green and pleasant-seeming at the foot of the Mountain.

FINALLY DIKAR goes down into the Far Land, four of the

Bunch with him, and they fight and kill a small troop of Asafrics. The Boys bring back to the Mountain a man and woman of their own people. Johndawson and Marthadawson. From these Dikar learns of how the people of America are enslaved; and he learns that America's greatest need is for a leader against the oppressors.

Johndawson has brought to the Mountain a curious device called a radio with which he can listen to the talking of the Secret Net, a far-flung band of brave men who risk death and worse to keep hope alive in the hearts of the Americans. One day this radio tells how Normanfenton, who may be the leader America so terribly needs, is a prisoner of the Asafrics and on a night very soon will be brought along a road not far from the Mountain. Dikar decides to go down to where Normanfenton will pass and see if by chance the Bunch can rescue him.

Down there Dikar is captured by the Beastfolk, men and women who, having escaped the Asafrics, skulk in the wild

Fiercely the Bunch charged the
Asafric guards of West Point.

woods around the Mountain. Hunted and starving, these have become as mindless and savage as the beasts. They are about to kill Dikar when Marilee, who has trailed him unseen, saves him and makes friends with the Beastfolk.

The next night Dikar leads the Bunch down from the Mountain. Aided by the Beastfolk, they hide in the dark tops of trees, and from there they rain arrows on the trucks carrying Normanfenton and the Asafric soldiers who guard him. Leaping from the trees the boys savagely attack the soldiers; and Normanfenton is rescued.

By dawn the Boys are back on the Mountain, with them Normanfenton and four of the Beastfolk—Nat and Walt, Ruth and Marge; and in the woods of the Far Land they have left no traces that might give away the secret of the Mountain.

In that gray, cloudy dawn, it seems to Dikar that he hears again the Voice of long ago:

"…In some tomorrow we cannot foresee, America will live again, and democracy, liberty, freedom, shall reconquer the green and pleasant fields that tonight lie devastated."

CHAPTER 1
BOSS OF THE MOUNTAIN

I "IN SOME tomorrow we cannot foresee,'" Normanfenton repeated Dikar's recollection of what the Voice said that dreadful night long ago, "'America will live again….'"

For days Normanfenton had lain very sick on a cot in the Boys' House, but now he was better. He and Dikar had walked deep into the woods, while Dikar told how the Bunch came to the Mountain, how they'd lived here, and why he had led the Bunch down from the Mountain.

"The good Lord grant," Normanfenton whispered, "that at last that tomorrow has come."

"I—I'm not sure I really remember the Voice, or if I only dreamed it." Dikar's nearly naked body was sun-browned, his hair and curly, silken beard bright golden in the sun, his eager eyes blue as the sky. "But I am sure that if we just stay here on the Mountain, safe an' happy, while those things are goin' on down there, we will be doin' awful wrong." He stopped talking. Normanfenton wasn't listening to him.

A strange, far-off look was in Normanfenton's deep-sunken eyes. His thin lips were moving, but Dikar could not hear the words they made. The words weren't meant for Dikar. They were meant for Someone neither he nor Normanfenton could see but Whose nearness Dikar sensed in the sun's warmth, in the birds' singing, in the earth-smell of the woods.

They had come into a level part of the woods where there was hardly any brush. The dark trees marched away from them into a dim and enormous space that was filled with a strange, almost frightening hush. The trunks of the trees rose, without branch or leaf, to the rustling roof of the forest. In places, there far above, frost had thinned and painted the leaves so that the sun, striking through, made patches of flaming color, brilliant reds and yellows and glowing purples. One of the light-beams struck full on Normanfenton.

Clumsily built as he was, there was something about him that reminded Dikar of the giant oak in the Clearing, something of the same gnarled strength, of the same enduring patience. He was naked above the waist, and his tight-drawn skin was criss-crossed with scabbed grooves where Asafric whips had cut, the marks of Asafric chains were still raw on his bony wrists; but his great, black-bearded head sat proudly on his bony shoulders and the suffering and sadness lined deep into his face was not suffering nor sadness for himself.

It seemed to Dikar that very long ago he had seen a face like Normanfenton's on a wall—in it this same tender sadness. Words echoed inside Dikar's head: *Oh Captain, my Captain, the fearful trip—*

A scarlet bird streaked under the forest roof. A white rabbit scampered across the leaf-strewn forest floor. The words slipped from Dikar and the remembrance of that long-ago face faded away. Normanfenton stirred, turned to him.

"Yes," Normanfenton said gravely. "If we just stay here on the Mountain, safe and happy, we shall be doing something awful wrong."

"Then let's get started! Let's go down to the Far Land an' start fightin' to take back America."

"Softly, lad, softly." A gentle smile came to Normanfenton's lips. "That's an army they've got, son. Those blacks are the best soldiers the world has ever seen, and the best equipped. Yee Hashamoto, the Viceroy—the Boss of the whole business—is as shrewd and cunning as he is cruel, and the Yellow officers under him are no man's fools."

"But—"

"And so we must plan carefully, very carefully." Normanfenton's shoulders were stooped a little now. "I must— Do you mind, Dikar, leaving me alone for a while?"

"Sure I'll go," Dikar answered. "Sure, Normanfenton. Anyways, I ought to go see how the Boys are gettin' along with the new little houses they're buildin' for you and the four Beastfolk." He started away, his feet making no noise, his bow, an arrow fitted into it, ready in his hands against the chance that he might come upon a deer.

The ground started to slant downward and the brush became thicker, so that Dikar couldn't see very far. It was cool here, where the sun never reached, and the earth-smell was blacker, the forest smells tangy with the spice of berries and of certain leaves his feet crushed—Dikar stopped still, suddenly, not a muscle moving, head canted a little, nostrils flaring.

AHEAD OF him, hidden by the netted greenery of the bushes, there was sound of a big body moving. It might be a deer, but the wind was from Dikar, and a deer would have scented him and fled. A human then? But none of the Bunch would make so much noise moving through the woods.

Whatever it was, it was coming toward him. The fingers of Dikar's left hand tightened on the half-round wood of his bow. The right hand drew the shaft of the arrow back.

Close to Dikar the bushes threshed. A shadow darkened the interlaced leaves of the brush. The leaves parted.

"Oh!" A girl screamed tinily, staring at Dikar with big, frightened eyes. "You—" Not a Girl of the Bunch, but Marge, Nat's mate, only her head visible. "You were going to shoot that thing at me."

"Not your fault I didn't," Dikar said gruffly, lowering his bow. "You have no right bein' here. You were told to stay in the Clearin' unless one of the Bunch is with you."

"I know." She pushed through the bush into the little space where Dikar was. "But—but I had ter be alone. I just had ter."

When he'd first seen Marge, in the cave in the Far Land where he'd been trapped, she'd been covered by dirty rags, her hair tangled and dirt-matted, her eyes dull and without hope. Now, dressed only in a skirt of long grasses and leafy breast circlets, she was white-skinned, no tired heaviness any longer in the way she moved but a slow grace. Her hair, short to her shoulders, had been washed and brushed with straw stubble till it was alive and shining, its reddish glow gathered into the single, brilliant spark of the scarlet flower she'd placed in it.

Pale and thin her face was from starving, but it was high cheek-boned, full-lipped. There were grimy streaks on it.

"You've been bawlin'," Dikar observed. "What's the matter?"

A sob swelled in the shadowy hollows of Marge's neck. "Matter?" she gulped. And then, fiercely: "Nat's the matter. That sweet husband of mine. He—he's been bangin' me around again. He kicked me. Look." She put her left foot up on a moss-covered stone beside Dikar, parted the reeds of her skirt with quick, angry fingers. "Look at this."

Dikar bent to see, and her arm lay warm against his chest.

On the pale round of her thigh, high up, there was a dark blue mark.

"Kicked me there." Marge's voice was low, husky. "An' why? Just because I was sayin' how wonnerful I think you are."

Her head twisted to look up into Dikar's face, very near, and her lips were a little parted and very red, and her eyes were like deep, green-flecked pools. "That's no lie, Dikar. I do think you're wonnerful." She swayed a little and was leaning against him, her skin hot against his. "I could go for you in a big way, honey."

"Nat shouldn't have kicked you," Dikar said gravely. "I'll have to tell him that's a Must-not of the Old—" He whirled at a sudden crash of the bushes behind him.

It was Nat, his big chest matted with black hair, his little eyes red. "I figured you right, you damn tramp," he rumbled, deep in his throat. "You and your mealy-mouthed boy friend. Sneakin' off—"

"Nat!" Dikar snapped, hearing Marge moan with fright from where she'd fallen when he turned. "I don't understand what you're sayin', but I don't like the way you're sayin' it." The cords in his neck were tight. "Marge didn't sneak anywhere. She came to the woods to be alone an'—"

"Alone!" Nat laughed shortly, but there wasn't any fun in his laugh. "Alone with you, you mean."

"That's silly." Dikar wanted to punch the black-stubbled face that leered at him. "She didn't know where I was and even if she did, why should she want to find me?" He could not punch Nat here. It was a Must that any fighting should be done in the Clearing, before the whole Bunch and according to the Rules. "We met accidental."

"You're a liar," Nat said flatly.

THAT WAS a Fighting Word and if any Boy of the Bunch had said it to him Dikar would have had to dare him to a fight before the Bunch. But Nat was a stranger on the Mountain. Maybe he didn't know he had said a Fighting Word.

"Marge me met accidental," Dikar explained patiently, "an'

she was showin' me the mark you made, kickin her. We do not do that on the Mountain, Nat. We do not hit a Girl.

"What the rule is in the Far Land I do not know, but here on the Mountain you will obey our Rules. You will not kick Marge again. You will not hit her. I tell you not as Dikar but as Boss—"

"Boss, hell!" Nat snarled. "You're not my Boss, mister, and what's more—"

"I am Boss of all who live on the Mountain." It was hard to talk low and calm, but Dikar made himself. "As long as you live on the Mountain I'm Boss of you an' of Marge—"

"An' you can take her any time you've a mind to, huh?" Nat grunted. "If you think you can put that over on me, mister, you've got another guess comin'." His hands were knotted into fists at his sides and the muscles in his arms were bulging. "You yellow-bellied, lyin', sneakin' wife-stealer, if you didn't have them arrows in your hands I'd—"

"Try it!" Dikar threw bows and arrows from him. "Try it, I dare an' double-dare you." All of a sudden he'd forgotten that he was Boss, forgotten the Rules, in his blinding rage. "Come on and see whether you can," he said, thick-tongued, his fists up to meet Nat's lunge.

"I've got them, Dikar!" a clear voice called. "I've found the healin' leaves for Marge's hurt." A slender, lithe Girl was between them, rounded limbs warm brown, brown hair rippling in an ankle-long mantle about her, eyes gray and cool.

"See." She held out a bundle of dark green leaves. "They're hard to find this time of the year an' I had to look far, after you told me to get them." Marilee turned to Nat. "You steep them in hot water, Nat," she said, "and then you bathe the place with the water and all the soreness will go out."

The dark Beastman stared at her. "Yeah. Yeah, I know. That's witchhazel." He took the leaves from Marilee, saying, "Thanks." Then he was saying to Dikar, "Gees, guy! Why didn't you tell me your wife was here too?"

"But I didn't—"

"You ought to hurry," Marilee interrupted Dikar. "The quicker you bathe the hurt, the better. Go on, Marge. Go with Nat and he'll take care of you."

Marge looked kind of funny as Nat helped her get up. She looked kind of angry. But Dikar forgot all about her when the bushes came together behind the other two and only Marilee was left here with him.

He put his arm around Marilee, drew her close to him. "How did you know to bring the healin' leaves?" he asked. His heart was pounding with her nearness to him.

"I was in the top of that tree, right over there, sunnin' myself, when you met Marge." Marilee shivered a little, "Oh Dikar! I'm afraid for you."

He laughed. "Silly. Nat's no one to be afraid of. I can handle—"

"Not Nat, Dikar. It isn't Nat I'm afraid of for you."

Dikar's brows wrinkled. "Not Nat. Who then, Marilee?"

"Marge," Marilee whispered.

"Marge! Why should I be afraid of Marge? She's only a Girl."

Marilee kissed him for answer, and then was laughing, and no matter how much Dikar teased she only laughed the more.

CHAPTER 2
ARMY WITH BANNERS

"COME IN," Normanfenton's slow, tired voice said the next morning. "Come on in, Dikar. You've kept us waiting long enough."

Dikar had stopped in the doorway of the little house the Boys had built for John and Marthadawson, waiting till the outdoors brightness should die out of his eyes and let him see inside. All he could make out, as yet, was four shadowy shapes, and, to one side, a bunch of little yellow lights. The yellow lights were the bulbs of the radio Johndawson had brought from the Far Land. Above the shelf on which were the bulbs and the other strange parts of the radio, Dikar knew there was a big round hole in a black wall, and from this there came a flickering whistle like the trill of a certain brown-feathered bird that nests in the Mountain's woods.

"I'm sorry," he said, stepping inside. "I had to settle which of the Boys should go huntin' today an' which had to stay in the Clearin' an' put up the racks for the Girls to dry the skins on."

He could see them now, Johndawson sitting near the radio on a stool made from a half-log, the others around a table. "Then Bessalton, Boss of the Girls, had a talk with me about how much more berries an' fruits an' meat will have to be fixed up for this winter than we've always done, an'— Well, there were a couple other things I had to take care of."

"This being Boss seems to keep you very busy." Johndawson smiled. He was tall as Normanfenton, but his hair was all gray and he had no beard. "I wonder how the Bunch would get along if anything ever happened to you."

"Oh, they'd get along all right," Dikar answered. "Someone else would be chosen Boss, that's all. Most likely he'd be a better Boss than I've been."

"You're very modest, old man," Walt said. He had changed almost as much as Marge since Dikar first saw him in the Beastfolk's cave. He was still little and thin and pale, but he was very clean now. Like Johndawson, he'd scraped off the matted beard he'd had and you could see that he wasn't much older than Dikar himself. He and his wife Ruth were a lot different than Nat and Marge; Dikar liked them a lot better. "Well, pull up a stool and join our Council of War."

A big piece of grayish-white birch bark was spread on the table, its curling corners held down by little stones. On the bark Walt had drawn with a burned stick a kind of picture of the Mountain and the Far Land around it. Not really a picture, because you couldn't know what all the lines and queer marks meant unless you were told. Walt called it a map.

"I know what a Council is, of course," Dikar said, sitting down between Normanfenton and Nat, "but what is war?"

"Fighting," Normanfenton replied. "Fighting and killing, not one man against another but whole nations. All right-thinking men hate it, Dikar, but sometimes they have to take part in it to keep other and worse things from happening to them and their dear ones, or to free themselves of these worse things."

Dikar nodded. "That's what we're going to do against the Asafrics. War."

"Right," Walt said. The whistle from the radio broke off, started again. Johndawson hunched up, listening to it. "Righter than rain." Walt's face was all tight-lined, but it looked as if there were a light inside it, shining through. "At last we're planning to war against them, instead of snapping at their heels and then cringing beneath their lashes."

"We've decided one thing, Dikar," Normanfenton explained, "while we were waiting for you. All through this state forest," his bony forefinger pointed to tiny bunches of wriggy lines on the map that meant the thick woods surrounding the Mountain, "men are hiding."

"Like Nat and Walt were," Dikar said, nodding, "when Marilee and I found them."

"Exactly. Give them leadership, and they'd make a nucleus for the force that we must build if we're to accomplish anything more than the sporadic raids such as your Bunch carried out in rescuing me. We're going to try and get them together."

"Swell!" Dikar exclaimed. "I'll go down there tonight an'—"

"The hell you are," Nat snarled. "They'd eat you up before you had a chance to open your mouth. That's my job. Soon as it's dark, I—" A choked sound from Johndawson cut him off.

EVERYONE TWISTED around. The radio's whistle stopped. Johndawson stared at the round place out of which the whistle had been coming, his face taut.

The sudden quiet throbbed in Dikar's ears. "What have you heard, John?" Normanfenton asked, low-toned. "Tell us."

Johndawson's gray lips moved but made no sound. Then they moved again and his voice was flat, queerly frightening.

"That was National Prime," he said. "The chief of the Secret Net. He was speaking directly to all stations of the Net. He was telling them—" His wrinkled hands closed hard over the edge of the radio shelf. "He was repeating to them a proclamation the Viceroy seems to have made yesterday.

"Yee Hashamoto's always issuing proclamations," Walt grunted.

"Not like this one." It seemed to Dikar that Johndawson didn't want to tell them about it, was using all his strength to make himself do it. "It starts off with a warning that the Asafrican Confederation's Supreme Council is displeased with the state of things in the North American Province. The sporadic outbursts of rebellion, the constant sabotage of railroads and highways, in factories and mines and oil fields, have cut our production too far to be further tolerated—"

"And so they're lengthening the hours of enforced labor still more," Walt put in. "Probably abolishing all days of rest. I heard rumors—"

"No." Johndawson shook his head. "No, Walt. Hashamoto is demanding that every American take an oath of allegiance to the Confederation, that we vow implicit obedience to its edicts and renounce all acts of rebellion."

"So he demands it," Nat growled. "So what? He's been tryin' ter put that over for years."

"We're given a week to decide whether we'll take the oath or not," Johndawson kept on, as if he hadn't heard Nat. "If we do, unanimously, an amnesty will be granted to all previous rebels. Further, the Asafricans will permit us to institute a system of self-government, nominally autonomous but strictly supervised by the Confederation and subservient to its edicts."

"Complete and abject surrender," Normanfenton exclaimed,

"dooming America to be a vassal state, an enslaved colony, forever. Our people will never consent."

"If we do not"—Johndawson seemed anxious now to finish—"in a vote to be taken one week from today, or if we do and thereafter a single incident of rebellion or sabotage occurs, a new policy of dealing with us will be instituted.

"First: All persons now held in concentration camps and prisons will be put to death. Second: No Americans will be permitted to live in individual homes. Families will be broken up. Men will be herded in one set of barracks, women and infants in a second, children between the ages of two and twelve in a third—"

"Great God above!" Walt groaned.

"Any community where this or any other Asafric order is resisted," Johndawson continued, with great effort, "even by one person, will be bombed mercilessly until every house in it, every living being, has been destroyed. But that's not all."

"Not all! Isn't it enough?"

"Enough, Norman?" The gray-haired man's mouth twisted. "No matter what they do to us, if we still have refused to accept the status of slaves, they haven't yet accomplished the efficient exploitation of our country for the benefit of their millions, have they?"

"No." A sudden horror leaped into Normanfenton's eyes. "How?" he cried sharply. "How do they mean to do that, John?" But Dikar knew he'd already guessed the answer.

"HOW?" JOHNDAWSON gave it. "Shipload by shipload, they will bring over their own hordes to take possession of America. District by district they will populate our cities and towns and countryside with their black- and yellow-skinned masses. District by district they will empty America of Americans, carry our men and women and children to the starved deserts and flood-drowned plains of Asia, to the fever-infested, insect-ridden jungles of Africa, to the earthquake-racked islands of the Pacific."

"So that's the choice they've given the people of America," Normanfenton whispered. "Eternal slavery or exile...."

"They'll fight," Nat broke in hoarsely. "Cripes, Americans is different from them cattle over there. They'll never give in. They'll fight till they're all killed out."

"We'll know soon," Johndawson said, heavily, "whether they will or not. Hashamoto gave a month for them to answer him, but—" All of a sudden the radio was whistling again.

"Hush," Johndawson hissed. He was tensed, listening.

The rest were listening too, though no more than Dikar did they understand what they listened to. A rustle of leaves came in through the windows. Girls were singing at their work in the clearing. Boys, bringing in an arrow-slain deer, called happily to one another. The windows were bright with leaf-flecked sunshine. But in here was only shadow and pale faces, and the unending thin pipe of the radio.

Johndawson started translating out loud what the radio was saying. " 'My friends of the Secret Net'—National Prime—'for years we've lived in constant, imminent danger of death. For years we have endured such hardships as men will willingly endure only for the sake of their God or of a country they love only next to their God. Each morning for years we have heard the roll of our dead.

" 'Because they died, my friends, and because we lived with death, the spirit of liberty did not die in America. Because of our work, the Asafrics have enslaved only the bodies of our people, not their souls. All the fearful years we have kept alive in our oppressed countrymen the desire and the will to fight for freedom.

" 'And so, fellows of the Secret Net, when we heard this ultimatum of the Asafrics we knew that on us had been laid in great part the burden of determining how the ultimatum shall be answered. Our duty, if there is no longer any hope of release, is to urge our countrymen to choose the lesser of the two evils with which we are confronted.

" 'Terrible as it would be to live forever as slaves, would it not be better so to live in this land where we were born than to be torn from it and carried off to die in exile. This question a little while ago I put to you, and now you have all flashed your votes to me, and here is the result.'"

THE FLICKERING whistle stopped. Breath hissed from between someone's teeth. Dikar's heart was pounding against his ribs and his palms were wet with cold sweat.

The whistle started again—and stopped. Johndawson said nothing.

"Spill it," Nat grunted hoarsely.

The voice in the room wasn't Johndawson's. "Three hundred and fifty-seven voted. All but two said—surrender." Johndawson's hand made a curious sort of movement, as if he were pushing something away from him.

Walt laughed. "They'll do as the Secret Net says." His laugh made Dikar feel cold all over. "That's the end, gentlemen," Walt said, "of our Council of War."

"Well," Nat said, shrugging, "I guess we're pretty lucky we're here on the Mountain. Seein' how the kids been safe here so long. I guess we can get away with it too."

Normanfenton wasn't moving, and wasn't saying anything. He no longer reminded Dikar of the great oak in the Clearing. He was more like one up near the top of the Mountain, from which lightning had stripped the bark and the leaves so that its wood was all gray, the life all gone out of it.

The lump in Dikar's throat, that was keeping him from talking, broke. "Look," he said. "Look, Johndawson. Didn't they say they're givin' up because there's no hope, no more use hopin'?"

Johndawson nodded wordlessly.

"But—" Maybe he was wrong. He must be wrong. These men who knew so much about so many things he couldn't even understand—they must be right. "Oh, never mind."

"Say it, Dikar." Normanfenton was looking at him a queer way. "Say it."

"I—I was just wonderin'. If there was hope… If we could give 'em some reason to hope—"

"If we give them a reason to hope!" Normanfenton whispered. All of a sudden he jumped to his feet, his eyes shining, his face shining. "You're right. You're all-fired right, Dikar!"

He swung around to Johndawson and his long arm was pointing to the radio and his voice was loud and clear again. "Send it out, John. Send it out all over the Net, all over America. Tell them that an army is forming to battle the Asafrics, an army with banners.

"Tell them—tell them that the first blow will be struck tomorrow. Tomorrow night. Say that if they listen tomorrow they will hear the sound of the army marching, the sound of Freedom's host, marching—"

Johndawson grabbed the round black handle of a little orange-red bar that was hinged to the radio shelf. He jerked it up and down, fast. Blue sparks crackled around the bar, sparks of blue light that didn't seem as bright as the light in Johndawson's face.

"An army with banners," Walt said softly.

CHAPTER 3
SEEK THE FAR LAND

"**B**UT DIKAR," Marilee exclaimed. "What can you do by tomorrow night big enough so that hearin' of it, the people of the Far Land will get back the hope they've lost?"

All day Dikar had stayed with the others in Johndawson's house, talking and planning and so he hadn't till now had a chance to tell her about it all. "It's got to be awful big," she went on, "bigger even than takin' Normanfenton away from the

Asafrics. It's got to be something only an army could do, an' we few are no army."

Right after supper Dikar had asked Bessalton to excuse Marilee from cleaning up and the dishwashing, and they'd come here to their own little house in the woods beyond the Eating Place.

"No, we're no army," Dikar murmured, lying close by Marilee on their bed of pine branches while he watched the grayness of just-before-night creep silently in through the open doorway. "But we plan to do what would be a big thing for even an army."

"What?" Marilee's head rolled on his arm that pillowed it, and her breath was warm on Dikar's cheek, and the smell of her breath was sweeter than the smell of the drying pine-needles. "What do you plan?"

"I love you, Marilee," Dikar said dreamily. "More an' more every day. I love you."

"Dikar!" Her hands pushed against his side, hard, pushed her up to a sitting position. Her eyes flashed angrily; her mouth quivered between anger and laughter. "If you don't stop teasin' an' answer me, I'll—I'll—"

"You'll what?" Dikar demanded, sitting up too. "What will you do, Marilee?"

"I'll stop lovin' you."

"No." He smiled, putting his great hands on her warm arms and holding her so. "That you can't do. You can't ever stop lovin' me or I you as long as the streams run down the Mountain an' the trees reach upward to the sun. It is because they are what they are that streams run down an' trees reach upward an' it is because we are what we are that we love each other, my Marilee."

Her eyes filled with tears, and then they were big and frightened. "Why do you say that?" she cried. "Dikar! Why do you look at me like—like you're goin' away tonight an' never coming back, an' are afraid you'll forget what I look like?"

"Silly." He smiled, but he kept on looking at her the same

way. "I *am* goin' some somewhere tonight where you cannot go with me, but I'll be back in the mornin'."

"You're goin' away," Marilee whispered. "You're goin' down into the Far Land, Dikar."

"Yes," he answered, low-toned. "I'm goin' down into the Far Land tonight an' you must not follow me like you did that night we first met the Beast-folk. Do you understand? You must promise me, cross your heart, that you will not follow me. I must think only of what I've got to do an' not worry that you're trailin' me. Promise me that, right now."

"If you'll tell me what it is you go to do. It's somethin' about your plans for tomorrow, isn't it?"

"Yes. Look here, Marilee. You know how, when we have snowball fights in winter, one side builds a fort with snow an' the other side tries to capture the fort?"

"Of course I do."

"Well, there's a place called Wespoint not far away from here on the river Johndawson's told us about, an' the Asafrics have made that place into a fort big almost as half this Mountain. It's there the soldiers live who rule all this part of the Far Land around here.

"They keep lots of guns there, little guns like the soldiers on the trucks had an' guns big as trees, like those that made the thunder I remember from the long-ago Time of Fear before we came here to the Mountain. It's a very strong fort, Marilee, so strong that, only an army could capture it, but tomorrow night we're goin' to try an' capture it."

"WE'RE GOIN' to—!" Marilee gasped. "But Dikar! Even in our snowball fights we always pick lots less Boys an' Girls for the side that's in the fort because the fort makes that side so much stronger. There at Wespoint all the hundreds an' hundreds of Asafrics are in the fort an' we'll be just a few tryin' to capture it. Just the Bunch."

"Not just the Bunch, honey. Nat's goin' down to the woods below the Mountain to try an' get the help of the Beastfolk who're hidin' there, an' we're pretty sure we can get 'em to help us."

"But even then we'll be awful few, an' we'll have only bonarrers an' knives against their guns."

"We have guns too. The eight long guns Johndawson calls rifles an' the nine little ones he calls revolvers that we brought from the fight down at his house in the Far Land. They tell me there are a lot of old soldiers among the Beastfolk who'll know how to use them."

"Eight rifles an' nine revolvers! It's crazy, Dikar! It can't be done."

Dikar's fingers tightened on Marilee's arms, and in his face the lines tightened. "It's crazy and it can't be done, but it's *got* to be done. The only way we have even a little chance of doin' it is by pullin' some stunt like the one we pulled to rescue Normanfenton. To do that we've got to find out all about Wespoint, an' that I can do best of all. That's why I'm goin' down to the Far Land tonight."

"But if the Asafrics catch you—"

"They won't," Dikar said, hard toned. "Look, honey." He was, getting to his feet and pulling Marilee up with him. "We've argued like this all day, just the five of us. If more knew about it we'd argue longer an' do nothin'. That's why we're callin' no Council of the Bunch but keepin' it secret from 'em till the last minute, an' that's why I'm askin' you just to give me your promise not to trail me down in the Far Land."

"I promise, Dikar," Marilee said. Then her arms were around him, holding him tight to her, and her lips were on his lips, burning.

And then she was whirling away from him, was plucking his sharp hunting knife from where it hung.

"Marilee!" Dikar cried. "Don't!" But he saw now that she'd snatched from the wall his bow and quiver of arrows too and was holding the weapons out to him.

"How can I keep you?" she said, deep-throated. "Go fast an' safe, an' come back fast an' safe to me."

As Dikar went out into the darkening woods, there was a great gladness in his heart that he had Marilee for his mate.

THE MOUNTAIN loomed above him on his right, a vast and rustling blackness. Girls' laughter, Boys' happy shouts, came from his left where the Bunch played games by the light of the great flames on the Fire Stone at the end of the Clearing.

A moment or two later Dikar caught the smell of newly cut wood. By the wavering, leaf-shadowed firelight, he saw he'd come abreast of the little house just built for Nat and Marge. Maybe Marge wasn't letting Nat go. Dikar decided to make sure, veered toward their house. A curtain of deerskin hung over the doorway.

Dikar called, low-toned, "Anybody inside?"

He heard someone moving inside and then, just the other side of the curtain, a whisper, "Who is it?"

"Dikar. Has Nat gone?"

"Sure." The curtain pulled aside and dim firelight stroked Marge's white form. "Sure he's gone," she whispered. "Come on in."

"No," Dikar answered. "I—I have to—"

"Scared?" Her hand caught his arm. "You mustn't get cold feet now, after bein' smart enough ter send him away?" Her eyes had a hungry look in them and her low voice was queerly husky. "You mustn't be scared of me." Her lips were half-parted and moist.

The clinging touch of her hand made Dikar feel creepy. He reached his own free hand across to it, pulled it loose. "Please, Marge," he said. "I've got somethin' important to do. I haven't got time—"

"You haven't!" She jerked her hand away. "You damned pup." A word Dikar didn't know spat from her suddenly white lips. "So I'm not good enough for you, huh?"

"Why Marge," Dikar said, puzzled. "You're no different to me than any of the other Girls. I—"

"Damn you!" she shrieked and her hand slapped stinging across his cheek. It started to slap again but Dikar caught its wrist, twisted it just enough to make her arm so stiff as to hold her away from him.

"I don't know what's makin' you act like this," he said, tight-mouthed, "and I haven't got time to find out. I've got somethin' important to do, an'—"

"Important!" she panted, the hunger in her eyes turned to hate. "Go an' do it, then, but don't come crawlin' back ter me when you're done. Beat it, d'you hear. On your way." She jerked loose and the skin curtain dropped.

Dikar stared at it, rubbing the slapped place on his cheek. All of a sudden the whole thing struck him as very funny and he laughed aloud. Then he turned and hurried off to where he'd told Normanfenton and Johndawson to meet him, a little clear space near the latter's house.

THEIR FACES, just visible in the starlight, were drawn and anxious. "We've been talking it over, Dikar," Normanfenton said. "We're wondering whether we're right in letting you go down there alone. Do you understand what the Asafrics will do to you if they catch you?"

"I understand it won't be anythin' nice," Dikar answered, quietly, "an' I don't want any more talk about whether I'm to go or not. You said you would show me how to tell my way by the stars an' that's all I want to hear."

"All right, son," Normanfenton said. "If you're bound and determined. You remember we showed you on the map that West Point lies a little northeast of where you'll be when you've climbed down the vine-cable?"

"That's right."

"Now then, look up at the sky, the way I'm pointing." Dikar did so, and Normanfenton went on to show him how the stars made certain pictures in the sky, how he could find one star that was called the North Star, and how by that star he could always tell which way to go.

Dikar listened hard, so hard that when he heard the threshing of someone moving around in the bushes he didn't even wonder who it might be.

Then Normanfenton had finished and Dikar was saying goodbye to him and to Johndawson, and he was alone again, going down toward the edge of the Drop and the place where he would climb down to the Far Land.

It was black dark here, but he knew by the slant of the ground how to reach the place where a streamlet leaped far out over the edge of the Drop and fell to the rocks below, hiding behind its fall the rope of vines by which he must climb down to the Far Land.

The golden sparkle of the stars broke through the thinning end of the forest, and then Dikar was out of the woods. The stream was at his feet. He could see the thick, twisted rope of vines that slanted down from the tree where its upper end was fastened, to vanish into the waters just where they leaped out over the Drop.

Bending to take hold of the rope, Dikar felt the skin at the back of his neck prickle. He sniffed. There was a smell of the breeze that ought not to be here, the smell of a human. Muscles along his jaw-ridge knotted. One of the newcomers to the Mountain must have been here at the edge of the Drop not long ago. He must find out which one, when he got back tomorrow, and order punishment for him.

Thinking this, Dikar lowered his legs over the lip of the cliff, caught them about the rope and slid down fast through the smother of water, stopped his slide as soon as he could get breath again, started going down more slowly, hands and legs working together in smooth rhythm.

The rope swung back and forth with his weight. It twisted around so that Dikar saw one minute the pale, rough face of the cliff, the next the foaming waters streaking down, to smash themselves on the tumbled, giant rocks below. Dikar wanted to look down at those rocks, but knew he must not. They were terribly far below, and between him and them was only this thin rope of vines. Even the thought of the awful emptiness beneath him dried his throat with terror.

Down he climbed, slowly, the rope swinging more and more as he went down so that now at the end of each swing Dikar could look up along the cliff and see its top, and the star-dusted black of the sky.

Something blotched the stars, just beside where the stream foamed white over the cliff-edge. Dikar swung under the veiling waterfall, swung out past it. It was a girl peering down, something flashing in her hand. As he swung back, Dikar carried memory of her with him. She was short-haired. She was Marge!

He swung to where he could see her again. She was bending down. The thing she held was a knife. It was reaching down into the seething water—reaching for the rope.

"Don't!" Dikar yelled. "Don't!"

She kept on reaching.

Her voice came screeching thinly down to him. "Laugh at me, will you? Laugh now, why don't you?" Dikar, swinging back under the water, couldn't see her, but he could feel a quiver in the rope, a quiver that told him she was cutting it.

He looked down. The stones were still dreadfully far below.

CHAPTER 4
THE DEVIL WEARS GREEN

IT FLASHED through Dikar's mind, too late, that it had been Marge in the bushes while he was talking to Normanfenton, that she'd heard enough to learn that he planned to climb down here, had hurried here while they talked of the stars and been hiding in the woods when he got there. He'd heard her, even smelled her, but hadn't paid attention to it because he could not dream that anyone on the Mountain would want to hurt him.

There was no way he could save himself. Even if he could swing himself to the face of the cliff before the rope was cut through, there was no handhold there.

"Marge!" he yelled up. "Wait, Marge—" He swung out from under the waterfall yelling, "Don't cut it, Marge," and saw that she wasn't cutting, that she'd lifted and swung around to the woods.

Another Girl leaped into view, clutched at Marge's knife-hand. A Girl whose long hair swirled about her. Marilee!

Dikar started climbing up again, his haste tearing his muscles, tearing his breath from him. He swung out from under the water's veil. Looking agonizedly upward, he saw the Girls locked together on the very edge of the cliff, their bodies straining, their feet slipping in the water. He swung back, and this time did not swing out on the other side far enough to see up.

Dikar couldn't see what was happening up there. He couldn't see what was happening to Marilee. He could only climb, frantically, breath sobbing from him.

A scream cut through the roar of the outleaping waters. Down through the torrent a dark something fell. It shot past Dikar, went spinning on down, a screaming Girl who plunged into the brawling spray of pale waters on the rocks so far below.

She had whirled down past him too fast for Dikar to see who she was. Marge—or Marilee.

For an endless, sickening moment the strength was out of Dikar's hands and legs. His grip on the rope was loosening. Then he had his strength back and was fairly hurling himself up the shaking rope, up into the smother and batter of the waterfall, and then he was kneeing solid rock under rushing water, was heaving erect.

Half-blinded, he saw the form before him only hazily, but he could make out an upraised arm, the flash of starlight on polished steel. His hand dashed the blinding wetness from his eyes.

"Marilee!" Her name burst from his chest in a great shout of thankfulness. He was crushing her quivering body to him, sobbing out his relief and his joy into the fragrant smother of her hair. "Oh, Marilee."

"I didn't break my promise," he heard a small voice say. "I really didn't, Dikar. I promised not to trail you down into the Far Land, but you said nothin' about what I should do on the Mountain. I wanted at least to know that you climbed down safely so I trailed you down to here, stayin' far back behind you so you wouldn't know I was doin' it. If I hadn't—" She broke off. Dikar stopped her shuddering with the tight hold of his arms and his kiss on her cold lips.

"No." Her hands on his chest pushed her free of his hold. "Don't kiss me." Her eyes were big in the pale oval of her face, big and staring. "How can you kiss me, Dikar, when I've just killed a Girl?"

"Listen," Dikar said. "The Old Ones taught us that killin' is wrong, but the Old Ones themselves killed the Asafric soldiers to save the Bunch, an' that wasn't wrong. What you just did isn't wrong, because you had to do it to save me. You had to kill Marge to save me," he repeated, "an' that wasn't wrong."

"Poor Marge," Marilee whispered. "Poor, poor Marge." She was staring at the edge of the Drop over which she'd seen Marge fall.

"How did you know yesterday to be afraid of her for me?" Dikar asked. "How did you know that she would try to kill me?"

Marilee's eyes came back to him. "I didn't think she'd try to kill you, but I knew she'd hurt you some way, you bein' what you are an' she what she was."

"What she was? I don't understand."

"MARGE WAS sick, Dikar. Not in her body but in her mind. Ruth told me that Marge an' Nat once had two little children, a boy an' a girl. One night Marge came home from somewhere they call church meetin, an' found that the Asafrics had taken Nat away because he'd been doin' somethin' for the Secret Net that he hadn't told her about. The Asafrics had burned down their house, an' in what was left of the House Marge found her children dead.

"Nat escaped from the Asafrics an' sent for Marge to come to him where he was hidin' in the woods. She went to him, but she blamed him for what had happened to her children an' hated him, Ruth said. To get even with him Marge started bein' in love with every man she saw an' if they wouldn't be in love with her she hated them too an' did everything she could to hurt them.

"Nat had an awful time with Marge, Dikar, but he stood for it because she was his wife an' he loved her."

"Loved her, Marilee? A queer way he showed his love for her, bangin' her around."

"Nat is a rough man, an' he isn't very smart. He thought that was the way to cure her.... I—I don't know how I can tell Nat—"

"You mustn't!" Dikar said quickly. "He must never know how she died, an' the Bunch must never know, or this thing will always be between him an' the Bunch. We'll just let everybody think she wandered off into the woods an' fell over the edge of the Drop. Don't you see that's best, Marilee, for Nat? an' for you?"

"Yes," she whispered. "Yes, Dikar. I see."

Dikar hated to leave Marilee with that look of pain on her face, but every moment he stayed here would make leaving her even worse. Swiftly he bent and got his hands on the rope and saw that Marge's knife had barely scratched it; he started down again, climbing into the black dark of the Far Land.

Down in the Far Land the woods were very like the woods of the Mountain, the sounds and the smells of them the same; but there was a feel of fear in these woods and there was a strangeness that made Dikar think of the dreams he sometimes had in which endlessly he ran from a blind and voiceless some-thing that pursued him.

So that he might watch the stars and know his direction by them, Dikar traveled not on the ground but in the top of the forest, running along boughs, swinging from one treetop to another by his long arms. All the Bunch could go as fast this way as on the ground, and faster.

A very long time Dikar went like this through the night. He could not go straight because he had to go around mountains higher than the Mountain from which he came, and he had to wade or to swim across streams, but always he guided himself by the North Star.

Once the Beastfolk smell came very strong to Dikar and, startled, he made a wide curve to get past it. Once, high in a tree, his reaching hand found a nest, and there was a sudden furious beat of wings about his head, so that he missed his hold and fell, and barely caught the tree's lowermost bough in time to save himself dropping five times his own height to hard ground.

All of a sudden Dikar came to the edge of the woods.

He was halfway up the side of a mountain. Right below the tree bough on which he lay, a wide road glimmered pale in the starlight, and beyond the road was a drop.

Dikar looked down that drop, and gasped. Down there was water! Not a stream like those on the Mountain, but water wider than the Mountain is high. It was black as the sky, and it had no ending.

"When you come to the River," Normanfenton had said, "you'll be very close to Westpoint."

This was the River.

"Go North along the River," Normanfenton had told him. Dikar started going along the edge of the woods, a little in from the road. He moved more slowly now, took more care not to make any sound, because now he was near Wespoint and the Asafrics would be watching to see that no one was too near.

PRETTY SOON he came to the end of the woods and had to go down. The mountainside slanted steeply down to the road and the bushes were not very high. Then there were no bushes and the steep ground was all queer flat stones that slid on each other when Dikar tried to walk on them.

He grabbed backward for the last bush and held on to it while he looked around for an easier way to go. Below him was the road, where he would be seen from a long distance. The steep slant above Dikar was covered with the little, sliding rocks. Ahead was a shoulder of the mountain, around which the road curved.

Sound was coming from beyond that curve, a humming kind of thunder, low down and rushing toward him. Dikar had heard that rushing sound not long before, waiting in the treetop for the rescue of Normanfenton. It wasn't thunder. It was the sound of a truck.

It was very loud now, just around the mountain's shoulder. There was sudden light on the road. Dikar pulled on the bush to drag himself back behind it. The bush came to him instead, and the stones were sliding out from under him, and he was slipping down to the road with a terrible clatter of stones around him.

The light hit him, blinded him. He couldn't get his feet under him. Something screeched crazily, right over him, and there were shouts all about him. Dikar stopped sliding, jumped up.

"Stand still or I shoot!" a high, thin-voice yelled. Dikar blinked into light coming from two great round things. The light was blotted by the figure of a man, coming toward him. The man was black against the light, and Dikar could make out that he was shorter than any of the Boys of the Bunch and that in his hand he was holding one of the little guns called revolvers.

Dikar stood very still, because he knew what the revolver could do to him.

The man stopped in front of Dikar. He had a queer, frightening smell. His voice was thin and high-pitched like a Girl's and it was very frightening too. "What are you doing here?" he demanded. "How did you get through our pickets?"

Dikar was too scared to say anything in answer.

"Sullen, are you?" The man got taut all of a sudden, as if he'd just made out something surprising about Dikar. "So! You are almost naked—armed only with bow an' arrows and a knife. The tale Captain Senshi of the ambushed convoy told was true, then. It is too bad he's already been executed. But Colonel Wangsing will be interested—very interested." The man chuckled; then he was yelling, "Bomo! Gullah!" and other words Dikar couldn't understand.

Two other men came running from behind the light, very big, their smell different from the first one's, stronger and even more frightening. One of them snatched away Dikar's bow and quiver of arrows and plucked his knife out of his apron cord. The other grabbed Dikar's arms from behind, pulled them together in back of him. Dikar felt something cold snap around his wrists, and the man let go. Dikar tried to pull his wrists apart. The cold thing bit into them, held them together.

"Yess," the first Asafric hissed. "The commander will be very interested in knowing that a band of naked savages do roam these woods. He will want to know where they are hiding—" Dikar was glad now that he hadn't been able to talk. Maybe he could fool the Asafrics into thinking he couldn't talk; that way he could get out of being made to tell about the Mountain. "Bomo—" Once more the Asafric made sounds that seemed like words but were no words Dikar had ever heard before.

The two others took hold of his arms, pushed him toward where the light came from. The light wasn't in his eyes any more and he could see that the short man, who must be the boss, was yellow-faced, flat nosed, his eyes narrow and slanted, his clothes green.

Bomo and Gullah wore green clothes too, but they were blacks. Their faces were shiny, their lips thick and purplish, their, eyes small and red and fierce.

The truck to which they pushed Dikar was much smaller than the ones that had been filled with soldiers guarding Normanfenton. Its sides were very high and painted green, and sticking up out of its middle was a bigger gun than any Dikar had seen yet. A third black sat in front of the gun. The yellow Asafric got into the truck and sat down alongside of this one. The two other blacks opened a door in the side of the truck behind the gun and made Dikar get in. They followed and sat down one on each side of him. Their boss said something, and the truck made a terrible noise and was suddenly alive and moving.

A scream tore at Dikar's throat, but it made no more than a rasping sound. He was scared. He was more scared by the truck than he had been when he saw Marge cutting the rope above him, or when he saw the Asafric coming at him with the revolver in his hand.

CHAPTER 5

WALLS OF WEST POINT

ONE OF the Asafrics jabbered something and the other laughed. They weren't afraid of the truck, Dikar told himself. They knew it couldn't hurt them. If it wouldn't hurt them it wouldn't hurt him. He was still cold, his skin was still wet with the sweat of that moment of terror, but he was no longer too scared to know that the truck was turning around in the road, was laying its lights on the stony mountain shoulder from behind which it had come.

It roared around the shoulder—Dikar's mouth dropped wide open and something that was not fear caught at his throat.

Far ahead a hill loomed against the gold-sprinkled sky and out of the hill grew a house, high and straight-outlined and grim but somehow strong, somehow beautiful.

Gazing wide-eyed at this, Dikar realized that this was a thing

Americans had built. Things like that I too can learn to build, he thought, and so can the Boys of the Bunch. Then he remembered that though the house had been built by Americans, the Asafrics had it now. He remembered that it was the fort called Wespoint. Its beautiful strength was strength against America.

The truck ran faster than a frightened deer, toward the fort. The road curved, and curved again, and into the truck's lights there leaped pale shapes like huge half balls. Sticking out of these shapes Dikar saw guns like this one in the truck.

The great, gray house was high and dark over the truck. The truck stopped. Black Asafrics, holding rifles, sprang out of the shadows, huddled around it. A yellow-faced Asafric without a rifle appeared. He started talking to the yellow-faced one in the truck.

Officers, Dikar thought suddenly, remembering that Normanfenton had told him the bosses of soldiers were called that. The yellow-faced men were the Asafric's officers.

The two officers talked in words Dikar didn't understand. The soldiers, eyes little and red and fierce in their shiny black faces, peered at Dikar as if they'd never seen anything quite like him before. The new officer went into the house. The first one got out of the truck, stood by it, smiling to himself as if he'd done something smart.

The other one came out again, said something to him. Bomo and Gullah made Dikar get out of the truck. All four of them went into the house together, the officer in front, the two blacks on either side of Dikar. The tremendous door closed, and it seemed to Dikar that it shut out all the world that he knew. That it shut out all hope.

Instead of the vast, high space Dikar expected, he found himself in between gray stone walls that ran on and on, no further apart than the ends of the two long rows of cots in the Boys' House. The roof over his head was no higher than the roof of his and Marilee's little house. In the roof were stuck lighted bulbs very much like the ones of Johndawson's radio.

They threw shadows on the walls and the shadows ran along and dipped in and out of many doorways that were closed by wooden doors.

The air in here was so thick that it choked Dikar. The smells of the Asafrics were so strong that they made him sick. The feet made sound on the stone floor, all together. *Thud, thud, thud.* The sound rolled away and came back, and it was a very dreadful sound because it was out of the Time of Fear, long ago, the sound of marching.

THEY MARCHED on and on, and came to the end of the long, narrow space. Here there was a kind of rough hill that Dikar had learned, in Johndawson's House in the Far Land, was called stairs. They went down the stairs. At the bottom they came into a stone-walled room where there were a lot of Asafrics. Someone yelled and the Asafrics jumped up and stood stiff and straight, all except the one who had yelled. He came to the officer and jerked his hand up to his forehead and down again.

The officer talked to this one a minute, and went away with Bomo and Gullah. The Asafric took hold of Dikar and made him go across the room and through a door studded with iron. There was darkness beyond it. Out of the dark came smells; of wet stone and dead animals rotting, of dirty men.

The Asafric pushed him ahead. Their feet made squidgy sounds on a stone floor that was wet and cold and slimy to Dikar's feet. There were other sounds all around him, little whimpers and moans, and someone sobbing. Dikar's eyes got used to the dark. There was a very little bulb in the roof of this place and by its dim light he saw that he was going between two long rows of up-and-down iron bars.

Living men were behind the bars. It was they who made the little creepy sounds. They had the shape of men, but their faces, hairy, twisted, were the blind and terrible faces out of nightmares.

The *thud, thud* of marching feet came toward Dikar and the Asafrics. Another Asafric was approaching them. He had a revolver stuck in his belt and alongside it hung a bunch of little irons. His hand grasped a short, thick club. As he came nearer Dikar noticed that he was brown-faced, not black like the other Asafrics.

"Washton," the Asafric with Dikar said, "this one fellah special prisoner foh Colonel Wangsing. Something happen to him, all our skin get flogged off. Unstan'?"

"Yassuh, Sahgent," Washton answered, his eyes gleaming white in the dimness as he goggled at Dikar. "Ah unnerstands. You wan' him put in a cell by hisself?"

"That be best."

"Nummer 'leben is empty. Down heah." Washton started going back the way he'd come. Dikar and the other Asafric following. They stopped again. The brown Asafric picked out one of the little irons from the bunch at his belt and stuck it into a hole in a plate that was fastened to the bars here. "D'yuh think he needs de han'cuffs kept on?"

"No. I take 'em off." Dikar felt the iron bands come loose from his wrists. Washton pulled at the bars and about four of them swung out together, like a door. A hand on his back shoved Dikar through the opening and the bars clanged shut behind him.

Dikar stood still, rubbing his aching wrists and breathing hard. He heard whimperings all about him. He heard the sound of the Asafrics' feet going away. The door through which he'd been brought in here thudded shut. Dikar whirled around, grabbed the bars, shoved at them.

They didn't move. Dikar pushed hard, but they didn't move. He shook them, and they made clanging noise, but he might as well have been trying to shake the thickest tree trunk on the Mountain.

He twisted, ran along the bars—banged into a wall of solid iron. He ran the other way, four steps banged into another wall. Fingers seemed to be choking him as he spun and ran straight back from the bars and had hardly got started when a third wall stopped him, this one of wet, slimy stone.

Dikar spun around, leaped for the bars, grabbed them with his great hands, twisted them, shook them. "Let me out!" Dikar bellowed, above the sound of the bars. "Let me out of here. Let me out!"

A yowl answered him, high-pitched, wordless, the yowl of some mindless beast. Other bars clanged in the dimness. "Out," Dikar shouted. "Let me out," and there were other cries and other clanging bars and Dikar's shouting was only one sound in a shrieking, gibbering, caterwauling chorus.

CHAPTER 6
MIDNIGHT RIVER

"**S**HUT UP!" someone yelled, up near the door. Where the yell came from there was sudden quiet, and then a dull thud as of wood on bone. A scream shrilled, and afterward it was quieter, so that Dikar could hear the pound of running feet and the sound of blows.

Washton came in sight. He was running along the bars across the corridors from Dikar's cage. His club struck through the bars, and Dikar saw the head and the body it belonged to, sink down. Now Dikar's were the only bars that clanged, his the only voice that shouted.

Washton twisted around, jumped toward him. Dikar's hands darted out through the bars with the swiftness of a snake's strike, grabbed Washton's club-wrist and his other arm in a rip that squashed green cloth into flesh.

Pain twisted the brown Asafric's face. "Let me out," Dikar panted. "Let me out of here or I'll tear you to pieces." The club fell to the floor.

Washton's eyes seemed about to pop from their sockets. A whisper came from between his lips. "Lemme go. Dey're openin' de door. If dey see dis dey'll put udder men in heah an' I won't be able to do nothin' foh you. Lemme go, quick."

Surprise at this brought Dikar back to his senses. Killing Washton couldn't get him free, not with all those other Asafrics guarding the only way out. Washton jerked loose, grabbed up his club from the floor, turned toward the door that was opening now.

"Trouble, Washton?" a voice called. "Need couple fella help?"

"Nossuh," Washton called back. "Dis new bird just took a notion to raise a ruction, but ah's got everything under control now."

"You keep dem fella prisoner quiet, you hear me, or I tell big fella captain flog you."

"Don' worry, Sahjent, dey'll be quiet, beginnin' right now." The door thudded shut. "Phoo," Washton whistled, turning back to Dikar. "Yoh shoh come near ballin' up de detail." He looked furtively about him, came closer to the bars. "But yoh gimme a chance to bop dese udder poh guys to sleep, so's ah don' hafta worry 'bout dere seein' how I get yoh outta heah."

"Get me out—" Dikar gasped. "Who are you?"

"Benjamin Franklin Geo'ge Washin'ton Smith's de name ah was christened," the Asafric whispered. "But ah'm known as Ex-eighteen to de Secret Net."

"But—but you're an Asafric soldier!"

"Shoh. Shoh ah is. Dat's de beauty paht of it. See, w'en de Asafrics fust came, dey figgered us cullud people would want to jine up wid dem against de whites, and dey sent out word we'd be welcom. Dey foun' out dey figgered wrong.

"Dey foun' out we wuz Americans fust an' cullud after. But dah wuz some of us got de notion dat we cud mebbe fight 'em better from de inside, so we did jine up."

"But suppose they found you out?"

"Dem what dey fin's out," Washton said, "takes a long time to die, but dem what dey don't jus' keep on wukkin'. Lots uh de sabotage dat's been happenin' is de wuk of cullud men. But me, ah reckoned dat so long's I wuz in his heah foht, de bes' thing ah cud do wuz fin' out all about it, whah at de machine-gun nes's an' de big gun 'placements is, an' whah at de sentry posts is, an' everyt'ing like dat. 'Bout a month ago dey transferred me to dis prison-gyard, but—"

"Wait!" Dikar broke in, excitement shaking him. "You say you know all about this fort?"

"Shoh ah does, but what's de use? Dah ain't nobody to who what ah knows is any good an' dah never will be now, after dat las' proclamation. Dah ain't even no America no mo'—"

"Yes there is!" Dikar broke in, his voice hoarse. "There's still an America, Washton, an' there's an army formin' to fight for it. An Army with banners!"

"Glory be to the Lawd!" Washton's hands lifted above his head, palms upward. "An army with—"

"Hush," Dikar hissed. "Hush up an' listen to me." He hung to the bars with his hands and talked fast. "That army is goin' to try to capture this fort, tomorrow night. They need to know all about it, an' you can tell 'em. You got to get to 'em an' tell 'em."

"Shoh. Shoh I'll tell 'em. I'll get you out an'—"

"No! You mustn't waste time tryin' to get me out. I don't matter. Listen. I'll tell you how to find 'em—"

"You'll show me how to fin' 'em," Washton broke in. "Dat'll be quicker an' surer." He was fumbling his little iron into the hole in the plate on the bars.

"De Lawd forgive me foh doubtin' Him," he chanted, "w'en I was give dis detail in heah, an' fixed a way to get out a heah, an' den de only ones dat wuz sont in heah wuz so crazy dah wahn't no use gettin' 'em out. Ah shoulda knowed He'd sont me here to fix de way an' in His own good time he'd send me de pusson t'wuz impohtant to get out."

THE BAR-DOOR swung open and Dikar started to go out. "Wait!" Washton whispered, pushing him back. "It's in dis cell." He came into it. "Dat's whah ah put yoh in heah." He'd left his bunch of little irons hanging from the hole. "Stay here an' lissen," he whispered, "an' if you heah someone openin' de dooh f'om de gyard-room, yoh call me quick."

He went on into the cell and Dikar stepped a little way out of it. Dikar was trembling as he peered through the dimness at the face of the iron-studded door way up there, and he could hardly breathe. Listening with all of him, he heard only a mutter of voices beyond the door, but from inside the cell he heard the thud of Washton's feet, heard a scrape of stone on stone.

"All right." Washton was pulling Dikar back into the cell, was pulling the bar-door closed. "All's ready." He stuck his hand through the bars, twisted the bunch of little irons, took them in and fastened them to his belt again. "Dat'll maybe hol' dem a few minutes we'll need bad." He grabbed Dikar's elbow, pulled him toward the back of the cell. "Come on. We gotta hurry."

There was a big, square hole in the stone floor of the cell, and the thin stone that had covered leaned against the back wall. "Down in dah," Washton whispered. "Jump down. Hurry! Foh de Lawd's sake hurry!"

Dikar jumped down.

His feet found earth before his head went down below the cell-floor. Washton jumped down alongside him. Together they pulled the thin flagstone over and let it down, stooping down into the hole under it It scraped into place, and the blackness was so thick it was like thumbs pressing against Dikar's eyeballs.

"We's gotta crawl disway a space. I'll go fust, but you foller me close." Dikar felt Washton start moving forward. Dikar stooped, found a tunnel, and was crawling after Washton.

In a couple of seconds the narrow earth-lined burrow bent sharply. When Dikar got around the bend it wasn't earth he was crawling on, but stone rounding down like a trough, wet and slimy as the cell-wall had been, and the smell here was sickening.

"Dis heah is a old sewer," Washton's whisper came back to him. "Ain't used no moh. When ah was just a kid, ah he'ped build de new one an' close dis one up, so ah knowed jus' whah it wuz an' dug right to it. It runs down to de River. Oh Golly! I never thought to ask— Can yoh swim?"

"Yes," Dikar gulped, thinking of the Bathing Pool in the woods. He was choked up and sick and dizzy and it was all he could do to keep crawling. The sewer pitched downward, more and more steeply, till Dikar was holding back to keep from sliding into Washton. He crawled on and on, only the sounds Washton made below him telling him that he was not alone.

After awhile there was a new sound far ahead, a gurgle of water. It got nearer, and the slant of the sewer lessened, though it still ran down. Water splashed, right ahead.

"Stop!" Washton called back. "I got to get my shoes an' some my cloe's off. I can't swim in 'em." After a little time Washton said: "Okay. Come on," and they were crawling again.

"Keep yoh haid up, boy," Dikar heard. "High's yoh can." He lifted his head a little and it bumped against the roof of the sewer. His hands, then his knees, went into the cold water. He heard Washton splashing, ahead of him. The water was cold, so cold that it hurt. It came up along his arms, his thighs, lapped against his belly.

Abruptly he bumped into something. It was Washton— Washton was motionless, right ahead of him.

"What is it?" Dikar gasped.

"It's high tide," Washton's choked tones came back to him. "De river fills de whole sewer." Teeth chattered through the words. "We's gonna have to dive unner an' I don' know how much furder it is. I don' know can I hol' my breath dat long."

"We haven't come this far," Dikar said, "to get stuck. I'll go ahead and see how far it is, an' then I'll come back an' get you."

"All—all right. Yoh go ahead."

It was a tight fit, but Dikar managed to squeeze past Washton's quivering, cold form. He crawled on, and the water came up over his head. He backed a little, filled his lungs with the thick, foul air, went forward again, crawling fast as he could under the black, icy water. The cold was in the very marrow of his bones. His lungs were bursting with held breath.

There was a glimmer of light in the water, vague, foggy. Dikar pushed forward faster. Black lines striped the misty glow. His head banged against something; his groping hands seized iron. Iron bars.

Iron bars closed off the end of the sewer. They closed Dikar off from the River and the way back to the Mountain. They trapped him in here to die like a rabbit in a caved-in burrow.

This truly was the end.

CHAPTER 7
LEAD US TO TOMORROW

DIKAR'S BRAIN swelled till it seemed to be bursting his skull. His chest heaved agonizingly, his fingers closed on the bars, wrenched at them. The rust-roughened, misshapen iron cut his flesh and the pain of that merged with the great pain that was his body.

Dikar's feet found purchase on the stone of the sewer floor. His banded muscles were ropes tearing his bones apart. The iron gave a little, a very little, but there was blackness in Dikar's open eyes. Blackness was welling up within him, and the iron's strength was draining his strength from him.

The time was short.

A grating sound was water-loudened in his ears. The pound of his blood was a gigantic hammer inside his head. He had no strength longer to fight the bars. No strength longer to hold his breath—

Something pressed against his side. Something touched his hands. He was falling down into a swirl of black waters. He was falling forward into a black oblivion, losing his grasp on the iron, losing himself in despair and defeat—

Breath burst from his tortured lungs and suddenly, miraculously they pulled in air.

Cold, clean and crisp, the air knifed Dikar's chest, tingled in his blood, drove the blackness from his brain. He could see a glint of golden light on tossing, black waters, a vast black loom high above him.

"Yoh all right, boy?" Dikar heard a sputtering whisper. "Are yoh all right?" It came from a face bobbing in the water, very near to him, a brown and anxious face.

"Washton," he gasped, treading water. "You didn't wait for me to come back. You came an' broke the iron."

"Shucks," the brown man whispered through the gurgle of water. "When yoh didn't come back ah had to come after yoh, didn' I? But it wahn't me broke de lock of de gratin'. Ah couldn't never uh done dat. Yoh had it loose w'en I got to yoh, only yoh wuz pullin' instead uh pushin'…. But we's t'rough, dat's de main thing, an' we's got to get 'way from heah befoh some sentry spot us. Which way, boy?"

Dikar's gaze climbed up the immense blackness that rose sheer from the River's edge till it reached the star-sprinkled, glorious sky that he'd thought never to see again. He found the star patterns that Normanfenton had shown him, found the North Star. "This way," he murmured, and started swimming.

The cold water stroked Dikar's sides and he felt like shouting with the joy of being free again. Beside him swam Washton, shadowy in the River, and Washton was his friend. To be with Washton was good, like being with one of the Bunch.

"WHAT'S YOH name?" Washton asked, swimming alongside him. "Yoh know yoh ain't tol' me yoh name yet."

"Dikar."

"Dikar what?"

"Just Dikar. How much further do you think we ought to swim, Washton?"

"Stop a minute." Washton lifted his head, treading water, peered at the dark land along which they'd been swimming, peered back the way they'd come. "We's come furder dan I t'ought; tide mus' be runnin' out. I guess we's pas' the las' line of the fort sentries. Go any furder we might run into some patrol from Highlan' Mills. Dis is good a place as any." He started swimming again, angling for the shore and Dikar followed.

They climbed up on a shelving beach, shook water from them, started climbing. The rocks were steep here, but there was plenty of place for hand and foot and they got to the road atop the drop without much trouble. The road was empty when they darted across it; they plunged into bushes the other side of it.

Washton glanced back. "Golly," he exclaimed. "Look at the marks our wet feet left out dare on de concrete. Any car comes along, dey'll know we's passed his way."

"Don't worry about that," Dikar answered, slipping through the bushes. "We'll soon be in the woods." He makes an awful lot of noise, he thought, even more than the Beast folk. "Then we'll climb up in the trees and go that way, and nobody will be able to track us."

"Huh!" the other grunted. "Climb up? Foolishment yoh is talkin'. Maybe ah looks like a monkey, but ah sho can't climb around in de tops of the trees like one. Ah's havin' trouble enough gwine along dis flat groun' wid de sticks an' stones cuttin' mah stockin' feet."

"You can't— Well, we'll just have to go along the ground then." This was bad. If the Asafric trackers were as good as Wangsing seemed to think, they'd trail them to the Mountain. "An hope no one does come along before our footmarks dry."

They reached the edge of the woods, went into its shadowy blackness. Dikar stopped. "I'd better go back, though, and wipe out the marks we left coming here from the road, so some tracker don't pick 'em out. You wait here."

"All right," Washton whispered. "But don't be too long. I—It's awful dahk, heah, an' it's just come to me dat dey says dese heah woods is ha'nted."

"I'll hurry," Dikar whispered, slipping away. The traces of their passage were plain to his eyes: bent twigs, trodden grass, stones disturbed. He followed them closely to the edge of the road, started to return, brushing up the grass-blades with his fingers, replacing the stones, doing as well as he could to straighten the bushes.

He whirled to a sudden burst of threshing in the woods he'd just left. That fool Washton was—

"Who dah!" a startled voice called from the dark forest edge. "Han's up or I shoot."

Shoot; Washton had no gun. Dikar stooped lower beneath the screening brush.

"HOL' YOH fiah, soldier," he heard Washton say. "Ah's a friend. Ah's Private Washington, Fust Compn'y Prison Guard."

"Advance, friend," the other voice said, "an' gib countersign."

Dikar worked forward, his movements making only a whisper of sound. "Ah ain't got de countersign," Wash-ton was answering. "Ah's just' projeckin' round, seein' could ah fin' a high-yaller pretty. Ah's all alone."

That last, Dikar knew, was for him, to tell him the Asafric hadn't seen him, that he had a chance to slip away while Washton kept the soldier talking. Dikar could see them now, two figures blacker than the forest darkness. A single ray of light glinted from the Asafric's pointing rifle.

The Asafric was still suspicious and hostile. While Washton lied glibly, Dikar was gliding through the bushes, angling away from the two toward the woods behind the man with the rifle. Just as he reached the nearest tree and ran up its trunk, the black soldier announced: "I take you to captain fella. Start marchin'."

The bough along which Dikar crept swayed under his weight, rustled. His lips puckered, gave forth the sleepy twitter of a wind-disturbed bird. "Golly," Washton was pleading. "Yoh ain't gonna turn me in, is yoh?"

Dikar dropped from the bough he'd reached, straight down on the shoulders of the Asafric. His heels kicked the rifle from the soldier's hand. His thighs clamped on the black's startled throat, and then they were crashing down to the ground.

Washton snatched up the rifle and pounded its butt down into a heaving chest.

There was crunch of bone caving in. Dikar felt the body beneath him go limp. He rolled away. The rifle lifted and fell again. The head on the ground was distorted, ghastly.

Dikar jumped up, blurted, "Come on!" and they were running into the woods, away from the thing that lay unmoving in the forest brush.

"Golly," Washton gasped. "Ah thought ah was a goner den."

It was weary, endless, that journey through the forest. Bad enough it would have been if they could have gone straight, but Dikar insisted on leading Washton long distances in the beds of streamlets, even though this took them out of their course, insisted on walking across whatever stretches of hard, bare rock he could find in the darkness. A number of times, when they came to fallen trunks or low trees, Dikar made him climb up on these and make his way along them as far as he was able.

"We're leaving tracks they can follow anyway," Dikar explained, "from where they find that sentry we killed, but by doin these things we're makin it harder for them. They'll have to wait for full daylight to start, an' maybe they'll not be able to find the Mountain till night. That's all we can ask."

"IT IS all we can hope for," Normanfenton agreed, when they'd reached home at last, and Dikar had told his story to the Council of War sitting together again in Johndawson's little house. "But it means that the secret of the Mountain is a secret no longer, that succeed or fail in what we attempt tonight, there is no longer any safety for your Bunch here on the Mountain. It means the end of your life on the Mountain."

"It means we've got to succeed," Marilee said, her eyes flaming. Dikar had found her waiting sleepless for him at the edge of the Drop when he came up over it in the dawn, and she'd brought hot food in here for him and Washton to eat while they talked.

While Dikar told his story she was binding cooling herb-leaves on his wounds and was caressing him furtively with tender, proud hands. "An' it means that there will be no argument now that the Girls can't go with you, since you can't leave us here for the Asafrics to find. We must go along."

"That can't be helped," Johndawson agreed. "But of course you'll stay back out of the fighting and—"

"We'll stay out of no fighting," Marilee flashed at him. "We're few enough as it is, even with the Beastfolk Nat has gotten to promise to help us. There's no Girl in the Bunch who cannot steal through the woods as silent as any Boy, who cannot handle a bow and a knife as well as any Boy.

"We worked together with the Boys, an' played together with 'em, an' it is our right to die together with 'em, Dikar," she turned to face him, "I dare you to say it is not our right."

Her eyes flashed.

"It is your right," Dikar said gravely, "I cannot say it is not. You Girls of the Bunch will be figured in on our plans for the fightin' the same as us Boys. But there's somethin' I've just thought of.

"While the Asafrics are only just started trackin' me an' Washton, they may guess that our hidin' place is here on the Mountain an' send planes to see what they can find out. I want you to go an' tell the Bunch that they must act all day today like the 'Ware plane' cry had been given.

"No one must be in the Clearin' an' nothin' must be left lyin' around there to show that people live on the Mountain. There must be no fires lit today. There must be no woodchoppin'. Go quick an' see that the rules are carried out."

As Marilee hurried out to obey him, it seemed to Dikar that a light had gone out of the house with her. "That's most likely the last order I'll give as Boss of the Bunch," he sighed, looking after her. "Because, Normanfenton, when we leave the Mountain tonight it is you who'll be Boss of us, an' of all Americans."

The tall, sad man's gnarled hand dropped gently on Dikar's

shoulder. "God grant, my boy," he said gravely, "that when I come to the end of the task He has laid upon me I shall as richly deserve His, 'Well done, good and faithful servant,' as you do, having come to the end of yours."

There was a moment of silence in that greenwood room. The bony, gray hand pressed hard on Dikar's shoulder and fell away, and Normanfenton turned to Walt, who'd finished marking on a map and stood waiting.

"Well?" Normanfenton asked.

Walt's hands closed hard on the edge of the table, but it was Nat who answered, his voice hoarse and rasping like a crow's caw. "There ain't no well about it. The way they got themselves fixed up, with their picket lines an' their machine-gun nests, we ain't got a chance of takin' that place."

"That's right," Walt agreed. "If what this man tells us is true, an army equipped with all the modern devices of war might capture it after a long siege, but for our few to attempt it is plain suicide."

"The wisest thing we can do," Johndawson said, his face gray and empty of life, "is to flee from this Mountain and try to get through to another hiding place. We'd need a miracle—"

"Then we'll work a miracle," Normanfenton cut in, "if that's what we need. Gentlemen!" He stood, tall and gangling, his shoulders stooped, and his voice was quiet. "We are here not to discuss whether or not West Point can be taken, but to decide how we shall take it."

Deep in his somber eyes a fire glowed and it seemed to Dikar that, very slowly, the eyes of the others caught that spark.

CHAPTER 8

WAR CRY!

IN THE dark of the woods Dikar knew that to any but a wildcat's eye he must seem a part of the tree whose rough bark pressed his back. He knew that the Asafric who paced the wide sentry path that ran all around the outer works of West Point could not see him. But Dikar was afraid.

What Dikar feared was that the Asafrics had caught the smell that was so strong in his own nostrils, the smell of the Beastfolk who waited, far back in the woods for the time to take their turn in the plan the Council of War had made.

The smell was so strong to Dikar that even though Norman-fenton and Johndawson and Washton had told him over and over the Asafrics could not smell it, he still could not believe this. He could not believe that the soldiers had not heard the Beastfolk noisily following the advance of the Bunch from the Mountain. He could not rid himself of the dread that the Asafrics were fully warned, that they had laid a trap for the Americans.

It must be so.

Suddenly Dikar stiffened. An owl had hooted, faint and far away. The sound was repeated, a little nearer, and once more, nearer still. The hollow night-voices ran swiftly toward him through the blackness, and now it was his turn and Dikar hooted.

The Asafric stopped short, turned his head toward the sound. Dikar's skin tightened across the back of his shoulders and his bow came up, arrow nicked into its cord. The hoots ran away from him through the forest night.

The sentry shrugged uneasily, started walking again. Breathing once more, Dikar counted the owl-hoots till they ended.

He smiled grimly in his covert. All the Boys of the Bunch were in place. Each had sighted his quarry.

The Black was hardly ten steps away now and in the glimmer of starlight he was a perfect target. Dikar's lips puckered, sent into the night-silence the shrill, far-carrying whistle of the treetoad. It ended with the twang of his loosed bowstring.

An arrow shaft quivered in the Asafric's green breast and the soldier's knees folded. He fell, the loudest sounds of his death the thud of his body on the ground, the clink of his rifle's barrel on a stone.

There had been other twangs, other thuds, in the still forest. Twenty-one times in that moment winged death had struck. A gap twenty-one times a hundred steps in length was made in the outer line of West Point's defenses, but the only pounds had been these small, quick ones.

That was the beginning.

Darting to the motionless body on the path, Dikar thought how strange it was that so many men could die so silently, how much stranger that the Bunch, whom the Old Ones had taught to kill only for food should have killed so many men. But there was a greater need for this killing than hunger.

DIKAR UNSNAPPED the bullet-filled belt from around the flaccid corpse, plucked the rifle from the ground. Breathing hard, he darted back to the tree that had given him covert, pounded the heel of his hand against its trunk to make the thumping sound of rabbits stiff-legged in their midnight dance. Then he whirled, sensing a presence that had been heralded by no sound.

"Dikar," the vague figure breathed. "Oh, Dikar. I was so afraid he saw you when you hooted."

"But he didn't, Marilee." His arms ached for her, but there was no time for that. "You must hurry." He thrust rifle, bullet-belt, into her hands. "You know what you Girls are to do. Take these back to Normanfenton for the Beastmen who know how to use them; tell him he can start bringin' 'em up now as far as this patch. Hurry, Marilee."

Her lips burned on his and then she had flitted away, but there were other shadowy forms here now, and from the smaller of these came an excited whisper.

"I got mine in the neck, Dikar, an' he went down pullin' at the arrow. He—"

"Hush, Billthomas," Dikar hissed. "That's gone an' past now, an' we've got to get movin'. You got your knife in your hand?"

"Yes, Dikar."

"An' you Carlberger? Your knife ready an' your bonarrer slung so you're free to move quick an' noiseless?"

"Yes, Dikar." He could see only that they were slim and not very tall, but he knew they were all beardless, striplings. How was it with the older Boys of the Bunch, Johnstone, Henfield, Patoshay and three more? Were they gathering each their own couple of youngsters?

The *chrrr* of an angered skunk broke from Dikar and was repeated from the darkness six times. He had his answer.

"Don't talk," Dikar whispered. "Don't even breathe if you can help it. What we've just done was like pickin' berries compared to what's ahead."

"Let's go," little Billthomas exclaimed. "What are we waitin' for?"

Dikar made the treetoad whistle again and they started across the sentry-path. Three shadows making no more sound than the shadows of the leaves about them, they filtered through the woods. Beyond the woods there were only bushes on which the stars laid their betraying glimmer. But the enemy would have had to be very near to know that these humans stole through this undergrowth.

The bushes frayed out, and now there was nothing but a hillside covered with long, dry grass. All the Boys' woodland skill could not keep this stuff from rustling as they snaked through it. Dikar's throat went dry. His forehead was banded with tight iron. On that long journey through the woods, yesterday, Washton had told him what a machine gun could do.

He touched Billthomas, crawling next to him, with a quick hand. Billthomas stopped, lay flat. The rustling that Carlberger made was silenced. Dikar lifted his head, slowly, till his eyes were just above the grasses.

The Asafric smell that had stopped him came from the pale half-round of a stone machine-gun nest, mounding up out of the hillside. He could see the guns sticking blackly out of long, narrow slits in the round wall. He could see, low down, a square, yellow glow that was the open doorway.

Let the soldiers within one of those pillboxes get the slightest hint of danger, Washton had told him, and an iron curtain would close that doorway, blazing light would flare across the hillside and the guns flail it with a rain of bullets. Dikar and his fellows would die but, worse still, the alarm would be given to the hundreds in the fort. They would come awake—and the surprise attack on West Point would have failed.

"Your only chanct," Washton had explained, "is to get inside dat pillbox and kill de eight sojers dat'll be in dere befoh dey knows whut's comin' off."

TWO THINGS the Boys had in their favor. The Asafrics in the pillbox depended on the picket line for warning of attack, and because of what had just been done they would get no such warning. And the Boys crawled through the dry grass with hardly more sound than the wind made, sliding by over their heads.

They made even less sound than the wind, moving again at the signal of Dikar's touch. Head down again, Dikar no longer could see the pillbox, but after a while he could see a yellow glow filtering through the blades of grass.

The frightening smell of the invaders was strong in his nostrils, but the noises that came with the smell were not voices; they were only the noises that people make when they sleep.

The light was very bright. Dikar's head lifted again. His eyes blinked right into the doorway itself. He sprang up, went through the doorway, saw a huddle of sleeping forms, felt rather than saw the other Boys leap in beside him. One of the Asafrics stirred. His head lifted and his fierce little eyes stared into the eyes of Dikar.

The soldier's mouth gaped open for a shout. Dikar's knife slashed across the black throat. Another form stirred, started to lift, sagged down with Dikar's knife buried to the hilt in its breast.

Dikar tugged his weapon loose, twisted to meet the next enemy. There was none. There was only a tangle of black corpses on the cots and on the pillbox's stone floor. The two other Boys, their naked skin red-painted, their knives dripping red, were staring at Dikar.

"We—we've done it," Dikar stammered, not believing it himself yet. "We've done it." He was sick, remembering the feel of his blade sinking into a man's flesh. "We've taken the—"

Billthomas' mouth twisted and he started laughing. His eyes horrible, his face grimacing, he laughed, thin and high and so loud that it must be heard even in the great building at the middle of West Point.

"Cut it," Dikar snapped. His open hand slapped hard across that frightening, crazy laugh, stopped it. Billthomas' eyes didn't look so terrible now, but Carlberger was staring at his own knife, his Adam's apple gulping in his throat.

"Pull yourselves together," Dikar gasped. "We've got to—"

A rattling, loud chatter from outside cut him off. Terror froze Dikar. The shape had made this same noise, the black shape that in his dream-memories swooped out of the sky down on a long line of trucks carrying children and flew away again, leaving wreckage and still corpses behind it. He turned, sprang to the doorway of the pillbox, stuck his head out and saw white light laid on the hillside, just where it rounded from sight to his left.

Rain was beating down the grass there—there was no rain. A figure sprang up from the ground, was outlined black against the light, a naked Boy with full-bent bow. The figure crumpled down again, the life out of it.

"Patoshay," a voice said, and Dikar realized it was his own voice. "His squad weren't as lucky as we were." The chattering rattle died away, but the white light stayed bright on the hillside and from within the pillbox a strange, tinkling, insistent noise was coming that Dikar had never heard before.

He whirled. Carlberger was gaping at a little red box on the inside wall. "It's coming from that, Dikar," the youngster gasped, pointing at the box. "Look! It's alive!"

On top of the box a little something, between two shiny round things, was fluttering and it was this that made the sharp noise. Dikar jumped to it, struck at it with his knife, struck again. The box split open, showed rolls of orange red wire inside. The noise had stopped.

"It won't hurt us now," Dikar gasped. "It's dead."

The rain-spatter outside stopped suddenly. Billthomas stuck his head out of the doorway, pulled it in again, and his face was as gray-white as the stone behind him.

His voice held terror.

"They—they're coming," he gasped. "The Asafrics."

SOMEHOW DIKAR was back at the doorway, was looking out. Out there in the white light, where Patoshay had died, three Asafric soldiers were coming at a trot, rifles in their hands, bags that looked very heavy slung to their belts.

One of the Asafrics shouted, jerked his rifle to his shoulder. It jetted flame. A bee hummed past Dikar's ear. He pulled his head in, glanced up for the iron curtain Washton told him about, saw it and pulled at it. It came down with a clang.

"That'll stop 'em," Dikar panted. "They can't shoot through that an' they can't shoot through these walls."

"They can shoot through those holes when they get close

enough," Carlberger said, thrusting a shaking hand at the slits out through which the guns stuck. "When they get close enough they'll shoot through them an' kill us."

Dikar sprang to the one that would face the Asafrics, stooped a little, saw them. They were still coming, but they were bent way over and moving slowly, as if they were scared. They *were* scared, he realized all of a sudden; they were scared of these machine-guns.

But Dikar knew they didn't have to be afraid of the machine-guns. No one in here knew how to shoot them.

Dikar's bow was in his hand, he was fitting an arrow to it. He knelt on the sort of stone shelf that held the gun's spread legs, aimed his arrow through it, loosed it. It hit the ground short of the Asafrics, but that told him what he needed to know. That was how far the thickness of the wall would let him send an arrow.

There was room here for only one to handle a bow. "Get at the other holes, you two," he ordered, very quietly. "In case they work around. Don't let an arrow go until they've come within thirty steps."

The Asafrics came on slowly. Dikar waited, blood thumping in his temples but his fingers very steady on the wood and the cord of his taut bow. A black reached the spot where Dikar's first arrow had fallen, passed it.

Dikar's bow twanged.

The Asafric pitched forward into the long grass, was hidden. Dikar knew he had not missed. He slapped a third arrow into place, looked for the other Asafrics. They had vanished.

Breath hissed from between Dikar's teeth. He couldn't have killed all three with one arrow. Where were the others then? The grass out there was swaying against the wind. Of course. They had dropped down into the grass. They were crawling up on the pillbox the same way the Boys from the Mountain had.

Dikar let his arrow fly. It hit in back of the place where the grass was moving. The Blacks had already come too close for him to hit them, low down as they were. Now he couldn't even see the grass moving to show where they crawled. They'd gotten so close that the edge of the shelf cut off his view of them. The machine-guns, slanted down outside the wall, could have raked the ground, but the attackers were safe from arrows.

"They'll have to rise up to shoot into here," Dikar spoke his thoughts aloud. "They'll be so close then it won't be any trick to plug 'em. Watch carefully, fellows, an' keep your bow-strings taut."

They waited.

The iron curtain over the doorway cut off sound from outside, and no sound seemed to come in through the slits. Dikar could hear only the heavy breathing of the other Boys, the *thump, thump* of his own heart. This waiting was hard, harder than the fighting had been.

SOMETHING ROUND, black, small as a ball, shot up across his slit; sound, gigantic, deafening sound, blasted into the pillbox. A red flame-sheet across the opening blinded Dikar. A new choking smell was in his nostrils. Smoke eddied in the slit and cleared away—and then there was another black ball, another blast of sound, another sheet of flame.

The Asafrics weren't going to rise up and try to shoot in here. The black balls were the bombs Washton had talked about. The blacks were lying safe in the grass, and were throwing them at the slits. Sooner or later one of the bombs must come through and explode inside here and then there would be no one left in here alive.

Well, Dikar thought, we've tried, anyway. We've tried our best.

"Dikar!" Carlberger screamed from the slit through which he peered. "There's more Asafrics, hundreds of them, coming out of the woods. The rest of the Bunch must have been licked even before they got started. Look, Dikar. Come here an' look. The Asafrics are running down the hillside. They're shootin' their guns—"

"Shoot your arrows at 'em," Billthomas yelled. "Shoot as fast as you can, fellows. Kill as many of 'em as we can before we die ourselves."

"That's right," Carlberger yelled, laughing wildly. "Fight 'em. Fight 'em till they have to kill us to make us stop fightin'. Shoot your arrows, fellows. Shoot fast an' straight!"

CHAPTER 9

THUNDER IN THE NIGHT

DIKAR BELLOWED, whirled and leaped across the pillbox. His hand shot out, struck Carlberger's shoulder and sent him sprawling.

"No," Dikar yelled. "Don't shoot. "Don't shoot, you fool kids." Billthomas goggled at him as if he'd gone crazy. "They're not Asafrics. They're our friends, shootin' at the Asafrics with the guns we sent 'em by the Girls."

"Friends," Carlberger repeated, staring up at Dikar from where he'd fallen atop a dead black. "I—how do you know, Dikar? I saw 'em an' you didn't."

"You said they were shootin' as they came." Dikar was pulling at the iron curtain over the doorway, trying to figure out how to raise it. "Asafrics wouldn't be wasting bullets on this stone house." The iron started to slide up and machine-gun chatter came through the opening, but there was no crack of rifles. "So I know they must be Americans shootin' at the ones who were tryin' to kill us."

Yellow light spilled out over someone lying crosswise in the grass just outside, a silent rifle jammed against his shoulder, Dikar grabbed for his knife—saw who it was.

Johndawson's head turned to him. There was a red streak across the stubbled cheek, but the gray-browed eyes were shining. "Dikar, my boy!" he exclaimed. "You're all right!"

"Yes." The light reached another man in the grass beyond Johndawson, a man covered with rags the color of dirt, his head a mass of dirt-colored hair. "But I've seen Patoshay die," Dikar said huskily. Beyond the Beast-man, he saw other black forms in the grass, starlight glinting on the iron of their rifles. "An' I suppose Steveland an' Halross are dead with him."

The rifles were all pointing in the direction of the pillbox from which the death spray had stopped coming. "Why aren't you shootin' at the soldiers who killed 'em?" Dikar demanded.

"Because it's out of range, and if we tried to get nearer we'd all be wiped out." Johndawson hitched a little closer. "Too bad that one held out. We're stopped cold. The other five were taken as easily as you took this—"

"Are you sure?" Dikar broke in.

"Of course I'm sure. We'd just reached the picket-patch when we heard the firing break out. Washton scouted ahead, came running back to tell us that only one nest was resisting. Those of us who had guns came at the double-quick, picked off the Asafrics who were lobbing bombs at you—"

"Good thing you did," Dikar muttered. Then, "We've got six of the seven pillboxes that Washton's map showed guard the houses where the Asafrics live, in a curve from the River to the woods. That means we've got six times eight more rifles, an' six times three machine guns, with plenty of bullets for them all. Why do you say we're stopped? Why can't we go on the way we planned?"

"The biggest reason's that that pillbox is right spang in the middle of the line, and we can't go on and leave it behind us. That's the first rule of warfare—"

"Then we've got to take it," Dikar interrupted. "An' quick." He dropped to his knees, started crawling out into the open.

Johndawson caught hold of his arm. "Where are you going?" he demanded. "What are you up to?"

"I'm goin to fix those soldiers who killed Patoshay. Listen," Dikar whispered, his lips white with thinking how the bullet storm had beaten his friend to the ground. "You see how that star there is just startin' to drop behind a thick tree-bough. Watch it, and when it shows again under the bough, have your men start shootin' at the pillbox again and rushing toward it so as to make the Asafrics start shootin' back at you again.

"Get as close to the farthest reach of their bullets as you can an' keep makin' believe you're goin' to rush further, but don't do it. Understand?"

"Yes, but what will you—?"

"You'll see." Dikar wrenched free, was creeping fast around his own pillbox. He came to what he was looking for, the corpse of an Asafric soldier.

THE BAG Dikar took from the dead man's belt was very heavy with the hard, round things it held. The grass through which Dikar crawled, circling far down the hillside and around the white flood of light, was sharp-edged, cutting, and its rustling was terribly loud in his ears.

His course rounded over the swell of the hillside and he saw the white mound of the pillbox from which had come the bullets that killed Patoshay. Dikar started climbing the hill again, keeping just beyond the edge of that fatal blaze of light.

A shot rang out from where he'd come. Someone shouted. There were more shots, cheers.

Rrrrrcht rrrrrcht—a machine-gun started its chatter. Another joined it. Those guns were on the other side of the pale half-bell; on this side there was nothing.

Dikar sprang to his feet, ran straight for the pillbox, plucking an iron ball from the bag he carried. His teeth found the pin Washton had told him about. He reached the pillbox, peered in through the silent gun-slit in this side. He saw five Asafrics crouched low over their chattering guns. He pulled the pin with his teeth, threw the bomb in through the slit, pulled another's pin and threw that in. Then he dropped to the ground.

Dikar heard a dull thud. It wasn't very loud. It wasn't loud enough. The bombs hadn't gone off.

Something was missing. It was the terrible white light. The night had closed in on him. The Americans' shots were still cracking, but the machine-gun chatter had stopped. Queer. Dikar pushed hands against the ground, pushed himself up along the stone, got his eyes to the slit again.

Smoke stung his eyes. Through his tears he saw only blackness inside the pillbox. There was no sound from inside there. No voices. No movement. But there was a smell of blood and of burned meat.

An arm was laid across his shoulder. "You've done it," Johndawson said. "You've done it, boy. You've wiped them out, complete."

There were other men around Dikar, when he turned. Normanfenton. Walt. Washton. Men, rags fluttering about them, were streaming out of the woods and across the bare hillside. The men were cheering. Even in the dim starlight Dikar saw that their hairy, starved faces were alight.

"Walt!" he heard Normanfenton snap. "John! Don't let them all crowd together. Get them split up, an even number to each pillbox. Distribute the rifles and ammunition you find there, and have the gun crews start unfastening the machine-guns so that we can take them along with us."

Johndawson and Walt ran away "We've found enough old soldiers in the lot," Normanfenton said to Dikar, "to make crews for all the eighteen machine-guns we've captured. There isn't a man in the outfit who doesn't know how to handle a rifle. We've got our army now, two hundred desperate fighting men, and thanks to you and your Bunch, we've got them armed."

"Two hundred." It was Washton who spoke. "Shoh, Gineral. Yoh'so got two hunnerd sojers an' dey'll fight like wil' cats." He'd appeared from nowhere, it seemed. "But dey's still near two thousand down dere in de barracks. Dey's awake now, an' dey knows somet'n's up. Listen."

Normanfenton stiffened. From far off there came ringing, brassy notes. "A bugle," the Leader muttered. "Blowing *To Arms!*

Turning the garrison out. This is as far as we'll get by surprise. What we win now, we'll have to fight for."

"An yoh'd better win it foh de dawn," Washton added. "'Cause soon as it gets light enough, de planes is gonna start flyin' ovehead an' layin dere eggs on us, an' dat'll be de end uf us. Dey'll smash us to—"

"Here, you." Normanfenton whirled to a number of figures that were coming near. "You Boys! Run to the pillboxes and tell everybody to line up, right away, for an advance. Hurry!"

THEY DARTED away and the Leader turned to Dikar again. "They must have been awakened by the sound of the firing. I'm going to press the attack before they realize exactly what direction it's coming from. They can't know—"

"Dey does know," Washton broke in. "Dese guys telephoned— Oh golly!"

He was staring upward at a new sound in the air, a high-toned *wheeee* that made Dikar's blood run chill, though he didn't know what it was. It rose to a scream.

Then a crash.

Fire fountained out of the ground, halfway down the hill. A wind, almost solid, jolted Dikar against the pillbox. Then it was gone.

"They're shelling us," Normanfenton muttered. His hands cupped around his mouth. "Shelter, everybody," he shouted. "Everybody in the pillboxes."

Another *wheeee* screamed through the night, another fountain of fire burst up out of the ground, nearer. Normanfenton had Dikar by the wrist and they were running, Washton beside them, down the long line of pillboxes, shouting that order. All around them were men running.

The air seemed full of the fearful screaming of the shelling. The hillside was alive with flame as they tumbled into the last stone nest and crushed into a jam of men who stank with the Beastfolk smell.

"We're safe here," Normanfenton panted. "The concrete will protect us." The sound the shelling made outside was like a drumming thunder now. "But we'll never get our men alive through that barrage. It will hold us here till daylight and then the bombing planes will finish us off."

Washton pulled down the iron curtain, his face greenish instead of brown. "Oh golly!" he chattered. "Ah done tol' you de big guns is fixed so's dey only kiver de River, but ah clean forgot de anti-aircrafts on de roof of de main buildin'. Dat's whut's shootin' at us, de Archies up dah on de roof of de biggest house in de reservation."

"The biggest!" Dikar grabbed his arm. "Washton. Is that the house we escaped from?"

"Shoh! Shoh it is. But—"

"An we're right near the River here!" Dikar swung around to the Leader. "Normanfenton! I'll stop those Archies for you." He raised his voice: "To me Boys. To me, Boys of the Mountain. There's work for us."

The thunder was rolling over the pill box. Normanfenton jabbered something at Dikar, but Dikar had eyes only for the naked Boys who pushed to him—Bengreen and Johnston and Fredalton and Danhall.

"We're here, Dikar." Johnston, red-beared, freckle-faced, spoke for them. "What do you want us to do?"

"I want to lead you to a place you may never come back from," Dikar answered. "I want to lead you to a place where this fight must be won or lost—and if it's lost, we will be lost, all of us, with no hope of livin'. Will you follow?"

"Lead, Dikar," Johnstone smiled, "an' we follow. You know that. You know you didn't need to ask."

"I know," Dikar agreed, pride swelling within him. "All right, then! We're swimming the River. Make sure your knives are fastened so you don't lose 'em. I'm afraid we'll have to leave our bonarrers, though. With the cords wet, they'll be no use—"

"Hey, mister," someone called hoarsely from back in the

crowd. "Here's the Asafrics' raincoats on the shelf here. They'll keep your bows dry if you wrap 'em up in—"

"Good," Dikar snapped. "Pass 'em to us. We'll wrap our bonarrers an' tie 'em to our backs." Twenty willing hands were helping. Normanfenton touched Dikar on the shoulder.

"You've done wonders, boy," the Leader said. "But I can't see how you expect to—"

"I can't either," Dikar answered. "But we'll make a good try at it." He jerked away, pulled up the iron curtain from over the doorway. The thunder of the shelling rolled in, deafening.

"LOOK," DIKAR shouted to the Boys. "You can count the time between when the shells fall, in the space from here to the River." One crashed as he spoke. "One, two, three, four," he counted and a thunder-peal drowned the "five."

"You see? We've got to get across that space an' into the River in the time you can count four. I'll go first, then Bengreen, Danhall, Johnstone an' Fredalton, one by one. Meet me in the River when you get there."

"*If* we get there." Brown-haired Fredalton grinned. "I never won a race yet on the Mountain, but I bet even a deer can't run as fast as I'll run when it comes my turn."

Dikar looked into Normanfenton's tight-drawn face. "We'll stop those guns for you," he cried. "The minute they stop, you bring your men on." A shell crashed as he said this last and Dikar whipped around, was out of the pillbox, was running across ground so torn up it was like no ground he'd ever seen. He dived into the black River.

He came up just in time to see Bengreen spring, out of the heart of a flame-fountain into the River. The thunder was deafening, the thunder of the Asafric shells. Danhall plunged into the River, the water splashing high over him.

"What a belly whopper he took," Bengreen chuckled, treading water beside Dikar.

"Here's Johnstone," Dikar panted. "Now Fredalton, an' we'll all be through." Shell-sound rolled away. Another shell crashed down. "The kid must have missed his turn," Dikar muttered. A third shell spouted flame above them.

"Fredalton never could run as fast as the rest of us," Johnstone said. "He couldn't run fast enough to—" Thunder blotted his voice out.

"He's go—No!" Diker yelled. "Here he is!" A dark shape hurtled from the bank into fire-reddened foam. "He got through." A head came up out of the water and it was black-haired, brown-skinned.

"It's not Fredalton," someone gasped. "It's Washton."

"Shoh nuff it's me." The brown man grinned. How did yoh-all expec' to find yoh way widout me to show yuh?"

"I was wondering about that," Dikar murmured.

"Well," Washton answered, "Ah's heah now, so less get stahted."

"Come along, fellows." Dikar gave himself to the stream. This swimming wasn't like last night's, he thought, trying not to think about Fredalton. Last night had been black; tonight the glare of the shells flickered like red heat-lightning overhead. Last night had been quiet; tonight the thunders of the guns rolled overhead, the thunders that must be silenced if America was to have a tomorrow.

Those thunders were still rolling when they reached at last the place where Dikar last night had strained at an iron grating and almost drowned. The thunders were still rolling, but the stars were paling in the sky to which the vast black wall rose, and across the sky was stealing the first faint leaden light of the dawn.

"Lemme go fust," Washton whispered. "Ah knows just whah Ah left my bunch of keys, an' somebody else might kick 'em away. Dey's gonna come in mighty handy."

They did. When the five Americans had crawled up the long sewer, had climbed up into the cell of Dikar's terrible memories, a key from that bunch opened its door so swiftly that the Asafric who'd taken Washton's place had no time "to cry out before

Dikar killed him. Another key opened the door at the end of the corridor, and the Boys leaped through, knives ready.

There was no one in the room beyond that door.

"Gineral call mus' have blowed," Washton grunted. "Ev'body out under full arms." His white grin flashed across his face once more. "Oh golly! Dat means dis whole buildin' ain't got nary sojer in it, 'ceptin de ones wuhkin de Archies on de roof. It means we's done gonna get to de roof widout havin' to fight no one. It means we's gotta chanc't, a good chanc't, to get away wid dis crazy stunt."

CHAPTER 10

OUR GREEN, OUR PLEASANT LAND

THEY HAD climbed up and up, it seemed forever, up hill after hill of stone stairs. Now there were no more stairs, and they were huddled against a door, and from beyond the door came the thunder of guns.

A window in the wall behind them was paling with the dawn.

Dikar got his hand on the handle of the door, turned it, opened it slowly. He saw a wide, flat space. He saw guns bigger than any he'd ever seen before. Black against the paling, ominous sky, their mouths belched lightning and thunder as sweating blacks served them.

"Let's go," he whispered, and he was through the doorway and the other Boys were through it and beside him; they were drawing taut the cords of the bows they had unwrapped sometime during their long climb.

An Asafric saw them. His mouth opened in a scream the thunder drowned and he pitched forward, an arrow in his throat. Dikar was snatching arrows from his quiver, was sending them flying at the milling mob of green-clad soldiers as fast as he could, and each was finding its mark in black or yellow flesh. The guns were silent, suddenly. The big guns were silent, but revolvers were barking lead at Dikar and the Boys.

He snatched at his quiver, found no arrow there. "Come on," he cried and, knife in hand, he was running across the roof, straight toward the few Asafrics who were left. He glanced sidewise and saw only Johnstone, red hair streaming, running beside him.

The others—something searing hot hit Dikar in the shoulder. His left hand hung limp, but his right drove his knife into an Asafric. He twisted, was borne down under the man's body. He heaved it off, rolled free, saw a contorted, yellow face, saw a revolver jabbing at him. Then a black something was between Dikar and gun-flash, was tumbling....

Dikar was on his feet; he hurled himself at the Asafric officer, batted aside the gun and got his hands on the man's throat. Something snapped between his fingers. The eyes were glazed suddenly, the body hung heavy from his hands.

Dikar let it drop, wheeled to meet the next attack. There was none. No one else stood erect on that roof. A silence, terrible after all that noise, surrounded him, and a terrible gray light lay on the twisted bodies that crowded the rooftop.

He was alone. His body was netted with pain, his flesh torn by bullets and knives. There was no strength any more in his limbs. But the guns were silenced.

Dikar's tired eyes dropped to the roof at his feet. Washton lay there, eyes open, brown forehead lined deep with agony, hand pressed to a side from which blood welled between the fingers. It must have been he who had jumped between Dikar and the Asafric's revolver. He had taken the bullet that was meant for Dikar.

"You—you shouldn't have—" Dikar's voice was cut off by a new sound, a sort of roaring not far distant. He turned wearily to it, saw a great bird soaring, a plane taking off to fly over the Americans who must be moving now from their pillboxes, who would be a fair mark now for the death-thunders the plane could send down on them. There was another....

"DIKAR." THE Voice croaked at his feet. "De Archies... take me... to dem. Hurry."

Dikar bent, lifted the brown man, carried him tenderly to where the big guns, silent now, thrust their black barrels over the low roof-wall. Just behind the guns a clump of great, black horns opened mouths to the sky and a jumble of wires coiled from them to the guns.

Three planes were roaring overhead now, circling.

"Put... me... down," Washton gasped, each word a separate agony, "by de automatic... range finders."

Dikar realised he meant the horns. He obeyed. Washton's bloody hand came away from his side, fumbled with something at the base of the horns. There was a whirring sound somewhere. The guns were moving. They'd come alive and were lifting. Were swinging their barrels towards the circling planes.

"Dat lever," Washton groaned, pointing. "Pull... pull it."

Dikar was afraid of the moving guns, but he jumped to the stick at which Washton pointed, grasped it, pulled at it.

Thunder crashed. The guns belched fire, smoke. Little white clouds appeared suddenly in the sky where the planes were. The planes weren't there any more. There was only a rain of black bits from where they'd been, and in one place the black body of a man, whirling over and over in the air.

Dikar's legs buckled. He slid, slowly it seemed, down to the roof. He was sitting on the roof and he was looking at Washton. He started to say Something to Washton—didn't say it. Washton wouldn't have heard him. He was dead.

Consciousness ran out of Dikar like sand runs from spread fingers.

DIKAR LAY on a cool, white bed and Marilee sat on a chair beside him. "There aren't many of the Bunch left, Dikar," she was saying, "nor many of the Beastmen, but we've sent out word all over America that we've taken Wespoint from the Asafrics, an' there is hope in America again.

"From all over this part of the Far Land the people are flockin' in here an' there are many men among 'em who know how to fly the planes, an' shoot the big guns. We've just got news that the Asafrics are comin up from New York to take the fort back, but we're ready for them.

"The planes are ready for 'em, an' the big guns that cover the River, an' the Archies that cover the air an' the mountain passes through which the Asafrics must come. We'll meet 'em with the thunder of the guns we've taken, Dikar."

"Yes, Marilee," Dikar murmured, his voice still weak. "We'll meet 'em with the thunder of guns, Marilee. We'll be makin' thunder tomorrow, thunder of freedom, thunder of liberty that is not dead, that will never die."

"Thunder tomorrow, Dikar," Marilee whispered. "Thunder of hope, tomorrow, for our green and pleasant land."

ABOUT THE AUTHOR

ARTHUR LEO ZAGAT (1895-1949), like fellow writer Erle Stanley Gardner, was a lawyer who forsook his profession in favor of the uncertain life of a pulp magazine writer.

A veteran of the First World War who attended City College of New York and Bordeaux University, Zagat graduated from Fordham University Law School in 1929, with the intent of practicing law. But it was the beginning of the Great Depression, and so he turned instead to writing with his fellow lawyer, Nathaniel Schachner.

Their first collaboration, "The Tower of Evil," appeared in *Wonder Stories Quarterly*, Summer 1930. Ten others followed, all appearing in the top Science Fiction titles of the era, *Amazing Stores, Wonder Stories* and *Astounding Stories of Super-Science*. They also sold to *Weird Tales*. In 1934, Zagat struck out on his own, branching out to write for Popular Publications magazines, where he made a name for himself writing detective stories and contributing to Popular's trio of weird menace magazines, *Dime Mystery Stories, Horror Stories* and *Terror Tales*. Thus he became known as "The Horror Story Man." He was also prolific in *Detective Tales, Ace G-Man Stories* and *Strange Detective Mysteries*.

When he had more than one story in a magazine, Zagat used the pseudonym of Grendon Alzee—the last name a play on his initials. For Culture Publications' sole entry in the weird menace sub-genre, *Spicy Mystery Stories*, Zagat wrote as Morgan Lafay.

He is said to have written as Anton York, which was the name of the hero of Eando Binder's famous story about an immortal. Curiously, Arthur Leo Zagat was known to some of his colleagues as Leo, but to intimates as "Bob."

Few series emerged from his typewriter over a 20-year writing career comprising an estimated 500 published stories. His longest and most famous, Doc Turner of Morris Street, ran for nearly a decade in the back pages of *The Spider*. It was one of the most popular backup series in any similar pulp magazine. Featuring the ministrations of kindly old inner-city pharmacist Andrew "Doc" Turner, it was inspired by Zagat's period of working at his father's pharmacy while attending Fordham.

Zagat's stories starring Steven "Tiger" Carlin appeared in Street & Smith's *Detective Story Magazine* in the early 1940s. Carlin was assisted by an elderly neighborhood druggist, Richard Frost.

Zagat was also known for his fantasy serials written for *Argosy,* among them, "Drink We Deep," "Seven Out of Time" and the "Tomorrow" stories. He also appeared in *Blue Book.*

During World War II, Zagat served as Chairman of the Pulp Writers' Section of the Authors' Guild, a branch of the Authors' League of America, where his legal background proved invaluable. Zagat left to join the Office of War Information, dividing his time between his New York apartment and his desk in Washington, while continuing to turn out stories. After the war, he taught short-story writing at New York University and was heavily involved in tutoring returning soldiers in the art of fiction writing. He subsequently founded the Writers' Work Shop for Veterans.

A lifelong resident of the Bronx, Arthur Leo Zagat died of a heart attack on April 3, 1949, at the age of 53. Of himself, he once wrote: "I have had no adventures in far lands. I have worked in a drugstore. I have sold insurance from door to door. I have ridden in the subway and walked the city streets with eyes and ears open. I have read Mother Goose… I do not think of myself as an artist. I am a tradesman, a merchant of tales. It is the way I make my living, and I behave towards it as any man behaves towards his means of livelihood."

www.ingramcontent.com/pod-product-compliance
Lightning Source LLC
Chambersburg PA
CBHW061519020726
47502CB00006B/2142